D0864125

LOVE *story* *of* *the* TROUT

Award-Winning Fly-Fishing Stories Volume 2
Edited by Joe Healy

Fly Rod & Reel Books

OIL CITY LIBRARY
2 CENTRAL AVE.
OIL CITY, PA 16301

LOVE story of the TROUT

Copyright © 2010 by Fly Rod and Reel Books.
Individual stories copyright by the authors.
Used by permission. All rights reserved.
Cover and interior illustrations copyright Bob White

ISBN 978-0-89272-909-8

Library of Congress Control Number available by request

Book design by Chad Hughes

Printed in the United States
5 4 3 2 1

Fly Rod & Reel Books

www.flyrodreel.com
Distributed to the trade by National Book Network

v preface by Joe Healy, *Fly Rod & Reel* Associate Publisher

ix introduction by John Gierach

---

1 **the conversion of epstein** by Charles Gaines (July/October 1988)

11 **the dead man of wendigo brook** by Robert F. Jones (July/October 1988)

23 **ironman** by Jerry Gibbs (July/October 1990)

39 **nobody has to know** by T. Felton Harrison (July/October 1990)

51 **meyer the tyer** by Cliff Hauptman (July/October 1991)

65 **what it was** by Dave Hughes (July/Oct 1991)

77 **the championship of fly fishing** by Randy Oldebuck (March, April, May/June 1992)

111 **old masters** by Rob Brown (May/June 1992)

121 **michaud's fine rods & flies** by J. H. Hall (July/October 1992)

137 **love story of the trout** by Dave Hughes (July/October 1992)

151 **the key to all mythologies** by Jim McDermott (July/October 1996)

163 **labor day** by Gary J. Whitehead (July/October 1996)

173 **hobard's gate** by Seth Norman (September/October 1997)

185 **greenwell's glory** by Thomas McIntyre (September/October 1997)

197 **the shining path** by Michael Doherty (November/December 2008)

---

207 author biographies

Love Story of the Trout

preface

Joe Healy

66 "Time for something different." So began the greeting in the July/October 1988 issue of *Fly Rod & Reel* by then-editor Silvio Calabi. The "different" was the addition of literary fiction to the pages of the magazine. Launched in 1979, *Rod and Reel* (later renamed *Fly Rod & Reel*) from its first issue looked at fishing differently from other magazines in the field, by way of science coverage, pull-no-punches gear reviews and overall probing thinking. The goal was to engage readers in a new way.

Welcoming literature into the mix only confirmed the put-the-readers-first approach—entertainment has a place with entomology, technical-tackle and fly-tying pieces, angler profiles and destination features, the magazine was stating.

Readers applauded and the concept fit so well that *FR&R* went on to designate the summer volume its "Reading Issue" for many years, up to and including the introduction in 1994 of stories from the annual Robert Traver Fly-Fishing Writing Award, which the magazine continues to cosponsor with the John D. Voelker Foundation. The Traver (as we at the magazine call it) is the only international writing award that recognizes "distinguished original essays or works of short fiction that embody an implicit love of fly-fishing, respect for the sport and the natural world in which it takes place, and high literary values."

The "something different" stories published through the years in the magazine provided an abundance of great writing for this collection. Our reach goes back to 1988 for short stories such as "The Conversion of Epstein" by Charles Gaines and "The Dead Man of Wendigo Brook" by Robert F. Jones—no moss on these gemstones—and continues on to several Traver Award–winning works from 1996 to 2008.

Some are set in times gone by—you wouldn't meet the gaff-wielding Billy Selby in Jerry Gibbs' "Ironman" today, as tarpon-kill tournaments are thankfully now catch-and-release. Others are meta-phoric (this book's title story), bittersweet ("Hobard's Gate" and "The Shining Path"), farcical ("The Championship of Fly Fishing") or slyly humorous ("Greenwell's Glory"); and "The Dead Man of Wendigo Brook" is outright Gothic, in a Poe-esque way. But all are noteworthy, not to mention remarkable, for their staying power as terrific entertainments.

Reading these 15 stories will take you on wild, lively and memo-rable journeys, all united by fly-fishing.

introduction

John Gierach

I've never liked the term "sporting fiction." It makes the same kind of pointless distinction as "investigative journalism." (I mean, what kind of journalism *isn't* investigative?) I won't say the setting of a story isn't important—it can serve as anything from incidental local color to the central metaphor—but stories with some fishing in them don't constitute a separate genre and shouldn't be held to a different standard. Good fiction is simply good fiction, whether the action takes place among accountants, soldiers, stamp collectors or fishermen.

The iconic fishing short story is still probably Ernest Hemingway's *Big Two-Hearted River,* first published in 1925. On the actual 1919 trip to Michigan's Fox River that the story was based on, Hemingway was with two friends and it was, by his own account, mostly fun and games: three young men fishing and goofing around in the north woods.

But in the story the fisherman, Nick, is alone and haunted, although we never learn exactly why. In fact we know nothing about Nick before he arrives at the river, but we come to understand that he's returning to something he once loved and that may now be the only thing left that makes any sense. Of course we're never told that in so many words. In the best literary tradition, we're left to discover it on our own. On the face of it, this is a plainspoken and accurate account of a camping and trout fishing trip with what we'd now think of as antique gear. (That's what I took it for when I first read it and liked it age 13.) The language is so spare and the tone so matter of fact that it's impossible to put your finger precisely on the place where your heart begins to break; but unless you're made of stone, it does break. More to the point, the story has little or nothing to do with fishing, but at the same time it could not be successfully transplanted to any other venue.

Readers who fish love the idea that Hemingway changed the name of the river, but I doubt he did it to protect a fishing spot as some claim. I think he did it for the same reason any writer would have: because *Big Two-Hearted River* is a better title.

This piece successfully walks a dangerous line. If you're a fisherman writing a short story that centers on the sport you love, one of the many pitfalls is that you'll overload it with tackle and tactics. On the other hand, if you skip over the nuts and bolts or toss in too much unexplained jargon, the inevitable non-fishing reader won't know what you're talking about. (Believe it or not, there are those who think a nymph is a minor deity from Greek mythology.) Hemingway's great story is a rare hybrid: a work of literature that could also be read as a how-to fishing article.

Writing fiction is just that kind of minefield. There are countless decisions to be made—large and small—and a wrong step anywhere can make the story blow up in your face.

Do you want the intimacy of the first person or the larger canvas of the omniscient observer? It makes a difference.

Who are your characters and what are their names? "Ebenezer" says one thing; "Bob" says another. The same goes for "Bambi" as opposed to "Jane."

Will your plot be simple or complicated and how will it be resolved? Or will it be resolved? A plot with loose ends can seem realistic or leave the reader feeling cheated. A plot that's tied up neatly can feel either satisfying or preposterously artificial. Will your characters drive the story or go along as passengers? In college I was taught that stories are either plot-driven or character-driven, but in the real world that's a matter of degree. Plot and character play against each other like a fish and the angler who's hooked it. Without both there's no story worth telling.

A journalist has to play the hand he was dealt while the fiction writer gets to stack the deck, but the freedom of making it all up quickly becomes daunting because whatever else a story tries to do, it first has to be plausible. A reader comes to a story with a willing suspension of disbelief, but it's provisional and can't be trifled with. Think of it this way: In the supposedly true story, a guy in a rowboat loses his watch overboard and, a few hours later, cleans a freshly caught lake trout that has that very watch in its stomach—still ticking. But if truth can be stranger than fiction, then fiction has to be truer than the actual truth, so that in a good short story, the watch is probably *not* in the fish's stomach.

But then for better or worse, there are no actual rules, so as soon as you say a story has to be believable, along comes one that's delightful because it's so mischievously *un*believable. It's impossible to say what makes a good short story, although after the fact you can sometimes pick out what made a particular story good.

It's no secret that most fiction is based on real people, places and events to one degree or another. Fiction is like a bird nest: The finished nest is a product of the bird's imagination, but the raw materials are actual found objects from the real world. Sometimes, after many drafts, the original pieces become all but unrecognizable. Other times not so much.

A well-known fiction writer once told me you might as well go ahead and consciously base your characters on friends and family because that's often the only way to make a story ring true and you'll get grief for it whether you do it or not. "Even if you make up a character out of whole cloth," he said, "half the people you know will think it's based on them and they'll hate you for it."

That's what they mean by "write what you know." It may also be why some writers have fewer friends than you might expect.

the conversion of epstein

Charles Gaines

We finally left the dock at Cozumel at nine a.m. and were tossing around in a strait a thousand yards off the coast of Yucatan by ten. There was not a single trout angler in sight, and that was just fine with Epstein.

In fact, there wasn't any kind of fisherman in sight, though this was May and the middle of the annual sailfish run. A thirty-knot wind was blowing, there were eight- to ten-foot seas running in the strait, and nobody but José wanted any part of it. All those fifty-foot Strikers and Merritts and Hatterases sitting back there at the dock like a meeting of the board of directors of the Bass Wejun Company, and every one of their captains with something else to do today but fish. Including the guy Epstein and I had chartered: Emilio.

"Ees too windy. Maybe mañana," he had said, and gone back to cleaning the already-spotless cabin of the fifty-two-foot Egg Harbor he captained. It belonged to a man from Pennsylvania—a trout angler, Epstein was sure, who had instructed Emilio never to go fishing when the wind was blowing.

I'd reminded Emilio that we had to leave mañana, and also that neither Epstein nor I had yet caught a sailfish on a fly rod. That was what we had come down here to do, but for the past two days we had let Emilio and the wind keep us from trying, and had settled for catching sail after sail on twenty-pound trolling tackle.

Today was our last chance.

"Good-bye," Emilio had said to that, and closed the cabin door.

More seriously, it was fishing's last chance with Epstein. Epstein had given up fishing almost two years before. Until this week he hadn't touched a rod since a July afternoon almost two years before, when a long-simmering hatred for what he called "trout anglers" had finally boiled over.

We had been fishing emergers on a snobbish little brook in Vermont, the guest of George Talbot, a man I knew who was always talking about "riseforms" and his latest reading of Dame Juliana, but was otherwise, to my mind, okay. Not to Epstein's mind, however. He and Talbot had developed a strong antipathy for each other over the course of the two days we fished together, and I was much relieved at the end of the second day when it appeared that Epstein and I were going back to New Hampshire without any outright unpleasantness between the two of them.

Talbot and I had been taking down our rods, talking peacefully beside his car in the warm dusk with a bottle of Beam on the hood between us, when Epstein came galumphing out of the brook, his forefinger through the bleeding gills of a large brown trout.

"Look at this," he shouted to me. "Do you believe this fish came out of this pissant little stream?" He tossed the trout at our feet, where it pitched feebly a couple of times in the dust. Talbot looked at the fish, then up at me, his face pale.

"Do you intend on killing this lovely fish?" he asked Epstein without looking at him.

"You bet, pal," said Epstein happily. "Kill it and eat it."

"I'm sorry, but I have to ask that you let me measure it first."

"Be my guest," said Epstein proudly.

Slipping to his knees, Talbot pulled a retractable tape from his vest, straightened the fish, and measured it. "She's not legal," he said.

"We'll have to release her."

"What are you talking about?" Epstein demanded. "The limit is eight inches. That fish has to be over fifteen."

"Exactly eighteen," said Talbot. He was quickly constructing a little platform out of twigs. "I think she'll be okay if we can just get her back to the water without *touching* her anymore." He looked up at me, ignoring Epstein. "We have a regulation here that we only kill fish between eight and sixteen inches. Or, of course, anything over twenty inches...."

"*What?*" thundered Epstein.

"Of course, most of us haven't killed a fish of any size in years." Talbot slid the trout gently onto the little stretcher he had made and stood up carefully. "I think she'll be all right, don't you?" he asked me.

"Well," I said, "it's bleeding from the gills."

"Let me get this straight," said Epstein weirdly. We were both following Talbot as he catwalked toward the stream, holding the trout stretcher gingerly aloft. "That fish is two inches too long to be legal, and it's also two inches too *short* to be legal? Is that right?"

" 'Legal' isn't exactly the right word. It's just the way we all agree to do things here on the Passacowadee."

I hadn't liked the sound of Epstein's voice, so I said, "Look here, Talbot, I really don't think that fish is going to make it...."

Epstein interrupted me by suddenly hopping in front of Talbot and snatching the trout off the stretcher. "The way I see it," he said, looking from Talbot to me and back again, his eyes glittering, "we've got two classic trout-angler problems here: Number one," he held up the fish by its tail, "is this trout going to live or not. And, number two, he's two inches too long for those of us here on the Passacowadee."

Talbot wanted the trout back. He reached for it but he was too late, because just then Epstein stuck the fish's entire head into his mouth and bit down. Holding the tail with both hands, he gnawed away furiously, snorting and huffing like a grizzly, and spitting out trout blood and pieces of flesh, until finally he had chewed off the head—which he spat on the ground at the feet of the pale, hypnotized Talbot. Epstein grinned wolfishly. In his last civilized utterance of any kind to a trout angler, he had said in a deceptively kind voice, "You see how easy it is to solve these little trout-angling problems if we just put our heads together?"

Of course it was not everyone who fishes for trout who drove Epstein to give up the primary passion of his life, but only that percentage (growing daily, he believed) who qualified in his mind as trout *anglers*. Epstein's trout angler had rules to govern every pleasure, and that was what Epstein most despised about him. But he also hated the fellow's stuffiness and academic bent, his pipe and tweed hats, how vulnerable he looked in waders, his sheepish enthusiasm for following other trout anglers, his womanish sentimentality, the prissy way he ate and drank, his physical cautiousness, and his obsession with minutiae: little flies, little rules, little tools hung all over his vest, the invention of little tactical problems to make trout fishing seem harder than it is.

In the last year or so before he quit fishing, Epstein had begun to see trout anglers behind every bush and tree. In West Yellowstone and Ennis, in Oregon and Idaho, in Labrador and Ireland—everywhere he went they were waiting for him, pursing their lips over some local rule, wading cautiously in shallow water with the help of a stick, making flaccid little casts, spooking fish they never saw, lighting their pipes and talking sentimentally. Talbot was just a merciful last straw. When pushed, Epstein would acknowledge that Talbot was not the most egregious trout angler he had ever met, just the last; and he would even express some regret at having thrown Talbot into the Sundown Pool of the Passacowadee.

But however good or bad his motives, Epstein had sworn off all fishing that day in Vermont—and not-fishing began to ruin his life. His marriage and his medical practice fell into shambles. He began to drink too much, and he developed an unnerving habit of picking fights with anyone in uniform.

I happen to enjoy the company of people who are actively engaged in wrecking their lives over something they like or don't like, so long as they are not members of my immediate family; but one night

Epstein's wife took me aside at a party and asked me for help. She looked up at me with her great, dark, Byzantine eyes and pleaded with me to "do something." We rarely saw the Epsteins socially, and I was moved. So I talked him into coming down to Cozumel with me. He had never done any saltwater fishing and I was sure he would take to it. For the first few days, though, he had found Emilio's pussyfooting delicacy about the weather, the cleanliness of his boat, etc., to be just another form of trout angling.

Fishing, it seemed, was about to lose Epstein permanently; and then we walked down the dock and met José.

José was sitting in a rusty lawn chair in the stern of a dumpy, homemade-looking thirty-foot boat called the *Gloria*. He knew no English and Epstein and I little Spanish, but we worked out the essential details in a matter of minutes. Epstein and I understood this clearly: that we had found a skinny, barefoot Indian with a potbelly who didn't give a rat's ass how much wind was blowing.

The *Gloria* didn't have sonar or teak decks or a shower. Neither did she have a few of the more necessary accoutrements to sportfishing—such as outriggers, a mate, or bait. But she did have an ice chest full of Dos Equis, and Epstein and I found a nice blue-skirted lure which we rigged without a hook on one of José's decrepit fifty-pound trolling outfits. As soon as we hit the straits, José turned up-sea, cut *Gloria* back to trolling speed, put on a Jimmy Buffett tape, and—drinking beer with one hand and spinning the wheel with the other, laughing and singing to himself and hopping around to keep his balance like a potbellied parrot—commenced to go fishing.

At first, Epstein and I couldn't stand up in the cockpit. But when we could, we let the lure out and sailfish started jumping all over it. Everywhere we looked behind the transom there were sailfish, herds of them, lit up and running over each other to get the lure. I gave Epstein the fifty-pound outfit and lurched toward the cabin for my fly rod.

"They're trying to eat the goddamn thing," Epstein shouted after me. All either of us knew about fly-fishing for billfish was what we'd read.

I staggered back into the cockpit holding the fly rod. "Just don't let them cut it off—it's the only lure we've got."

Epstein was crouched at the transom, his legs locked under it, whipping the boat rod up and down and making the blue lure, thirty yards back, leap and plunge. Through the waves we could see sailfish diving and jumping all around it. I tried false-casting and couldn't because of the wind, so I dropped the big red-and-white streamer into the prop wash and let the boat's momentum carry it back about fifteen yards.

"I'd better go tell José what to do," said Epstein. "Here," he shoved the boat rod over to me. "I'll tell him to throw the boat out of gear when I shout."

"How are you going to tell him that?"

"Small, small problem, amigo," said Epstein. "Size of a trout angler's reproductive equipment."

While he was gone, the boat quartered into a particularly big sea, yawed and crashed into the following trough. Behind me I heard glass shatter and Epstein curse, and then he was beside me again at the transom, grabbing the boat rod back.

"José is all set. I'm going to bring this lure in, so get ready and don't blow it."

I pulled the tip of the fly rod up into the wind to my right as far as I could without lifting the streamer off the water. Then I stripped line off the reel onto the deck, and hoped I could make one good cast. Epstein was reeling fast, and the blue lure skipped toward us, hounded by the sailfish. When the lure was about fifty feet away and still coming, Epstein said, "You ready?"

I nodded.

"José!" Epstein yelled, and just as the boat went out of gear, he yanked the rod up and backward over his head, lifting the lure off the waves and catapulting it toward us. Confused, the sails milled forty feet off the transom. I lifted the fly-rod tip another inch or two and pushed it hard forward. The streamer picked up, caught the wind, and rode it out perfectly to the sailfish, pulling loose line off the deck. When it slapped down I started stripping it back in foot-long jerks.

The streamer hadn't traveled a yard before a sailfish charged in a quick, silver furrow of water and ate it. I let go of the underside of the transom with my knees, reared back to hit the fish, and slipped. Epstein caught me and held me upright. "Hit him again," he said, and I did, three times, and we watched the backing pour off the reel.

"Why is there blood all over the deck?" I asked Epstein.

"A window broke in the cabin and I cut my leg on it."

"Isn't that an awful lot of blood?"

He was still holding me upright against the transom while I played the fish, and I could feel blood running down the backs of my legs.

"It's okay; just don't lose that baby. Can you believe this?" he whooped. The sail was tailwalking a hundred yards back, its lean, violet body snapping like a flag in the wind. "We have wasted our whole lives fishing in mudholes for guppies. I have just been made whole, goddamn it...."

"I have to puke now," he added after a moment. His voice was still so delighted I thought he was kidding. He wasn't. Without letting me go, he turned his head and threw up violently onto his shoulder and the deck. When he was finished, he coughed a couple of times and spat. "Deep-sea fishing!" he shouted hoarsely into my ear. "To hell with women and work!"

With Epstein holding me upright and with José handling the boat beautifully, I had the sail tired and circling just off the stern in eight minutes. When the fish moved under the boat I yelled for José to go forward. Taking me to mean the fish was ready, I guess, he threw the boat into neutral and popped back into the cockpit like a jumping bean, gloved for billing the fish and thrilled to death with everything that was going on—even, it appeared, the blood and vomit all over his deck.

"Go forward," I yelled to him and pointed to the fly line running directly under the stern, which at that moment stopped and refused to budge. The fish had run the line around the prop.

"Oh, no," Epstein said quietly and let me go.

"*Aiyeee!*" said José. He popped back into the cabin, reemerging in seconds in a mask and fins, and, before Epstein or I could figure out what he was doing, jumped overboard into the heaving sea.

Epstein and I looked at each other, then overboard. It was not a place anyone would want to be. Between the fish and the fly line was a foot of fifteen-pound leader tippet. Though we didn't say it, neither Epstein nor I believed that the tippet had not already parted, either on contact with the prop or at the fish's first surge. But within seconds, the line came unstuck and I felt it to be, miraculously, still connected to the fish.

Epstein pulled José back into the boat and José got the engine going and the boat turned upwind. Then he came into the cockpit and grabbed the sailfish by the bill. He pulled the fish half over the transom and Epstein started clubbing its electric blue head with a Coke bottle.

"Stop it," I said to him. "That's my fish and I want to release it." Even before I had finished the sentence I was sorry I'd said it.

Epstein paused with his hand raised, and looked at me. His face was set with a fierce new assurance, and his eyes had the same non-committal savagery in them that you see sometimes in animals' eyes.

"The hell it is," he said quietly. Then he clubbed the fish again with the bottle and José let it slide dead onto the deck.

Both of them straightened up then and grinned at me. Epstein had tied his T-shirt around his thigh, which had finally stopped bleeding. In real life he is a doctor, but he doesn't look like one. He is also an ex-college football player and wrestler, and an enthusiastic fistfighter and skydiver—a big, tough, trouble- and pain-addicted man. Later, back in Cozumel, not trusting Mexican clinics, he would disinfect and sew up his wound himself. It took thirty-five stitches to close the cut, and then we went out and drank a world of Cuervo Gold and said very little to each other.

One thing Epstein did say, late that night, was that he had found his religion. He said that very loudly at about three in the morning while staring steadily at a stuffed blue martin hanging in the lobby of our hotel. And I suppose I believed him. I haven't seen Epstein since that moment, but occasionally I hear about him and his fishing. Captain Bob Marsten wrote me recently that he and Epstein took a Striker, several tanks of tequila, and two hookers down to Chile this past winter to look for swordfish, but spent all their time shooting sharks and getting laid in the tuna tower.

I have learned for a fact that very little in life is simple, even fishing. But there for a moment or two in the cockpit of the *Gloria*, standing astride his sailfish, shirtless and hairy, new-looking and sweating and caked with dried blood and puke, Epstein was, I believe, a simply happy man. After he had grinned at me for a long time, he picked José up and hugged him. Then he sat the little Indian carefully back down on the deck.

"Muchas gracias," Epstein told him.

José ran up to the wheel, cracked a cerveza, turned up the Buffett, and winked at us over the stained shambles of his boat. He put the throttle in the corner and *Gloria* heaved forward. "More fish now, si?" he shouted.

Epstein squinted approvingly at him. "I'd say...164, maybe 165."

"What's that?" I asked him.

"Trout anglers that little bum's worth."

the dead man of wendigo brook

Robert F. Jones

Perhaps it was a trick of the water, a *trompe l'oeil* of the late summer light, or maybe just a hallucinatory vision provoked by hours of upstream nymphing. You know the feeling: cast, lift, reach, lift, cast—over and over, always staring, until the world fades away, sun and birdsong and roar of water, and all that's left is the endless dance of the strike indicator. But in that moment—one of those timeless Zen moments—I saw the dead angler clear, down in the depths beneath the floating red leaves.

I mean crystal clear, in detail. His waxen face with the hair floating vaguely in the current, pale eyes fixed upward on mine, the grizzled mustache trailing like eelgrass over a rueful smile, the blue collar-points waving above the fishing vest. I could see it all in that mirror-light of underwater, A shattered black rod gripped in the stiff hand, forceps twisting silver from a retractor pin, the bulge of fly boxes in the pockets. Leader snips dangling from a D-ring. Even the flies hooked into a fleece drying patch—dry flies—a Ginger Quill, an Adams, a Blue Dun, and a fourth I didn't recognize, the brightest of the lot.

As I looked, horrified, he rose from the bottom—lifted, it seemed, by the hackles of those flies on his chest, by some heavenly Mucilin or mystical Gink that urged him free of the roiling current's downward grip. I grabbed for him, got hold of the slippery vest, wrestled the current for a moment, felt the fabric slip from my fingers, then a sharp stab of pain in my palm. I flinched. He broke away and down again. One hand rose, limply, as if in farewell, and he rolled back into the depths.

I staggered off into the shallows, stunned and disbelieving. Odd things happen to the mind on trout streams. Illusions and delusions are the bedrock of our sport. Maybe I'd imagined the whole thing. Maybe it wasn't a man but merely a waterlogged tree stump, or a drowned deer. But I saw it so clearly. Then I remembered the pain in my hand. Sure enough, there was a fly stuck in my palm, dead center. It was the fourth of the flies I'd seen on his vest, the odd one. It was buried to the shank. I pulled at it tentatively and it came right out—barbless, thank God. Absently, I stuck it in my own drying patch, then sat back on the bank in the sun to watch the pool for the body's reemergence, but mainly to think.

What I decided, when the body failed to show again, may seem heartless and inhuman, but remember that I am a fly fisherman and the season was winding down. I decided to fish on. What else could I do? The truck was a good five miles downstream, and it was another ten from there by jeep to the nearest highway. By the time I got out it would be midnight—no time to organize a search party with grappling hooks for a man already dead and beyond help. I was fishing my way up Wendigo Brook, a little-known feeder of the Nulhegan River in the so-called Northeast Kingdom of Vermont. The region itself received little pressure from anglers—the locals are mainly "worm-flangers" who fish near the bridges, and then only when the rivers are discolored from heavy rain—and this section was virtually trackless except for logging roads used seasonally by the paper company that owns most of the land. I was packing in, light, with only a tarp for cover, and figured to be on the water at least three days. There was a highway to the north where I could hitch a ride back to the trail where my truck was parked. So far, the weather had been splendid—high, crisp, sunny September days; frosty nights full of owl hoot and coyote song and, toward midnight, a dazzling display of the aurora. The trout were fat brookies and cagey browns, bright and savage in their spawning colors. Why give that up for a dead man?

A fellow I know told me how he'd been fishing for spring steelhead up in British Columbia once when he came upon his partner, dead of a heart attack on the gravel. "I reeled in the fish that had killed him, released it, then laid him out with a stone for a pillow and his rod alongside him like a knight's lance," he told me. "Then I went back to the river. What the hell, the run was still on."

So I, too, fished on.

It was getting toward evening, time to look for a campsite and kill a couple of trout for supper. Ahead the stream wound down through a grassy meadow, one of those dried-out beaver ponds that stud the country up there, with plenty of standing, sun-cured drowned trees to provide firewood. I unslung my pack and spread the tarp under a big white pine, built a fire ring from a fractured ledge, gathered wood for the night, and laid a fire, then went down to the brook to catch supper.

Nothing rising yet, just the brown waters coiling smooth and deep under the high banks. I pulled the dead man's fly from my patch and examined it. A strange fly, this one. It was hair-bodied, kind of like a deerhair Adams a friend of mine ties, with a big, fat body resembling an Irresistible or a Rat-Faced McDougall. But this clipped hair was of a color I'd never seen before—all colors, it seemed, the more I looked at it. In that late afternoon light it almost glowed, refulgent and refractive at once. Blue and burgundy and mahogany, with glints of fiery green, as if copper wire were burning. A deep midnight luster in toward the hook shank, like the underfur of a fisher cat. It couldn't have been dyed, not with all those ever-changing colors, and I tried to puzzle out what sort of animal that hair could have come from. Not badger or moose or wolverine or skunk, certainly not squirrel or bear—not even cinnamon bear. Marten or sable, perhaps, but I doubted it. Hackle, wings, and tail were clearly from the same animal, and equally deceptive as to their true colors. The hook, too, was of a type I'd never seen. It was a size 12, I'd judged, sort of Limerick-bent, with a turn-up eye, japanned in black lacquer like a salmon hook, but of course too small for that purpose.

There was something archaic about it that called up images of LaBranche or Gordon tying late at night by lamplight, with a Catskill blizzard howling beyond the windowpanes, or perhaps Dame Juliana herself in some echoing abbey chamber with rush-torches guttering on dank, gray walls. Could it have been tied before stainless steel came on the market? Unlikely—the fly was not a bit tattered. Or maybe it just didn't catch fish—that would account for its pristine state. But then why did the dead angler have it on his drying patch? What the hell, I'd give it a try.

I knelt on the bank and worked the fly out with a few false-casts. I still had a short leader on, the same I'd been using while nymphing, since this was a trial run and the tippet was heavy enough to turn over the big fly. The fly was traveling overhead in the higher light and I could see it from the corner of my eye—glowing. A red-gold firefly, it seemed, above the oncoming dusk. I aimed to drop it on the deep run against the far bank, where a nice fat brookie ought to be lying, hungry and unselective as to his menu. He would fill mine. But before the fly even reached the water I saw a wake streak toward it. From my side of the water. Then another, from downstream. And another from far upstream....A huge, dark, golden-bellied shape leaped clear of the water and nailed the fly solid, a full foot above the surface. A big brown by the look of him. He'd won the race. The other wakes turned sharply and chased after the brown, who hit the water like an anvil dropped into a lake.

Thank God for the heavy tippet. So stunned was I by the ferocity of the onslaught that I failed to drop the rod tip as the hooked fish jumped, then jumped again. The lesser trout jumped with him—half a dozen, it seemed, all in the same instant. All aimed at his mouth, where I could see the dead angler's fly glowing in the brown's jaw. It was as if...But—impossible. It was as if they were trying to take the fly away from him!

I snubbed the brown around and horsed him in, panic gripping my heart. I hadn't felt like this since I was a kid, fast to my first big fish and frantic that it might get away before I could land it and go running home to show my friends. But when I netted him and lifted him to the bank he was too big to kill—too big a fish for my supper, far too handsome to die. I slipped the hook and sent him back. As he swam off, they followed, darting at his mouth in puzzlement—where was that good bug?

What the hell was this? My heart slowed down and I moved upstream toward the head of the run. Once again I laid the fly out, once again the wakes appeared from all directions. Once again a big trout leaped clear of the water to glom the fly before it hit. Once again the other trout chased it.

Once again he was too big to kill. This was getting upsetting.

I took five more fish on five more casts as the light failed, each the same as the last. Now we've all had similar, or roughly similar, experiences at times, particularly at dusk when almost any big bushy fly splatted on the water will take trout one after the other. I recall an evening on the South Platte in Cheesman Canyon when I took eight nice Colorado browns on successive casts during a caddis hatch, without shifting a step from my position in midstream. But this night there was no hatch, not that I could see. And each fish took the fly before it hit the water.

I'd often seen brook trout chase one of their number after it was hooked, but brookies are notoriously naive—some say suicidal—in the face of danger. These trout, as best I could see, were browns—the Einsteins of entomological discrimination. And not little ones, still learning their Adams from their *Baetis* from their Coachman, but fifteen- and sixteen-inchers from the graduate school of Selective Sipping. MBAs at least—Masters of Bug Assassination. And the big ones who nailed the fly were full professors, some even emeritus.

It was nearly dark by the time I wised up, cut off the dead angler's fly, and tied on a mothlike Grizzly Wulff. It took me well into full dark, float following fruitless float on the now-still, apparently trout-less water before a lone, ten-inch brookie foolishly gobbled the fly and sacrificed himself for my supper. I knocked him on the head and slipped his guts out, shamefacedly, then stumbled back through wet grass to light my fire. The dinner—fried trout, baked beans, cold Cling peaches from the can—left no memory of taste behind it, but I must have eaten it because I remember walking back down to the river to wash the pan. The water was strong and black as ice-cold coffee, but I needed whiskey. I lay against the pine trunk in my sleeping bag, sipping Scotch from the peach tin, my mind dancing like a skyful of mayfly spinners.

You've probably wondered as I do why certain flies that bear absolutely no resemblance to anything in nature not only catch fish but, at certain times and places, are the only flies a trout will look at. The Royal Coachman is perhaps the best example, though the Professor, Yellow Sally, Scarlet Ibis, and Umpqua Brat certainly rank right up there among the Great Inexplicables. But the Coachman, with its white wings, rusty hackle, bristly barred tail, and three-segment body of fluorescent red silk flanked by bumps of black-green peacock herl looks like something beamed down to your fly box from Alpha Centauri. I've heard it argued that the segmented body makes the trout think "flying ant," while the white wings are there only to help the angler keep track of the fly in fast water. I've got another theory, and it came back to me that night as I depleted my Scotch and pondered the fly I'd found—a fly I'd started thinking of as *Ephemerella incognita*.

Given that trout have been around for millions of years on this planet, making a living largely off aquatic bugs: During that time, many insect species have come and gone, while the trout in his various forms has remained pretty much the same. Could it be that deep in the trout's racial memory, taped on his genes as vividly as his spots and fin rays and mating instincts, are images of insects long since extinct? Images that, when presented in a certain light or temperature of water, by a certain curl of current over a specific type of stream-bed—sand or boulder or pea gravel—trigger a strike as inevitable as a salmon's fruitless leap at a newly erected dam on its preordained spawning river? Maybe trout still feed on a long-dead past, just as men do on books long out of print but nonetheless still compelling.

And perhaps this odd killer-fly I'd come by, this *E. incognita*, by sheerest chance happened to imitate some splendid bug of prehistory, some trouty equivalent of braised sweetbreads or oysters on the half-shell in an age of sawdust hamburgers....By the time I sloped off to sleep, the Scotch bottle was down by a good three inches.

Fog on the water at daybreak—a pearly peasouper through which the spires of black spruce and the cracked, bone-white fingernails of snags poked silent and dripping. Heading down to the stream for coffee water, I heard something splash away through the shallows. Moose, I thought. Their big, cloven tracks scarred the shore the full length of Wendigo Brook from where I'd entered it. After filling the pot, I went down to look for sign. I wish I'd never looked. There at the bottom of the run where I'd caught the trout the previous evening were the carcasses of seven big browns. Clearly they were the fish I'd hooked and released. But how? I hadn't played any to exhaustion, I'd hardly touched them in removing the barbless hook, and not one had swayed even slightly onto its side before swimming off strong and swift to cover. Now, though, they were just heads and tails connected with bare bones. Whatever had eaten them had some appetite. The skeletons looked like cobs of sweet corn that had been gnawed from end to end, machine-gun style. Big paw prints surrounded this scene of carnage, not the long, plantigrade prints of a bear or a bootless man, but round ones a good hand span in diameter, with sharp indentations as if from claw tips at the end of the toes. A catamount? If so, it was the size of a Siberian tiger—my hand span is nine and a half inches. Thank God the thing had finished eating before I came upon it....

I hurried back to the fire and stoked it up with my remaining wood. When the water came to a boil, I spiked my coffee with another inch of whiskey, then waited for the fog to bum off. I dug the .22 Colt Woodsman out of my pack, checked the magazine, and jacked a Long Rifle round up the spout. Not that it would do much good against a creature the size of that one, but it made me feel better to have the holster against my thigh as I packed and headed upstream as soon as I could see a hundred yards. I resolved not to joint up the rod until I was at least a mile away from that place, no matter how good the water looked.

But as the day brightened and the sun shone strong and jolly, my worry burned off like the fog. I felt like a fool with the pistol on my hip and put it back in the pack. There were trout rising every-where—in the pocket water, the riffles, along the undercut banks, in the long, slick runs and the deep blue-green bottomless pools. Would *E. incognita* work its wonders with every trout in the river already glutting itself on the blue-wing olives I now saw emerging? The naturals were no bigger than size 18 or size 20—a fraction of the size of the *incognita*. Even if I cast with utmost delicacy, as fine and far-off as I could manage, its impact on the water would probably put everything down.

I strung up, tied on, and cast. At first nothing happened. The feed-ing trout continued to etch their endless, interwoven circles on the water, and I was about to breathe a sigh of relief—last night's events had just been another of those rare lucky moments in a fly fisherman's diary of strange happenings. But then, *wham!*—another huge brown appeared out of nowhere and took the fly at the end of its float. In fact, the fly had been dragging abominably for half a minute while I stood there stupidly, relieved (falsely) that the mystery was explained. I played the fish fast but carefully, took great pains to ensure that I didn't so much as touch it while pushing the hook with a fingertip out of the corner of its mouth. Again, it swam off in full strength, even splashing me with a faceful of water as it tailed away. Thus began, ironically, the most frightening, frustrating day of my angling life.

I tried the *incognita* in the most unlikely trout lies—in dead back eddies, in boiling currents too strong for a tarpon, directly at my feet in seemingly fishless pools, even bounced it down a shallow gravelly riffle no more than ankle-deep. Wherever I dropped it, trout appeared, often as if from the stream bed itself, out of ancient redds long buried under glacial till, springing in seconds from alevin to parr to full-grown, hook-jawed, bloody-eyed lunker hell-bent on suicide at the spear of my hook. One such—a broad-shouldered five-pounder at least—actually zipped up through water only half his own depth from dorsal to ventral, scooting along the gravel on his pectoral fins like some giant wind-up toy. I'd see cohos do that on the Salmon River near Pulaski, New York, when the water was down and the fish themselves pursued by a horde of two-legged snaggers, splashing and falling down in their lust for a kill. But never the dignified brown trout. It was sickening—ignoble, repellent, downright hoggish.

And behind me, as I fished and tried not to look back, I saw fish after fish—all released as tenderly as possible—go belly-up in my wake. Every one that the *incognita* bit, died. Yet I couldn't stop fishing. Even as my mind shrank from what I was doing, as I cursed myself aloud as the Mengele of Meat Fishermen, the Pol Pot of Piscators, the Idi Amin of Demented Anglers, I kept casting, hooking, releasing, but killing trout—trout of such a size and beauty that if I'd seen some worm-flanger catching and killing just one, a day ago, I'd have seriously considered shooting the bastard and leaving him for the ravens.

Poison on the hook, I began thinking. What I took for lacquer was actually some kind of venom—like that black tar the Wandorobo hunters use in Africa, boiled down from the sap of the acocanthera and smeared on their arrows and spearheads, to kill even rhinos and elephants. But I too had been stuck with the hook. Maybe I too was dying—going mad first, unable to stop what I hated doing, compelled by the poison to continue. Maybe in an hour, maybe not until tonight, I would gasp hopelessly for breath like those splendid fish lying behind me, roll belly-up in my sleeping bag, eyes going white with death....

And what? Provide a midnight snack for that big, round-pawed carrion-eater I'd surprised by the riverbank?

That snapped me out of it. I looked at my palm where the hook had bitten me—my God, less than twenty-four hours ago—but the wound was healed as if it had never been there. Nor was the flesh tender when I probed it. Oh, I felt a little woozy, but that might just be a touch of hangover from last night's Scotch, plus the belt I'd had for breakfast. And I hadn't eaten a bite of lunch. It was already late afternoon. No wonder I was giddy—too much fresh air, too much sun, too much adrenaline, too much imagination. When I looked back downstream, I couldn't for the life of me see a single dead fish, yet just moments ago it had seemed there were dozens. Maybe I'd imagined it all. After all, I am a writer...

But the *incognita* was still clinched fast to my tippet. And with a pang of horror I saw that, for all the big fish it had taken today, all the spiky vomerine teeth that had raked it, not a wing was tattered, not a hackle point bent, not a tail whisk frazzled or a strand of dubbing trailing loose. With a shudder I cut the fly loose and threw it into the current.

Before it could hit the water, a huge brown surged head and shoulders up and onto it—snap, like a giant mousetrap, and he was gone. At that moment, a wind kicked up and, under its roar, I heard a low, throaty growl from downstream. I turned and ran....

I slept that night on a rocky islet in midstream, struggling out to it through currents that lapped over the top of my chest waders. There was ample driftwood jammed up at the head of the island to build a huge, roaring bonfire. I kept the Woodsman unholstered beside me while I ate a frugal supper of beans, Spam, and Bing cherries—no trout for me tonight; in the hours just past, I'd killed enough to last a lifetime. I also brought the Scotch level down another few inches, trying to quiet my raging imagination. To keep my mind off the day's events, I dug out a book I'd brought along, as I always do, to read myself to sleep. Usually it takes half a page or less, after a hard, fine day on the water, but tonight I feared it would take longer. *Keys to the Kingdom*, it was titled, by Zadok Mosher; "Being a Compendium of Myths & Legends Peculiar to Northeast Vermont." I'd picked it up in a fine little bookstore in St. Johnsbury that specialized in used books, long out of print. No date of publication was given, nor was the name of the publisher, but clearly it was an ancient tome—glossy paper, antique typeface, faded leather binding, excellent drypoint illustrations—the sort of book no one makes anymore. I settled down into my sleeping bag, took a wallop of whiskey and brook water, and opened the volume at random.

"The Monster of Wendigo Brook." Uh-oh. But I read on.

"The Wendigo is thought to be a myth of the Cree Indians of the western boreal forests," Mosher wrote. "A murderous creature, half cat, half man, that stalks its human prey through the treetops. When it catches an unwary Indian, alone in the forest, it swoops down and grabs him, lifting the hapless victim high into the air. Then ensues a pell-mell dash through the night sky, conducted at such speeds that when the Wendigo—dragged finally groundward by the weight and frantic struggles of its still-living captive—allows the victim's feet to touch the earth, the sheer friction sets his moccasins afire. The Wendigo, like a housecat, likes to show off its prey, frequently carrying it at chain-lightning speed around the camp from which the poor captive strayed. His kinsmen, huddled in their tee-pees, can hear him screaming through the night: 'Oh, my burning feet! Oh, my feet of fire!' In the morning, nothing is found of the victim but his scorched clothing and picked bones, usually under a tall tree at the top of which the Wendigo, like an owl, has made his meal.

"Such, then, is the Wendigo of the Cree. But the Abenaki of northern New England have their own legend—that of the Water Wendigo. Like its western congener, this creature too is a man-eater, though it much prefers fish. It haunts the virgin trout streams of that luckless country, hoping to find a dupe to catch fish for it. To that end, it ties a lure on whatever old hook it can find, using swatches of its own fur to disguise the fatal implement. This fur, the Abenaki say, is irresistible to trout and salmon, some of which have been known to crawl on their fins from lake to lake in pursuit of a lure of such devising. No sooner do they taste of it than they die. Whereupon the Wendigo dines on their corpses. But since the Wendigo cannot cast a fishing pole by itself, it needs a human intermediary to do its fatal business in its stead. This it handily finds, the Abenaki say, since what man would pass up the chance to catch a fish with every cast of his lure? Should the fisherman object to sharing his catch with the Water Wendigo, the Wendigo kills him along with the fish, then contrives to pass the lure on to another victim. No man has lived to tell how. Nonsense, of course. But when you hear a withered old Abenaki tell the tale, in a skin lodge of a still winter evening with the Aurora guttering overhead...."

That was enough for me. I poured another Scotch and resolved, then and there, to fish no more on Wendigo Brook—tomorrow or ever. Total nonsense, of course, as Mosher said, but I would not press it. I was lucky to get rid of the fatal fly when I did. I unjointed my fly rod and slipped it into its case, finished my drink, stoked up the fire, and somehow went to sleep.

The sun was already up when I awoke, so sound and dreamless had been my rest. It was a beautiful day, clear and warm with just an apple-bright bite of frost in the shadows, the brook tinkling and purling along its merry way over the time-worn rocks. I looked at my map and saw a quick way over the hills to the northwest that would take me to the highway in a matter of hours. I'd have to bushwhack, and there might be a few bogs and beaver ponds along the way, but any amount of hard slogging was a cheap price to pay to get away from this cursed river. Still, I'd better get myself around a good breakfast first—a couple of chunky little brookies, caught on a human-tied, unmystical fly for a change. I went over to where I'd left my rod-case leaning against a rock the night before.

The rod case was open, the rod assembled. The line threaded bright yellow through the guides to the tip-top. The leader led down to the keeper ring. Cinched in it, snug and bright, was the *Ephemerella incognita.*

Again I fled, to the limits of the island. I may well have been gibbering to myself as I ran. I skidded, half fell, down through the sharp granite rubble to the water's edge. My reflection shone clear on the still, cold water. I looked down, dreading what I should see.

The face of the dead angler stared up at me from the mirror of Wendigo Brook. The grizzled mustache wavered, shimmered in the current, the pale eyes stared up into mine—dead at first, then with growing recognition. The face I saw was my own....

ironman

Jerry Gibbs

That morning Billy Selby's inner alarm woke him at 5:45 and he lay quietly on his back waiting for his head to clear. Before moving, he began a mental check, searching for weaknesses in the day's program. He could find no flaw in the plan formulated last night, the moves to each new area timed to accommodate the crazy-quilt of local tides. There were backups in case the wind changed. The fish would be there. They would get them. It was only a matter of size, of weight, to keep their lead.

Don't you wish, he thought, then rolled to his right side, swinging his legs to the floor and standing in one fluid movement. He reached up, stretching the stiffness from his arms, back, and shoulders, feeling their soreness, the thickness of hands and arms from the previous two days of poling the skiff across the water. Not too bad, though, he thought; your wind's maybe not what it was, but you know the tricks now. He was sixty-three years old, had captained the largest blue-water craft and little inshore skiffs from the Canadian Maritimes to the Caribbean, and he was built like the trunk of a venerable oak.

In the pale light he looked with the usual wonder at his wife, sleeping lightly, a wing of blonde hair across her strong, high cheekbone, the fine ends moving slightly with her breathing. Then he turned and padded in bare feet to the washroom. He put the water on the stove for coffee, returned to their bedroom to dress.

"Hello," Lynn said, sleepily. "How was your night?"

"I thought you'd sleep. I'm all right. Fine."

"How're your arms?" she rolled over, the sheet tracing her long, slim length. Last night she had kneaded and rubbed the muscles in his arms and shoulders, knotted and cramped from poling, until they could relax.

"They're good. They'll be fine."

"It's going to be hot today."

"*Mmm.*" It was her way of telling him to wear shorts. He rarely did, usually dressed in khakis whatever the heat, still not liking the fuss with sunscreen after all these years, unlike the young guides who lived, bathed in the stuff. Smart, too; without it, you paid. He put on a pair of faded tan shorts and a short-sleeved shirt. He went to start their breakfast.

This was the third day of the tournament, the big one in the world of fly-rod tarpon events, and he had the lead. Correction—Phil had the lead. Phil Anderson was the angler; he was guiding. It would be good to win. It kept you up there even if it shouldn't have to be necessary, even though you had, in a large part, been responsible for starting the game in the first place, had fished the big names, all of them, guided them while they carved the benchmarks of the sport. Wins helped in your back yard, too, helped remind all the young turks coming along now. In this business you never rested. He smiled. Or in most any other.

When they'd finished breakfast and he knew it was time to go, he wished very much it was the next day or the one after. They gathered the dishes, and he went out to check the skiff.

He could have kept the boat in the water, but he never did, tournament or no tournament. He backed it out and saw Lynn leave in the car for the club.

They found Phil Anderson in the club dining room sipping a

coffee. He greeted them, smiling widely around his cup, long and lanky, shoving back a shock of sun-streaked light-brown hair. Swinging his arm behind him, he put the cup on a windowsill.

"God, I feel right today! You ready?"

"Going to do it today," Lynn said, too late to catch herself, knowing Billy hated that kind of thing. She took hold of his heavy upper arm a moment, holding it firmly. So many superstitions.

"Let's put her in," Billy said.

They launched the skiff on the old bumpy limestone ramp, and Phil brought the boat around front to the dock and tied up. The noise level had built slowly, and now it was a steady drone. They looked once again at the standings board, confirmed their closest competitor, already knowing who it was, and suddenly it was time to go. Lynn kissed them both for luck. They dropped lightly into the skiff. Selby cranked the big engine, gentled the throttle forward, cupping the rim of the wheel, steering out the channel without having to think about it, big hard hands moving the tilt/trim control of the engine, dropping the tabs. And then they leaped forward and were up on plane in seconds.

They left the main channel, cutting into a shallow staked pass that ran close to the first fat mangrove island.

They came to the first place. The sun was good, behind and to the right, so they could see well into the water, their shadows falling to one side of their intended direction. Billy killed the engine, raised it, and climbed onto the poling platform at the stern while Phil went to the forward casting deck. There he stripped off line, cast it, stripped it back, letting it drop in loose coils between his feet. In his left hand he held the fly, leader, the entire front taper, and some of the belly of the line in wide loops that could be sent into the air with one rod stroke, the streamer then presented with one, maybe two false casts. The speed was necessary to lead, and hit just ahead and to one side of the moving fish, and you couldn't afford any extra rod-waving—or even a fleeting shadow of aerialized line—entering the tarpon's angle of vision. Those small suggestions of danger would send the huge creatures fleeing in terror like threatened bait from the shallows.

Billy placed the foot of the forked pole firmly at the edge of the tiny channel that sliced into the bank they would work. Little puffs of gone-by, blue-green algae billowed up like autumn leaves, skimmed across the channel and floated away over the flat. He planted the pushpole, leaned a thigh against it, and the skiff pirouetted to the right. They stared down the flat in the thick silence of the wild place. High overhead a single man-o'-war bird wheeled and slid away across the sky.

For a little while there was no life on the flat, and they stood in a silence that Phil was first to break.

"Ray coming," he said.

"Yep," Billy acknowledged. "See anything behind it?"

Phil stared into the little muds behind the feeding ray but saw no other fish following, grazing for a free meal turned up in the ray's wake.

"Nothing."

"You see up ahead?" Billy asked.

"Funny water."

"Yeah. Let's take a look."

He doubled his efforts on the pole, pushing the skiff faster toward the bouncy surface just ahead, the disturbance often a tip-off to fish. You watched the surface as briefly as possible, trying to penetrate below it with your vision, down where the fish would show. Showed now.

"That's them." Phil said, low and tense.

The fish were moving right to left, dark blue-gray shadows, no real detail at the distance, except for size. They scanned the school, fast.

"Second fish is the biggest, but all small fish. Really small," Billy said. "They're weight, though...."

It was nothing they did, but something unseen that suddenly spooked the school, and the fish bolted ahead. Selby turned the boat right, back on course.

"Now you don't have to waste time on the little stuff."

Phil grinned. They worked well as a team. "Good start, so quickly. Now we just need size. Keep 'em rolling, Billy."

"Just tryin' to please, boss," he said, inwardly wishing Phil hadn't verbalized the business of a fast start. It was not a lucky thing.

They held on the bank, watching ahead for more fish, bigger fish. They came to a small channel that snaked into the flat, the water light sapphire blue. The edge dropped sharply, looking like a miniature western canyon wall with erosion-carved, distinctly stratified levels. They launched off the edge, floating across the deeper water as on air, motes of light sparkling deep in the clear water. The wall on the other side loomed up, climbing sharply, and they were on the bank again, the bottom rust-colored, broken with beige and spots of brilliant jade. The surface was silky smooth still, heaving gently. Then they saw the tarpon rolling.

There were many fish in the school. The backs and dorsals of five of them cleaved the surface, turning so slowly you could see clearly the great scales covering their bodies. They were on a heading that required Selby to turn only slightly, then move ahead faster to close within casting range. Now they could see the forms of the fish below the surface, growing closer. Three more fish broke again, moving gracefully, calm and steady.

"God, they're happy," Billy said, straining on the pole. "Get ready!"

"Lead fish...," Phil said.

"Yeah, now give it all you got."

The cast was away, line shooting out above the surface. It settled to the water, the streamer sinking, fluttering, then beginning to swim. The big lead fish moved its head and the bulk of its body followed.

"She's turning, keep it coming...," Billy crooned, low and steady. Then, "No, look at tha—"

With the lead fish still coming for the fly, a tarpon from the back of the school bolted forward. They could see it clearly, mouth opening, engulfing the streamer, turning its head while Phil struck, jabbing hard three times to sink the barb. The lead fish was big, but this one was bigger. It had wanted the fly badly, and now its reaction to the hook was as violent as its attack.

The fish went into the air short yards from the boat, gills rattling, mouth open, the unhinged side-to-side head-lashing warning of what would follow. Still shaking, it crashed back, ripped along beneath the surface, the fine braided backing burning from the reel, then came up again with its entire length clearing the water. It was down now, ripping line through the surface on a fully reversed heading. Before the line had a chance to straighten, the fish again blew up, Phil desperately trying to give a moment's slack with each leap to keep the tippet whole.

Billy pushed after it, slipping once on the remains of his forgotten sandwich, kicking it overboard.

"Crazy. Crazy-as-hell fish," he said softly.

The tarpon made its first long run now, going straight away from them. As it fled it went through the surface once in a high, shuddering leap, slamming back and running again, always straight away. Selby cursed, poling hard. The run slowed and the fish began turning right. For the first time, Phil was able to spool line. Then he realized the fish was circling. The tarpon came for them. Anderson put everything into reeling, then in a rush lost all he'd gained as the fish completed its circle and started away once more.

Leaning on the pole, Billy tried to close the distance between boat and fish. Phil couldn't do anything now. The tarpon stayed under, sometimes boring left and right in short flurries, but always holding the same general heading out into the bay.

After what seemed a very long time, the fish stalled. Billy slowly moved in, just a little, Phil reeling, pumping the heavy-butted rod, wet backing spooling up while his heart soared.

Though they were gaining line, Billy felt no confidence with this fish. Mainly he didn't like the way it ran always in one direction. The heading was away from the shallowest water where, with nowhere else to go, the fish would jump and, in jumping, tire itself. But for now the tarpon was coming.

The fish was close enough so the knot connecting the backing with the end of the fly line was out of the water. The line was tight, knifing straight across to the dark, clearly visible form of the fish. Then Phil felt the thudding jerks.

"She's going to come up!" he said.

It was the first time in a long while that the fish had tried to jump, and Billy wondered why it was doing so now. The fly line sliced the surface, rising above it, first the running section, then the taper, and then the bulk of the fish was in the air broadside to them. It lifted nearly straight from the water, huge etched scales on its side, silver flanks gleaming in the sun, one bright flat eye locked on them for a scant moment before the violent head-shaking began again.

The tarpon slammed back without grace partly on its side, then with no apparent effort plunged away, ripping backing through Phil's fingers. He opened them instantly to keep the line from cutting his flesh, letting the direct-drive reel take over, the handle spinning so violently it was no longer distinctly visible. The fish ran straight away from them, taking all the recovered backing and more. Billy put all his strength into the pole.

The fish bored ahead, and for a few moments they kept it from taking more line. Then Phil turned his ahead slightly so Billy would be sure to hear.

"Line's getting low, and he's taking more."

Billy was sweating hard, his breathing harsh. "Too deep now. I have to crank the engine."

He leaped from the platform, landing lightly despite his size. He slammed the pole into its holders, lowered the engine, and started it. They began motoring toward the fish just fast enough to let Phil pick line up. Billy had checked his watch when the tarpon took the fly. Now he looked at it again. They'd been on for forty minutes, a time that would have already brought many tarpon coming in steadily to the pressure of a rod.

For a while the water was too deep for poling, but they had closed the gap and now Billy killed the big engine and used the electrics to position them while Phil tried to find some weakness in the fish. He began to turn the tarpon once with pressure on the right side, the side in which the streamer was embedded, but the fish straightened again. All Phil could do was resist as strongly as he dared, keep the nagging worry of the pressure there and hope the fish would come to see that something as simple as letting its head turn and following the unyielding pull would diminish that foolish annoyance. That was the beginning. That was all you asked for at first. That one small act of acceptance by the fish was your opening, and you could not fail to act upon it. That was when you went to work in earnest, and you could never rest for a moment after that until it was over, one way or the other.

The lone hammerhead came from behind them and from the left so they didn't see it until it passed the boat, cutting right and left, sensing the tail and body beats of the troubled fish, trying to detect blood or odor that was not there.

The tarpon was ahead, moving right, the shark still off to the left and closer. Billy turned on the electric motors. It was a big shark, and it looked dark brown in the water until it came closer to the surface, cut the surface with its fin, which was lighter, paler in the air.

In the bow, Phil cursed the shark softly.

Phil increased his pressure. The fish did not turn, but it slowed perceptibly. The skiff sliced ahead smoothly and quietly. The hammerhead circled out and Billy cut between it and the tarpon, so when the shark turned again, it came for the skiff, sensed and probably saw it, and shot away. They watched its riffling wake on the surface after its body was out of sight. But it did not stay away.

When the hammerhead returned, it did so from the right, coming in to the skiff on a wide circle. The tarpon was on a course that would take it across the bow, right to left, when suddenly something—the shark maybe—spooked it so it bolted on its heading, Phil letting go with the rush.

"Better than close to Mr. Hammerhead," Phil said.

"Except that when the shark goes over there we won't see him, either."

The electrics were on full now that the tarpon had run, and Bill cut the skiff toward the hammerhead, which was tracking in the direction the tarpon had gone. This time he closed on it quickly. The shark was intent on the stress signals of the tarpon, and though it was close to the surface, breaking at times, it had not seen the approaching skiff. Billy left the motors, grabbed his push pole, and returned to the platform. At the last moment he turned the bow sharply left, paralleling the shark, then reared back on his feet and launched the pole like a javelin.

The pointed metal tip struck the shark on the back of the head—and bounced off. The hammerhead exploded, streaking off at right angles. This time it did not return.

"Nice," Phil said, waiting to see what the tarpon would do.

Bill turned the boat, easing over to where the pole floated.

"Shouldn't lose a fish to a shark that's under fifty feet away," Billy said. "If you can't throw the pole at him, you ought to be ready with something else. Maybe crank the big engine and run over him."

"It's a lot easier in shallower water, though," Phil said.

"Yeah, you're right. Better look to your fish."

Phil turned his concentration on forcing the tarpon back. Billy moved slowly to help him, the electrics humming low and steady.

They had gone six miles out into the bay, two hours into the fight, before the tarpon acknowledged the unyielding pressure and began to come. It turned, and Phil led it on, pumping steadily, taking line, then following its swing past the skiff where he had to let it go again. Billy kept the angle of pressure against the fish where it would have the greatest effect, and in a little while, Phil turned the tarpon again. Four times he turned the fish and four times led it nearer in the swing. And then, when they thought they would win, the fish would come no closer.

The tarpon stalled ten feet from the skiff. It held near the surface, plainly visible, blue and silver, the outlines of its fins and scales and eyes clear but abstractly mottled, fluid in the moving water that broke the light. Each time Phil turned and led the fish in its arc toward the skiff, when the distance closed to ten feet the tarpon resisted, swinging away. Billy tried using the electrics to move with the fish, to close ever so slightly on the swing, but the tarpon sensed it and turned more sharply away from them, maintaining its distance.

"I'm just going to have to wear it down," Phil said.

"Mean, stubborn sonofagun," Billy said.

He left the electrics and now took the gaff from its brackets. There had been no doubt that if they could take the fish, they would. This was a weight fish, the fish they needed for the win, and so there could be no releasing it as there would normally be, and the gaff that Billy freed was the killer gaff. It shone silvery in the sun, eight feet long, the maximum permitted by tournament regulations. The bight of the hook was six inches, and its thickness was a full three-quarters of an inch. The point had been filed into three facets. The angles where the planes met were sharp for quick, cutting penetration.

"Try him again," Billy said. He walked forward to where Phil stood.

Phil brought the tarpon around again, and this time it seemed slightly closer, but it still wasn't enough. Twice they tried, gaining inches. Time became the enemy now. With each passing minute the hook of the streamer opened the hole in the fish's mouth. With each effort to turn the fish, the strain would further weaken the fine tippet and the knots that joined it to the other parts of the leader. Billy worked ahead of his angler on the platform.

"Back to the edge—as far back as you can," he said. He was on his knees in the bow of the skiff, the narrow outline of the bow perhaps less ominous to the tarpon.

The fish came around once more, and Billy dropped flat, thrusting his feet beneath the walk-around gunwales to hold himself against what would come. The tarpon was swimming close, growing bigger, Selby beginning to reach. But the fish never came close enough. The tarpon moved slowly forward, and with the pressure Phil would not relinquish, the bow of the skiff turned with the fish. The tarpon stalled, finning gently, unwilling to complete its arc.

"Turn him!" Billy demanded. "Right now, bring him around."

Phil held the rod almost parallel to the water, his grip high on the butt of the rod, and slowly moved the fish. The tarpon let itself be led, just close enough. Selby arched his upper body out over the water, reached and hit the fish in the middle of the back.

He jammed his legs, anchoring himself, holding the fish the way it was possible to do with even larger tarpon, but not with this fish. Weary from the nagging, relentless pressure, but not broken, the tarpon erupted. It spun, and the gaff twisted in Selby's grasp, impossible to hold, Billy refusing to release, feeling the grip of his legs fail, the skin on his chest and stomach and shins abrade as he was ripped over the bow. He felt his sunglasses slapped from his face, pulled down around his neck on their loop as the fish dragged him underwater.

The rush dragged Selby twelve feet to the bottom. His feet and legs hit several times, once the ankle of his left leg slapping something hard and sharp, cutting. The fish's speed built an incredible crush of water against him. He tried to keep his eyes open, his vision blurred by the water and his rush through it. It lasted for seventy-five feet. Then the tarpon slowed and stopped. Billy kicked his way to the surface and gasped for air. He turned on the fish, tried to turn himself toward it, lever the tarpon over with the handle. He heard Phil start to yell something from the skiff, and then he was pulled under again.

The fish ran toward the boat, then angled away another seventy-five feet before it stalled. Billy came to the surface again, coughing, sucking air into his lungs.

"Let go, let him go!" Phil yelled at him.

Billy pulled himself along the gaff, the fish looking huge as he reached it. He could see the fly still in the tarpon's mouth. Now he reached the end of the handle, grabbing the iron, the hook itself, at the bend where it entered the tarpon's back, and then the fish went down again.

The gaff handle slammed Selby in the side of the head but he held the hook with one hand. He was over the fish now, seeing it gray and blue in his half blindness, terrifying in its strength and closeness. He held the hook, ignoring the screaming demand for air, worked his free hand forward, clawing, trying to lock on the fish's eye sockets, gills, mouth.

The fish ran for the boat, passed under it, the gaff slapping the bottom and then Billy's back rammed hard once against the hull. On the other side of the boat the tarpon stopped. The gaff handle broke the surface, Billy still underwater with the fish, still fighting for a grip on it when Phil reached the gaff.

The tarpon spun, lashing against the locked gaff, Phil still lifting, bringing them both in. Then the gaff's hook tore free, and the gaff circled back and up, the hook entering the lower part of Billy's right leg, going through the leg completely and cutting upwards through blood vessels and nerves. Billy came up on his back, his breath bursting in a terrible scream. In horror now, half out of the skiff, Phil worked to free the hook, then threw the gaff behind him. It clattered to the bottom of the boat.

Billowing clouds of blood colored the water. Phil caught the guide's uninjured leg, turned him, grabbed his arms, slid him in over the low gunwale. Billy lay on his back on the bottom of the boat, the long, ragged wound pumping blood, and it was clear that major damage had been done and that they must act very quickly. Anderson scanned the skiff, began to open hatches while the flow of blood continued, spreading brilliantly on the deck. Billy's head was aft, the leg elevated slightly by the angle of the skiff.

"Ah, hell," he said, voice dry. He moved away the hand that was holding the wound, keeping tissue together. He hipped and elbowed himself onto the aft platform, yanked open a hatch, and grabbed the oil rag. He rolled over again and tied the cloth around his leg above the wound. Phil came back and grabbed the small bait net. He slipped its handle beneath the rag as a lever to tighten the tourniquet. There was another rag in the compartment and he tied that directly over the worst part of the wound. Blood had pooled in the skiff but the flow was staunched, oozing slightly through and around the cloth.

Phil found cushions for under Billy's head and neck. He slipped another atop a tackle box, lifting the leg to rest, elevated. Then he raised the electric motors, dropped the main engine, and started it. They were on plane in seconds.

"You doing okay?" Phil asked.

"Sure."

"You want something? Water?"

"Yeah, that'd be good. Here, I can rear up and steer a minute."

"No, I'll get it."

He slowed the boat, dropping them off plane, left the helm for the cooler, got the jug of water, cracking it open. Selby drank deeply.

"Just keep it there," Phil told him. He grabbed the wheel, straightened the boat, and slammed the throttle all the way forward.

Selby watched the water as they ran. He held the net handle and from time to time turned it to loosen the rag and avoid cutting off blood flow completely to the leg. When he did that, the wound bled more freely, but not the way it had before. After tightening the tourniquet the fourth time, he tipped the water jug to his lips and drank again.

"God, I'm sorry," Phil yelled over the engine.

Billy lifted a big hand from the jug. "Nobody's fault. Something that happened." He let the hand drop. He leaned back, feeling tired, detached. The wound that had previously felt numb was now hurting, a throbbing hurt that came from deep in the leg and periodically stabbed searing pain up into his groin. He felt strangely outside himself, but his head was clear enough, and he began to think about how bad the wound might be and what it would ultimately do to him. He knew what it was going to do right now. It was tarpon season, he had been fully booked, and now he was out of it.

Maybe later in the year, he thought. There's a lot of good fishing later that almost everyone passes up. Should be in good shape again by then. Pick up a few fishermen you have to disappoint now. Disappoint, hell. Pick up a few bucks, too. You'll need it by then.

He was glad to see they were running in shallower water, passing the small mangrove islands, running light as though through air, getting closer, going home.

They were packed in at the club waiting for the boats and for the weighing, and the air was electric, bristling with excitement. Some of the boats were coming in fast, small toys in the distance, growing very quickly into the powerfully, exquisitely rigged machines they were. Lynn Selby stood outside the club with friends around her, feeling anxious, and then someone said there was Billy's boat coming, and she stood on her toes and saw it. She watched it carefully for a few moments, and knew something was wrong.

"It's Billy's boat," she said, "but Billy's not running it. Something must have happened."

"Oh, sure that's Billy," someone said.

"No. No, no it's not," she told him, not turning away from the skiff.

They came in fast, Phil landing the skiff well, shutting down, and reversing the engine hard to stop them quickly, and she saw Billy lying in the bottom of the skiff, the rag tourniquet around his leg and the thickening brightness of the blood everywhere.

"My God," she said, Billy looking at her now, smiling tiredly, and she went down to him.

"I'm all right, it'll be all right," Billy told her over her asking, her looking from him to Phil who was handling a line, now turning to her, everyone on the dock turning fast, Phil trying to tell her but Billy's voice coming through over everything, the old, deep rumbly voice not as strong as it normally was.

"Goddamn gaff," Billy said. "Pulled out of a fish...got me."

"Oh, Billy," she said, putting her face to his. She looked at the leg, touching it gently. The crowd pressed in. Billy saw a ring of faces with little meaning to him. Phil was hollering for some help, and two big men pushed through. Both were guides. Carefully they lifted Billy's bulk, moved him to the dock, and back into the shade. He didn't like it at all on his back, looking up at the crowd. In a short while he heard the ambulance siren rising, falling, growing closer and louder.

They had him on the stretcher quickly despite his size, and the crowd was pushed back, friends helping move the rubbernecking strangers. They went quickly down the dock. The one boat in the tournament they had worried about was coming in, its fish laid out silver and flat in the cockpit, broad tail curled up on the edge of the aft platform, massive scales sharply outlined in the late-afternoon sun. It was a good fish, probably enough to give them the win. Billy looked at the tarpon closely as they moved on. Good fish, for sure. But not nearly as large as the one he and Phil had fought. Not even close.

Later, in the hospital room, Lynn told him about the seventy-eight stitches, the nerves and the vessels patched, and some worry about his walking, which would be easy to believe given the way the leg pounded now like a world-class hangover. Then she began really putting her mouth on the fish. He watched her, looking lovely in her anger, working over the fish's lineage many generations past, its present character and ultimate reward, far better than any of his oldest cronies would have been able to do. He started laughing softly.

"You think it's funny!" she exploded.

"No. You. You've got a mouth. Some mouth." he shook his head incredulously.

She leaned on him, buried her face against his for a moment, then stood up, quickly brushing away a suspicion of tears.

"You're going to be fine."

"Sure," he told her. "It's not the fish's fault. Fish does what it's supposed to do. Even friend shark. Sharks got to eat too. That's what they're there for. To clean up."

He was somewhat groggy, as though he'd slipped down a few extra rumrunners too quickly after being in the heat of the day. "Tarpon are in the shallows trying to keep themselves going, keep their species going, fat and happy and sexy, and we're the ones who bust in on them." He found it hard to concentrate. "That's what we're for, just like any other predator. That's what we'll keep doing. That's what I'll keep doing."

"You get yourself healed first."

"Sure. This one won't get me. Don't you worry." He held her shoulder with one big calloused hand.

"I won't," she said.

Then he began drifting off, seeing the bright, color-changing water and the line of creature-shaped clouds curling crazily on the horizon, the sun strong overhead, very good for seeing fish. Then he was asleep.

nobody has to know

T. Felton Harrison

In the corner of his window C.B. sat and listened, in the purple before dawn, to turnbuckles clanging on the masts of the boats moored in the sound. They rolled in a stiff north breeze that only a day or so ago drove snow and ice before it and now brushed harmlessly against his cheek and billowed his curtains like cartoon ghosts. His hands being occupied with pre-fishing chores, C.B. had managed to deftly manipulate his favorite fishing magazine with the soles of his feet, so now he could better study a photograph that had caught his attention late the night before when his vision had been temporarily impaired by inadvertent overmedication (an honest, if not infrequent, mistake). It was of a fisherman in an ice-choked stream, surrounded by snowy banks, his clothing reminiscent of the Peary expedition, frost hanging from his mustache and a handsome steelhead coming to his outstretched, frostbit hand. The headline read DIE HARD.

C.B. pondered his own surroundings and wondered what the photographer would have entitled this predawn north-Florida beach-house scene. IT WAS SO COLD HE HAD TO WEAR SOCKS, maybe.

Tying in the last leader, he dropped the rig to the floor and stood to straighten his back and study the work laid out on the table. Three fly rods, one 12-, one 10-, and one 8-weight; each with a gold Harrison reel—two Los Roques and an Archangel—secured to its reel seat. Each had a size 4 streamer; one orange, one green, and one purple and red, the three most popular colors at the close of last year's ling season.

Ling have long been a sought-after game fish. In some places they are known as cobia, some places lemon fish, and in other places black salmon, but on the northwest Florida coast they were ling, and they held a special position among the local anglers. They were the first migratory fish to come through after the winter, and they came through in abundance. Even more important, they came close to shore, so every local fisherman had boyhood memories of catching them from the beach pier (where boys could afford to fish), and every small boat that could hug the beach could afford to hunt them. Then too there's something about sight-casting to large fish that tends to boil the blood of any true angler.

The season officially opened next week with the ling tournament. Boats would come from as far as Destin and Orange Beach, and not just twenty- and twenty-five-footers—even the floating hotels that normally stayed in blue water. They'd all parade up and down the beach, no more than a hundred feet out, in an endless regatta of game boats of every description.

But that would be next week. And that was why Jack and C.B. always went out this week. The stupid ling, as it turned out, knew absolutely nothing about the tournament and simply scheduled themselves by water temperature. No doubt this genetic ignorance accounted for their position in the food chain, but the timing almost always worked out well for Jack and C.B.

This year Jack owned the boat. Both men went through three-year cycles of boat ownership. One year to get over the euphoria of a new boat, one year to grow very tired of trying to stay ahead of saltwater corrosion before finally selling the boat, and one year to forget the pain of boat ownership and catch the bug all over again. As their affluence grew, so did the quality of the boats, and this year Jack had a handsome twenty-foot Whaler with an OMC outdrive and a spotting tower, which in this area was commonly called a ling tower.

The sky was postcard peach and orange as they rounded the point and began their first run down the beach.

As beaches go, few could compare to the snow-white sands of Santa Rosa Island. Above the high-water mark were the dunes, some fifty feet tall, smooth and steep, with waves of sea oats covering their sloping sides, and the occasional huddle of wind-twisted dwarf pine or magnolia.

The Gulf water was shallow and crystal-clear, with an emerald tint blending to sapphire blue farther out. Spotting a cruising ling in this water was not difficult—just watch for the telltale shadow moving across the bottom.

The technique for hunting ling was to position the boat between the first and second sandbars and slowly troll east to west, west to east, one man at the console, one man in the tower. Since it was Jack's boat, C.B. feigned nautical ignorance and wrangled the first watch in the tower. He chose the 12-weight to start, which was not just the result of wishful thinking, as fifty to sixty pounds was not all that unusual in this water.

Mercifully, the breeze dropped as the sun rose, making a good northerly cast a more reasonable proposition, and within minutes the first torpedo appeared off the bow.

"Twelve o'clock, sixty feet!" C.B. yelled.

Jack cut the engines and C.B. fired out a pretty good one, leading the fish by six or eight feet, and stripped in. Nothing. Now the fish was thirty feet out and moving fast. C.B. knew there'd be only one more shot at this one and he took it.

"Hookup!" The rod bent double as the black rocket went straight out to sea. C.B. left the drag loose and backing smoked off the reel. This was a big one and it was a worthy run. Jack turned the boat in the direction of the fish and idled forward. There was plenty of line but it'd be a bitch to crank it all in when the fish turned, so Jack followed at a respectable pace.

The fish began to tire and C.B. recovered a few yards before the second run. The fight went on, each run being a little shorter until the ling came close to the boat.

"He's a big one," Jack crowed. "I'm betting this one goes sixty pounds. You ought to keep him. There's a lot of bragging mileage on this guy."

C.B. thought a moment. "Nah, tag him. Maybe the next guy to catch him will get the message."

It wasn't until Jack grabbed the leader that C.B. saw it. Not twenty feet out and bearing down hard.

"Shark, Jack! Pop him loose!" But it was too late. Jack couldn't react before the shark had the ling in his mouth and cut it in two. Somehow the leader held and Jack managed to raise the remains of the slaughtered fish, no more than a head and some bloody meat.

"God *damn*! That son of a bitch! I can't believe he got it that fast. One brazen sonuvabitch. He must have been awful hungry."

To lose a fish like that at the last minute was something that rubbed Jack the wrong way, and in a big way.

C.B., on the other hand, was still staring at the mutilated ling, his remorse spilling out like the blood that oozed over the deck and the gunwales. It was his fault the fish was killed. In open water the ling would have escaped, but weakened by the fight and tethered to the line it had no chance at all. It was his fault.

"Hey," Jack shouted, "he's back!"

C.B. looked down, and sure enough, there was the shark going under the boat. It was a hammerhead and not all that big, maybe only five feet. In truth, it looked hardly longer than the ling it had just attacked, though much huskier. It was even possible, though of course unlikely, that the size of the ling had been overestimated in the heat of battle. In any event, the shark was unwanted company and it was time to move on.

"Let's just troll on down the beach a little and see what we else we can find," C.B. suggested. Jack nodded reluctantly, and threw the engine in gear. Jack hated sharks and moving away was, to him, a form of backing down from the animal, something else that Jack found particularly abhorrent.

C.B. looked down at the fish head on the deck. "Jack, why don't you go throw that thing overboard. It sure isn't any use to us."

"No way. I'm not about to feed that garbage disposal. I'll dump it later."

C.B. shook his head. "Suit yourself."

And as he looked up, there were two ling shadows off the starboard bow.

The engines slowed to idle and Jack strained to see the shapes that C.B. had spotted. They were there, all right, and not far off.

C.B. had already false-cast and the fly dropped just ahead of the cruising pair of fish. One turned to follow.

"Strip!" Jack shouted. "One of them is after you."

The fish took the fly and immediately turned and arrowed out for deep water. Just as quickly, a greyhounding shark shot from beneath the boat. The men looked at each other in disbelief.

As Jack screamed, "Pop him off!" C.B. snapped the delicate tippet and the ling was free to run for its life. They stood, staring out to sea for several seconds as if something spectacular was about to happen.

"I can't believe that bastard followed us down here," Jack said, and there was anger and bewilderment mixed on his face.

"I'll bet you he's done this kind of thing before. Somehow, before today, he learned that boats are a good source of an easy meal. You know that sharks are ignorant animals, even for fish."

"Wonder if he got the ling?" Jack said.

"I don't know, but why don't you take the tower for a while."

"No, you're doing good." Jack paused. "Besides, I think that toothy sack of crap is going to come back, and when he does, I've got a little surprise for him." Jack smiled and held up a six-foot gaff. He'd made it himself, years before, but it was mostly for show. It had an oversize stainless hook and a handle that was too long to be of much practical use, and it looked more like something from a medieval coat of arms than a fishing tool. As far as C.B. knew, it had never been used, and it sure wasn't any good in the present circumstance.

"What in hell are you going to do with that thing?"

"The next time that that four-eyed SOB swims under this boat, I'm going to stick this down and beat his pea-brain out of his ugly head." Jack declared this with such conviction that for a second, C.B. thought this was indeed a feasible plan. But that quickly passed.

"You looked strangely serious when you said that, Jack."

"I am serious, buddy. If that sucker comes back, his ass his mine."

C.B. grinned. "Time for a reality check, pal. You know, in your heart of hearts, that that really is an insane suggestion, don't you?"

"No way, C.B. I'm telling you, he better not come back, if he knows what's good for him."

"The old melon's gettin' a little soft out in the sun, pal. You're starting to worry me." That much was true. C.B. had known Jack most of his life, and he also knew that if anyone in the world would or could snatch a shark out of the water—or at least try—that person was Jack.

"Jack, they're too fast and too heavy and too strong. If you did snag him, he'd pull you over. And bear in mind that he would then be really pissed off."

"No, C.B., think for a minute. He doesn't weigh anything underwater. All I have to do is build up enough momentum so I can snatch him over the gunwales."

"And then I suppose you'll give him the Vulcan death grip just before he mutilates the boat."

"Nope. Then I use the attitude adjuster on him." This was the old ice hammer that Jack kept on board to subdue large fish, including sharks.

"But, Jack, that's what you use after the fish has been weakened in a long fight, and preferably while he's still in the water."

"You just gotta be a little quicker, that's all."

"I'd love to stay and discuss this with you at length, but there are fish out there and they're looking for this fly." C.B. fired out a cast and Jack looked in that direction to see two big ling that had almost swum into the boat during their conversation.

"They're hungry this morning!" C.B. hooked up as fast as the fly hit the water. It was an excellent fish, running hard and stripping line like a marlin.

C.B. wasn't sure what made him look down, but he did, and there it was, sliding out from under the boat for a meal. "Jack!"

"I see him. Don't worry. You just fight your fish."

C.B. was not a stupid man. He knew what he should do. Anyone would. But he was having a very good time with this ling, and it seemed less than fair that he'd have to break off another fine fish. After all, few people had this kind of luck; it was a better than average day for sightings and hookups.

The boat lurched and then came a sound that froze his heart. A terrible crashing, thrashing, and banging, followed by a splash. *Splash?* C.B. looked down from the tower to see a nightmare come true—an able-bodied hammerhead, tail and head twisting and contorting wildly across the deck as only a shark can, trashing the stern of the boat in rage and fury. The shaft of the gaff, which had been hooked somewhere in the shark's underside, was slamming into the gunwales with a commanding thud. It was instantly clear that this animal was ferocious, angry, and capable of doing great harm.

But why was Jack in the water?

"He knocked me outta the boat!"

"Sure he did! Pretty damn convenient, though, wouldn't you say? I mean, you out there and me and Jaws in here?"

"Just shut up and get down there before he completely wrecks my boat, will you."

"You think I'm going down there? No thanks, pal. That's your shark. You wanted him in the boat."

"You big sissy. He's only a fish. Now get down there and beat his brains out so I can get back in the boat. He may have friends out here."

"Well, they're only fish, Jack. But I'll gladly help you in over the bow so you can show me how to subdue the next shark you haul in the boat."

Jack gave C.B. the nastiest look he could under the circumstances and swam to the bow, where C.B. managed to scrape his chest pretty well pulling him in over the bow.

"I can't believe you couldn't take care of one little fish for me, C.B. It's not like I asked you to loan me your wife or something."

"I'm not married, Jack."

"Not this week, anyway."

"So when did this degenerate into character assassination?"

Jack looked at C.B. as if there was something particularly nasty that he wanted to say but was holding back through some shred of self-restraint. With calculated calm he said, "Let me show you how easy this really is, C.B."

Jack slid along the center console and reached around the edge, feeling blindly in the compartment beneath the wheel, and came up holding the formidable ice hammer. One end of the head was blunt and the other had a long, curved, serrated pick.

"How do you plan to get his head, Jack? He's not only got a mean-looking tail, but that gaff handle could take your head off."

"Easy, bud. I'm going up that tower and I'm jumping down on the bastard and putting this pick right through his head. After that I should be able to hold the gaff while he breathes his last."

C.B. looked at Jack with total astonishment. "That's your plan?"

"You got a better one?"

"Yeah, we wait till he dies."

"That could be an hour, and he's already taken a thou off my resale value."

"Would you do me one favor, Jack? Would you not dive onto the gaff handle? Even in your present diminished capacity, you can see what a mess that would make, can't you? I mean, it would be almost impossible for me to explain. You've probably never seen an aortic rupture, but let me tell you, the blood loss is so massive and sudden, we're talking buckets, gushing like a fire hose, probably eighty percent of your whole supply within seconds. You never saw such...and the pain—you don't even want to hear...."

"Okay. All right already. I get the point. So I'll swim around to the stern and come in over the transom. Will that make you happy?"

"I don't think happy is still one of the possibilities, but that sounds better, anyway."

Within moments Jack was raising himself onto the dive platform at the stern. The shark was no less lively than when he had been so rudely brought aboard. Jack carefully leaned over the transom in a position that would give him a clean shot at the shark and turned the hammer to the wicked-looking pick side. The shark wouldn't cooperate and kept lashing his head and body from side to side in strong jerks. Twice Jack started his swing but hesitated. Then, with great resolve, he raised the hammer high and came down on the shark with terrific force, cleanly missing the animal's head and driving the pick deeply into the deck.

Although there was an instant to attempt extraction, it was immediately evident that the hammer was in the deck to stay.

"Damn, damn, *damn!*" Jack howled, and quickly swam back to the bow of the boat. C.B. helped him up again but said nothing. There was a look of irreconcilable rage, an indifference to condolence, that had to be carefully considered here. C.B. felt it was likely that anything uttered by the lips of man would only exasperate an already volatile situation, but he had to try.

"Enough is enough!" Jack roared.

"Jack?" C.B. ventured. But Jack had already edged around the console and was again rummaging blindly in the compartment. C.B. prayed he hadn't already guessed, but he was only too right. From around the corner Jack pulled out a black case and unzipped a battered 12-gauge pump.

"Jack, buddy, think for a minute!" But it was too late. C.B. quickly lost count of the earsplitting reports, hoping against hope that each would be the last. In the deafening silence that finally came, C.B. looked up from where he was cowering on the forward deck to see Jack with the shotgun still at his cheek. Armed and insane, C.B. thought. Only in America. C.B. found himself rethinking his position on gun control.

"Jack?" No answer. Knowing the gun was empty, C.B. stood to

survey the carnage. The shark was definitely slowing down. C.B. could make out at least three good hits, one to the right side of the head, one to the shark's dorsal, and one to the back of the head—the latter being the only genuinely effective shot. All in all it was quite a gruesome scene. But the devastation to the deck and the transom, now there was something to write home about.

"Jack? Jack? You in there, pal?" C.B. could tell that Jack heard him, and better still, he could see that the rage had somehow been satisfied by the act of unloading his shotgun into the stern of his new boat. In fact, it was plain that Jack was now concerned with the boat and not the shark. That was a very good sign.

"It's okay, buddy," C.B. said soothingly. "The shark's dead. And the boat—I'm sure the insurance will cover it. You can just tell them that you were cleaning the gun and it accidentally went off about, what would you say, six times, maybe?"

Without ever moving the gun, which was still fixed in space, trained more or less on the shark, Jack swiveled his glazed eyes toward C.B. "I killed the boat, C.B. I shot my own brand-new boat to pieces."

"That's good, Jack. That's real progress. You've got an excellent command of reality. A lot of people would have trouble coming to grips with the fact that they just destroyed their own brand-spanking-new Whaler with small-arms fire. Of course, there's the bright side; they might make it into an ad. You know—'Even if you empty a 12-gauge into the deck, it keeps right on floating.' Of course, that could be premature, but not to worry, we're in easy swimming distance of the beach."

"C.B., what in hell have I done?" Jack moaned.

"Well, hopefully not too much to the controls, but you definitely altered the hydrodynamic qualities of the hull. But, assuming you somehow missed the bilge pump, I think we have a better than average chance of getting to shore under power. If you'd aim that cannon somewhere else, I'll give it a check."

Jack collapsed on his butt, the vacant look of defeat frozen on his face. C.B. relieved him of the gun and checked the chamber, just for luck, before returning it to the case.

"Look at it this way, Jack. It started out to be just another outstanding fishing trip and you turned it into an epic that we will relive again and again. We'll get a lot of mileage out of this one, pal."

Panic came over Jack's face. "C.B. you have to promise me something. You gotta swear, okay?"

C.B. shrugged. "Sure, Jack, sure. What is it?"

"You've got to promise me you'll never tell anybody about this. Not ever. You gotta give me your word, okay?"

"Sure, Jack. Are you kiddin'? Nobody will ever hear it from these lips. Nobody has to know a thing. My word on it."

Royal Wulff

Yellow Humpy

Goddard Caddis

Love Story of the Trout

meyer the tyer

Cliff Hauptman

Everybody knows the secret.
Everybody knows the score.
I have finally found a place to live
In the presence of the Lord.
                    —*Blind Faith*

I suppose it is the same with most of the so-called service profes-
sions where you spend most of your time dealing with the public.
You meet a lot of what you might call your eccentrics. I do not
know if the guiding business attracts more than its share of weirdos,
but it seems like it might. Maybe it is simply that the guiding business
caters more to the rich, and that it is just rich people who are stranger
than most. That has strong possibilities.

Naturally, you meet a lot of people who are memorable for their
good personalities too, but they do not stick out so much or so long. It
is definitely the ones playing with the shortest decks that hang in your
memory. There was one character that was an eye-opener above all
others. He was a one-of-a-kind oddball that I never could quite figure
out what to make of, though Dog-Nose took to him almost right
away. For my taste, he was more dangerous than any of the others.

There was nothing physical he was likely, or even capable of, doing to you; it was his way of thinking that was so alarming. But I should explain who this fellow was and how we happened to meet him.

It was back when things were really starting to pick up, just about when Dog-Nose's popularity and legendary status was reaching its crest, that we got a letter from one Meyer Fleigel, better known as Meyer the Tyer, who was himself something of a legend in his own time. It was not uncommon, back then, to be getting letters from the rich and famous. During those days, I and Dog-Nose guided presidents, writers, artists, luminaries of one sort or another, and what you call your captains of industry. The worst type, which we were called upon to host fairly regularly, was the so-called outdoor celebrity. This is your fellow who writes a regular column in one of the big outdoor magazines or has a radio or television show on the subject or authors a batch of books or whatever. It is this type who usually thinks he knows more than you do, even though he has never set foot in your particular bailiwick before in his life. He will come up after having been chasing tarpon or bonefish in Florida or South America or someplace and then claim that he knows all about catching Atlantic salmon on account of his vast experience with fish that are as about as similar to salmon as a penguin is to a grouse.

But we put up with that sort for the publicity we got out of them, and some of them turned out to be okay in spite of themselves. A few of this type came into the outdoor field from the side door, as it were. They were the ones who made fishing tackle or guns or clothing-related things for the sportsman, and many of them were only too eager to give away free samples to the likes of the Legend. Those fellows were the easiest to get along with, for although they were well-traveled and experienced in hunting and fishing on account of they could write off all their trips as business expenses, they were also regular people with a business to run and a fair understanding of public relations. And although Dog-Nose had a strict policy of never doing commercial endorsements of products, it could be worth a couple of arms, legs, and other bodily parts to a manufacturer to have Dog-Nose just using his product so other sports could see it. That made those fellows nicer to deal with on account of their wanting to do nothing that would get us ticked off at them. But I think many of them would have been genuinely decent sorts anyway.

But getting back to Meyer the Tyer, you have undoubtedly heard of him if you are any kind of serious fly fisherman. His salmon and trout flies are in the Museum of Fly Fishing down in Vermont along with the likes of Carrie Stevens, the Darbees, Theodore Gordon, and the rest. He was as famous as any of them and had, for fifteen years running, tied the fly that caught the first salmon of the year out of Bangor Pool on the Penobscot, which was traditionally presented to the President of the United States (the salmon, not the fly) as an annual ceremony. That is a remarkable thing in anybody's book, for there are many different anglers responsible for the catching of those fifteen salmon over those years, and every one of them happened to be using one of Meyer's flies. That is how legendary he was.

Actually, about six of those fifteen fish were caught by the same fellow, one Salmo Sam. who used to live down by the Bangor Pool in a hollow log in the first weeks of each season until the spring of '66, when the river flooded more than usual and swept the log out to sea with Sam inside it, dead drunk. A Nova Scotia–bound ferry, headed up the Bay of Fundy, busted up the log about a month later and discovered Sam drowned inside. Apparently the punky wood swelled up when it got wet and held Sam like one of those Chinese finger traps. That put a quick end to his six-year run of presidential salmon, all caught on flies tied by Meyer the Tyer.

So that was the caliber of Meyer's renown by the time he wrote to us about taking him out trout fishing on the upper Kennebec. The request meant not a pile of rabbit raisins to me but that yet another celebrity prima donna was about to saddle us with his adolescent behavior. But Dog-Nose was excited about the visit.

"Junior," he says to me, "you are about to meet a man who is like no one you have ever met before. I've read about this fellow and have looked forward to meeting him with great enthusiasm. I'll be interested to see your reaction to him."

"What makes this guy so hot?" I ask him. "I ain't seen you so excited about guiding anybody since that famous nymphomaniac Italian countess showed up."

"This is different," he says. "This man is not only a master of the fly tier's art; he is a world-class scholar as well. This unassuming immigrant, who ekes out his meager living in the millinery trade and ties exquisite flies for the sporting trade, is also an intellectual who writes wonderfully erudite works of philosophy."

"For the thinking trade?" I ask.

"It's just that we so rarely get to guide someone who has something to say about anything besides himself," says Dog-Nose with a look that could wither an anti-intellectual.

"Okay," I say, "I'll reserve comment until I meet this character."

Holy smokes! Dog-Nose was right. Meyer the Tyer was not like anybody I had ever met before. Here was an old fellow of about seventy-five years, dressed like he stepped out of those brown photographs from the 1920s. He wore black baggy pants and a black suit jacket over a white shirt, and on his head was a wide-brimmed black hat about as flat as a serving tray. For a hatmaker, you would think he could do a little better for himself. Pouring out from under the hat, which I never saw him take off his head once during those ten days he was with us, was a mop of stringy gray curls that hung down the side of his head like filamentous algae. And on his face grew a mustache and beard that would make the inside of a mattress look orderly and well-groomed. That is how he showed up for a fishing trip in the Maine woods. And that is what he wore for the whole ten days, except for the waders that we provided him. On top of all this, he spoke with an accent you could not cut with a well-honed fillet knife.

"Za plesha to mit chew," he says to me, shaking my hand upon arriving, and I honestly did not know he was speaking English at the time. Although I would love to be able to imitate his speech with the written word, as it were, it would take me forever to write it and you even longer to read it. So I will write what he said in regular English except where it makes sense to do otherwise, as when he utters his favorite profanity, "fockink scombeg," which was quite often.

It turns out, as I gathered over his stay with us, that this fellow is a Hasidic Jew (a religious order I am still not too clear on) from somewhere in eastern Europe who came to this country as a child and took up the family trade of hat-making. Back then, ladies' hats were big on feathers, and Meyer always had a supply of scraps and leftovers. Once while wandering around midtown Manhattan, he saw some salmon flies in the window of a fishing shop and was taken by their beauty and by the realization that here was a way to make some money from all the feather scraps he had. So he talked the owner into teaching him some fly-tying techniques and began to supply the shop with flies, never really understanding what they were used for. Finally the shop owner took him along to one of the famous Catskill streams and showed him how the flies were used. Of course, there are no salmon in those waters, but the owner showed him how to fish trout flies and how the salmon flies that Meyer had been tying acted in the water. Understanding that, finally, Meyer began to tie better salmon flies and eventually expanded into trout flies too. Before long, his flies were among the most sought-after in the country.

All that biographical background was told to us by Meyer during his stay. And I think I have gotten most of it right, although listening to him talk was a lot like having a conversation with another angler while you're both fishing noisy, fast water and standing about fifteen yards from each other. You can hear the sounds but you only actually get about every third or fourth word. So when you're finished yelling back and forth, you have got the general gist of the exchange but the details have all been washed downstream.

"So vot de fock shoot I know abot fishink?" he would say, and I would have to not only translate that but then decide whether he really expected me to answer the question. I have never heard a man ask so many so-called rhetorical questions in all my life.

In any case, the above question was intended by Meyer to illustrate the fact that although he was one of the most celebrated fly tiers who ever lived, he did not necessarily have much aptitude at the intended use of his creations, namely fly-fishing.

"I have had such tribulations in my attempts at fly-fishing," says Meyer in his gargly, throat-clearing accent. "So, like the trials of Job, why should it not lead me to a deep and unswerving belief in the Almighty at a time when I was beginning to lose faith?"

"You, a devoutly religious Jew, were losing faith in God?" asks Dog-Nose, getting into the question-asking mode himself, so that whole conversations began to sound like a quiz or a game show but with hardly anybody ever actually coming up with an answer.

"So what's so astonishing?" says Meyer. "Have not even the most pious throughout history suffered moments of doubts? What? One's faith should not waver when one hears of innocents dying, of children starving, of injustices being freely and routinely committed by ruthless and greedy fockink scombegs all over the world?"

(Just so you can fully appreciate the difficulty involved in my having to translate all this for you, that last bit would have sounded something like "rootless and griddy fockink scombegs aluffa de voilt?")

"And you're saying that your faith was restored as a result of fly-fishing?" asks Dog-Nose.

"Sure, why not?" says Meyer. "That and other things."

"What do you mean?" asks Dog-Nose, finally with a question that has some sense to it.

"What I mean," says Meyer as we both lean forward to catch this great crumb of wisdom like two guys trying to take off their pants while sitting down, "is that can one honestly believe it is possible for the world to be so screwed up without Divine intervention? Can purely random events so consistently produce such predictably focked-up results? There *has* to be a God to make such a mess, don't you see it?"

Dog-Nose and me both sit bolt upright like we have been goosed and stare at each other and then back at Meyer. Meyer, meanwhile, pausing for dramatic effect, pours himself a shot of Scotch, picks a blackfly off the surface of the amber liquid, and guides the rim of the glass up inside the tangle of whiskers hanging around his mouth.

"What are you saying?" asks Dog-Nose.

"Nothing new," says Meyer. "Throughout the Bible, God is

characterized as a vengeful, wrathful, all-powerful deity. Since the beginnings of Judaism, have Jews been worshipping God because He is just or because He is merciful or because He is loving or has a good sense of humor or is competent at doing his job? No, for crying out loud. We worship God because He will bust our asses if we do not cower before him and make him feel important. He is one powerful *sunemabitch*."

"Holy shit," I finally blurt out and grab for the bottle, "that's outright blasphemous to talk about God the way you just did."

"You think so?" says Meyer, after I just told him in no uncertain terms that I thought so. "You think I blaspheme when I acknowledge out here in the woods, naked in the full presence of God, that he is powerful and can squash me just as I squash one of these fockink scombeg blackflies that are eating me alive out here?" Meyer's arms are flailing around like a tipped-over helicopter gone berserk. "Why should you not believe that I am worshipping him by saying that? Why not consider that He is most appeased when we rail against Him, thus confirming His awesome power?"

Dog-Nose has a look on his face like he has just undressed the most beautiful woman of his life and she has turned out to be not only a mannequin but a male one at that.

"You think you know God?" continues Meyer, slathering himself with some kind of horribly stinky, jellied bug dope that he has scooped out of an ancient Krank's shaving cream jar. "Let me tell you about Him. You know those big, fat, sadistic Southern sheriffs with the mirror sunglasses and the bellies hanging over their pants? That is what God looks like to me, my friend. And that is what God is like. He is just like those sadistic bestids with an adolescent sense of humor. Am I not right?"

You have got to picture this scene. The three of us are camped next to a river that is running silky-smooth and soundless except for the occasional *plip* of a rising trout. It is late in the afternoon of a warm summer day, and the birds have begun to pick up their evening chorus. Blackflies are hovering around us as they nearly always are up here, and we are all sitting on camp chairs outside the tents in a clearing beneath towering evergreens. Except for the annoyance of the flies, which you can lessen considerably by applying some decent repellent, the place is a paradise on Earth, as peaceful as you could ever hope to find. And here is this hairy blasphemer in his black rumpled suit and white shirt, calling down the wrath of God upon us all. I don't know how Dog-Nose was taking it, but I personally was fully expecting Mount Katahdin, looming in the northeast, to erupt and send fire and brimstone down upon the heads of us lousy sinners and a tidal wave of mud and ash to come pouring down the river to bury us in an eternal tomb of cement.

"You see these gotdem blackflies?" continues Meyer, finally asking a question that I have no trouble determining as purely rhetorical. "Why is it not reasonable to believe that God has sent these to show us that if He were truly angry He could, in all His power, summon up a plague worse than these crappy little flies? To believe that God is that impotent would truly be blasphemous, would it not? But He is not angry; He is happy. He is having a good laugh at our expense by sending these focking pests to bother us. That is His sense of humor."

"That's certainly an interesting theory," says Dog-Nose, stretching his legs and smashing a blackfly on the side of his head.

"Theory, shmeory," says Meyer. "Did you ever notice how every time you settle down to some important task, you have to pee? You have to stop what you are doing just as you finally reach the most crucial point, or at the precise time when it is most disastrous to let yourself be torn from the complexity at hand. Just at that moment when you are most precariously holding the ends of fifty dozen tiny threads, either physically or mentally, that will absolutely tangle themselves into chaos if you let them go, you have to go pee. And is it not also true that if you are waiting for an important phone call, no matter how long you postpone the inevitable, the call will finally come when you are on the toilet? Yet you think this is chance? This is God, my friend. This is his sadistic, adolescent sense of humor. May I show you something?"

Without waiting for an answer, because of course the question had been rhetorical again, Meyer stood up and began to put on a pair of hip boots that were hanging from the branch of a spruce.

"Notice, my friends, how the water is like a beautiful mirror?" he says, lifting his chin toward the river in a gesture of pointing while his hands were busy with the boots. "And do you not see the tops of the trees, how still they are, as if awaiting the word of God? There is not a breath of air moving, not the slightest zephyr, am I correct?"

We nodded our heads in agreement, I and Dog-Nose, as we watched the now-booted Meyer, still wearing the black suit and wide-brimmed hat, begin to rig his fly rod. As carefully as though threading a needle, he worked the leader up through the guides one by one, and although I could not see how it was possible, the line seemed to constantly slip from his steady fingers and fall back through the guides so that he had to start all over again about six times until my insides started to feel like somebody was whitewater-canoeing in them, and I took the rod from Meyer and threaded it myself without any further ado. He thanked me with what you might call your enigmatic smile and took the rod.

"How is the wind?" he asks.

I and Dog-Nose tear our eyes from him and look around. Still nothing stirred. The world was not breathing, just like us.

"What fly do you recommend, my friend?" he says to Dog-Nose. And Dog-Nose says that since there is not much of anything going on out there, something generic like an Adams or Royal Coachman ought to be as good as anything. So Meyer digs a battered fly box out of his gear and takes out a size 16 Adams and holds it up. "Fine," says Dog-Nose, and as Meyer is tying it onto his leader, he looks up at us and gestures with his head and eyes that we should once again check the surroundings. The trees are dead still, the water flows unruffled. Meyer applies some flotant to his Adams and steps to the edge of the water. He glances again at the tops of the trees, and our eyes follow. Even the little flimsy tiptops of the hemlocks, as responsive to wind as feathers, are lying limp and still.

Meyer steps into the river to within a foot of his boot tops and begins false-casting upstream. There is the slurping rise of a large trout within an easy thirty-foot cast. Meyer sends the fly into the final backcast and brings it forward in a perfectly beautiful, tight loop headed right for the spot above the rise, and suddenly all hell breaks loose. A squall line comes down the river out of nowhere, bending the trees into wildly thrashing parodies of fishing rods fighting monster trout. The water in the glassy run turns into heavy rapids from the wind, and Meyer's line, having never reached its target, is stretched straight out behind him in the gale. Then, just as suddenly, it is calm again.

Meyer comes sloshing out of the river, soaking wet. "You see the wonderful sense of humor?" he says. He leans the rod against a tree, where it immediately falls on the ground, and after bending down to pick it up and picking up his overturned chair, which blew over in the wind, he sits down and pours himself another Scotch. I and Dog-Nose are speechless. The rod, for no apparent reason, slides across the rough trunk of the hemlock as though it is smooth as a birch and clatters to the ground again. Meyer just smiles.

Next morning there is a ferocious mayfly hatch on the river and the water is boiling with rising trout. We all of us don chest waders so as to get right out into the best spots and not be limited by the hippers. Again I am moved by a frustrating churning in my gut to help Meyer rig up his rod on account of the way he keeps dropping the line down all the guides after almost getting it to the top. How in hell he ever gets any flies tied is beyond me.

Dog-Nose positions Meyer out in the run and proceeds to instruct him on the best procedure for working the risers in his vicinity. Meyer works out a few yards of line. Out in the middle of the run there is a slight breeze, though nothing to inhibit short casts. I watch as Meyer false-casts and snags his backcast in a tiny twig about twelve feet above the water that I didn't even notice protruding out from one of the bankside trees. It is the only thing within twenty yards that could possibly interrupt the flight of his line, and he found it.

The fly has embedded itself in the twig well enough so that it cannot be shaken out, and Meyer has to snap the leader and put on another fly. He dismisses Dog-Nose's offer to tie the new fly on for him.

"What? You should pay for my misfortune?" Meyer says to Dog-Nose. "No, my friend, you go ahead and cast. Show me that those fish can be caught."

So while Meyer ties on a new fly, Dog-Nose goes to work shooting perfect loops over eager fish and landing four fat brookies before Meyer is ready to try again. It is something beautiful to behold. Even Meyer stops to watch the Legend at work and gives him a hearty round of sincere applause as the last trout is netted.

"Your turn," says Dog-Nose.

"I should be so lucky," says Meyer, and begins to work line out again. Just as he sends his cast forward, the fly hits his rod tip and ties itself there with about six inches of tippet. The rest of the line slaps down in front of him and drifts back with the current, tangling around his legs. "Ah," he says, "God's in heaven; all's right with the world."

Undaunted, he untangles everything and tries again. This time his backcast dips slightly and the fly touches the water behind him, coming up hooked to a small leaf that holds his forward cast up in the breeze, luffing and buzzing, and the whole loop of line collapses in a pile on his head.

"Fockink scombeg," shrieks Meyer, trembling and livid, the line draping down over his hat and shoulders like a prayer shawl, his fist shaking up at the heavens. "Pig-eating drek!"

"Whoa, there," I finally say, rattled by the profanity of this outburst, "it's one thing to call God a son of a bitch like you did last night, but don't you think this is going too far?"

Meyer looks at me like I am five years old and he is my grandfather and my mother just died. His eyes are filled with pity for the lack of understanding that are in mine. And he is deeply moved by my innocence.

"You do not understand what I have been saying, do you, my friend?" he says, lifting the line off his hat and letting it drop to the water, then putting his arm around my shoulder. "It is the passion and manner of my worship that upsets you."

"I ain't never in my life heard of anybody worshipping God by calling Him a scumbag," I say.

"Yet is it not, in fact, truly worship to so fervently acknowledge the power of God?" says Meyer. "What do you think worship is, anyway? You wince at my language. Yet who has ever said that God requires our good wishes or our compliments? No, my friend, God only requires our obedience, our devotion and our confirmation of His omnipotence. And what better way is there of appeasing Him than to show Him how much He has hurt us? He loves it. The more foul and violent my rages become the more passionate is my worship, and He knows it. If He were angry with me, He could truly punish me, but this is merely an expression of His divine sense of humor, and my lot is to provide His amusement."

"But what about loving the Lord thy God with all thy heart and all thy soul and all thy might?" says Dog-Nose in all sincerity.

"What are you, a rabbi?" says Meyer. "So when have I said I do not love the Lord? You think that just because I scream at Him that I do not love Him? He is the Lord, for heaven's sake. I *have* to love Him. He constantly does rotten things to me, but do you think for a minute he does not love me? He is the Lord. He loves every one of us. What you say to Him has nothing to do with anything. It is that you say it with conviction to the depth of your soul that matters."

With this, Dog-Nose, who had been listening with trout rising all around and bumping his legs, says: "There is in all this, Meyer, an appealing logic to your theology. But how do you know that God actually has anything to do with your failure to catch trout? How do you know you're not simply the world's worst fly fisherman simply by a pure lack of aptitude?"

Meyer smiles his patient smile and says, just as he did last night before the wind demonstration, "May I show you something?" And he proceeds to take the fly off the end of his tippet and put it in his pocket. Then he signals us to step back and starts to work out some line. With fifty feet of line out, he is casting the most perfect loops I have ever seen, setting the empty end of his leader down precisely on the centers of the rings caused by the still-rising trout. He hits the center of each ring, just before they begin to elongate and droop downstream, as though he is Robin Hood or William Tell or somebody hitting a bull's-eye with an arrow. Then he lets out some more line and some more until the entire thirty yards is whistling back and forth in the air over his head with the precision and beauty of a whole squadron of jets in formation, and he says, "Do you see that red maple leaf over by the bank? The one wriggling at the end of that little twig?" And me and Dog-Nose look and see that there is no mistaking which leaf he is talking about even though it is a hundred feet away.

Then Meyer, who has been keeping all that line over his head in an unbelievable series of false casts, lets go of that whole length of line and the very tip of his leader snaps against that little red leaf and pops it off the twig like it was shot with a bullet.

All in all, there was no denying that the man put on an exhibition of such casting precision and accuracy that it made Dog-Nose's earlier display look as clumsy and graceless as if it had been performed by a dancing bear.

Dog-Nose looked like he had been struck dumb for good, but broke out of his trance and asked Meyer: "I don't get it. If God were really out to make you the butt, why didn't He screw up that long cast and make you look foolish?"

"If He did that," answered Meyer, "how would He ever make you realize I am right?"

A very strange feeling came over me at that point. It was like the feeling you get the first time you do something new, like start a new school or take on a new task that you are not sure you are any good at but that everybody else is depending on you to do right. There was something in Meyer's logic that made terrible sense. And that is what was so terrible.

We fished all the rest of the day and the rest of the week without Meyer making one single successful cast while a fly was on his line. And we watched him worship God until the veins popped out on his neck and forehead, and his hands bled from punching them into the rocky banks, and his throat was raw from raging.

"The man is either a lunatic or a prophet," says Dog-Nose after Meyer's departure.

"What, he can't be both?" I say.

Love Story of the Trout

what it was

Dave Hughes

I'd like to tell you what I think, though you'll hardly care any-more. But first I'll tell you who I am—you might not care about that, either.

I'm an old one-armed man who once, just for a minute, thought he'd got what life meant and could have put it down in a burst of a few words, if pen and paper could have been gotten to quick enough. But they weren't around where I was then, out in the woods, so I shouted it out instead into the forest above the stream, thinking that would make me remember it. But when I gold hold of pen and paper later and tried to force it down, the words that were there when I had it had gone, and the ones left were only the ones I'd always had. They weren't very good ones then and still aren't.

Which is why I never became a writer, though I wanted to once but don't now.

Here's how it happened, if it happened.

I was young that summer, and everybody thought I'd go off to col-lege, but I didn't because anyone could see the war was coming and we'd be in it and there was no use learning a head full of stuff just to get it shot off as easily as somebody who didn't have anything in there. So I went all the way to the Northwest to work in the woods instead, up in Washington. I'd go to school if I ever got back. No use taking a chance on wasting it.

I got a job as a cedar-bolt cutter. "Way up in the woods," the boss told me was where I would work when he hired me, and that sounded great, like what I wanted to do, be alone way out there, up high.

But where he sent me, the mule with the first few things the company issued me plodding along behind the guy taking me out, he chewing tobacco and turning to squirt it on his mule's shoes and not talking to me, like a new guy in the woods wasn't somebody you wasted the few words you had on, was way down in a canyon, deep in some stream bottom. No sunlight got in there much.

Hardly ever.

It was all cut off by the canyon, and then by those trees that were packed so tight they made a canyon inside the canyon, and I was small at the bottom of it all where no sunlight got.

"Peckerpoles!" the guy said, and tossed my stuff on the ground—*thump!* He squirted tobacco on my boots. Then he whacked his mule on the ass and said, "Let's get outta this hole, Morrie!" Which was more than he'd spoke to me.

When they'd plodded off, him spitting tobacco and his mule letting off a series of farts as they went uphill, there was only the sound of the stream bouncing off its rocks and laughing at me. I walked over and pissed in it.

Then I buttoned up my pants and went to work, flailing a tiny clearing in those jammed peckerpoles for my camp.

B olt cutting was hard work, but there was nothing wrong with that. But there was something wrong with something.

For a month I couldn't figure it out. It rained some but that didn't bother me. I built a lean-to out of the canvas tarp the silent mule guy had thrown to the ground. I cut a cedar tree down into lengths and split a slab for a bench that I didn't sit on much because when I was in camp I prowled instead of resting. Something haunted me.

I dipped water from the stream in a black coffeepot, but always upstream from where I'd pissed, and I never did that again. The stream stepped right down through the woods there, like it was on a ladder of stones, stopped in front of my camp in a deep pool, then bounced through a riffle and stepped off again toward the ocean, not far away to the west.

The mule guy came back with supplies once a week but didn't talk much. The stream got to be my company, its laughing voice.

I spent my days cutting cedar bolts, fighting through that thick Washington underbrush with my crosscut, ax, and wedges, looking for cedars three and four feet through. I whacked them down, cut them into lengths, split the lengths into bolts that in winter would be floated out on high water and split into shingles at the mill.

The work was too dangerous to do alone, but the Depression was still on and men came cheap, and if they got hurt they either died or went away. I found out later what happened to the guy the boss sent into the canyon before me. But right then I was at the age when there was no chance I would get hurt. So I didn't mind working alone. And I didn't get hurt until later, either, in the war.

But something was wrong down there, then.

One Sunday I figured it all out in an instant. It hit me so that I slapped my leg. I was standing in the stream right in front of my camp, not sitting and resting but so tired I wished I could, when I saw the water well up in the shallow riffle below the pool. Something swam through there, out of the riffle up into the pool. It was a muskrat or something. I waited for it to come up for air but it didn't.

I tried to look down into the pool to see whatever it was, down where the water was deep, but not so deep I shouldn't have been able to see the bottom. The water was clear in the riffle but as black as my coffeepot in the pool, and I couldn't see into it. I looked up at the sky and the sun was shining somewhere up there, an hour or so on its way into afternoon. But the crowns of all those trees were so thick they blocked off the sun.

The pool reflected trees and darkness, not sky and light. That was why it was black. I looked back into camp. It was shady, and shade would have been good, but shade's only good if you've got sunlight to get out of. That was it.

Let's get some light into this goddamn canyon! I thought to myself; I almost said it out loud. That's when I slapped my leg.

I forgot about whatever it was that swam into the pool and spent my only day off all week hammering peckerpoles to the ground. I spent the next day doing it too, when I should have been cutting cedar. But once I'd figured it out I couldn't stop till light got onto that lean-to, and I had to cut a big patch because those skinny trees were so tall I had to cut them way back before any sunlight hit it.

When I got done it felt good, and I sat relaxed on the bench in front of my lean-to in the sun in the new clearing and surveyed the damage I'd done. I'd been closed in by blackness for weeks without knowing it, so it was worth it. Hell, I was from Iowa.

When the mule fellow brought my week's supplies he struck up an alarming amount of conversation. He aimed at the fire and spit tobacco onto my coffeepot, looked around at my new clearing, and said, "What you been wasting your damned time doin'?"

"Lettin' light in," I told him.

"Light?" he said. "What the hell you want light in here for?" He squirted at my boots but I leaped and he missed.

I cut another cedar bench and set it out next to the pool, where the inn from my new clearing struck too. When I looked into the water again I got surprised. A streak of light sliced right down through the water like a sunbeam cuts across a darkened room full of dust floats, lighting everything in its path and everything left dark as night in the water surrounding it, all the way to the bottom of the pool.

A big boulder was lit on the bottom, and the current sort of waved around it. Most of the water was still black around the boulder, outside that sunbeam, and I couldn't see anything there. But everywhere I could see, suspended in the ray of light around that rock, I saw big fish hanging, their bodies gray and long and thick-shaped, their tails wavy like the current.

Suckers! I thought. *Out here in the West just like back home they got sucker runs.* I didn't ever go fishing when I lived in Iowa, but a run of big suckers came up out of a lake every summer into the little creek. Me and my friends when we were kids stoned them, splashing around barefoot on slippery rocks and screaming and killing as many as we could.

I didn't think much more about these—who the hell thinks about suckers when you get grown up? But they were what I watched when I sat on my bench by the stream in the sun because they were what moved and we always watch what moves.

Once in a while one sucker would lift off the bottom and swirl around the pool, swimming fast and strong and I thought unsuckerlike, setting itself back down where it started, the others shifting nervously when it lit among them again. Sometimes a new fish would swim up out of the riffle, humping up the water like that first one had so now I knew what it had been, not a muskrat but a sucker. It would glide in, they would all shift around, then settle again with the new one in with them.

I worked hard all that week, the work going easier and me getting stronger and more confident in it because when I was in camp, I rested instead of prowling. I knocked cedars down and whacked them into bolts as fast as lightning strikes a tree and splits it and leaves smoke fuming from the split. I saw that happen once back in Iowa. It was good work and I piled it up.

When Sunday got there and the muleteer brought my supplies, I was sitting on the bench by the stream, watching the suckers. They were struck by the shaft of sun down on the bottom of the pool. There must have been almost twenty of them.

"Look at this," I said, and he tied off his mule and walked over to look.

"Suckers," I said.

He spat. "You're a sucker," he said.

"What do you mean?"

"Them're salmon."

"The hell you say!" I said. I'd heard of salmon before, but had never seen any. They came in cans, was what I knew about salmon.

"The hell they're not," he said. He turned away and threw my stuff to the ground.

When he started to head out I called after him, "Bring me something to catch one with." I meant a net, like I'd seen people throw for fish in Iowa.

"I'll see," he said and left.

What he brought was all wrong. There was no way to cast the sonofabitch. It was a skinny pole made of bamboo, a reel there was no way to let loose the click on, so the line would fly out, and the line was so thick it would scare a fish half an hour before the bait got there anyway. There was some gut at the end, and it was a good thing, because even a sucker wouldn't bite anything tied to that fat line.

But the bait was just a bunch of feathers wrapped on hooks anyway, stuck in a tin box. They weren't heavy enough to cast and there weren't any sinkers in the box. They smelled like mothballs and I doubted any fish would bite on feathers that smelled like that. But then I didn't know anything about salmon.

All this gear had got left in a bunkhouse corner by the guy who had my job before me, and got killed by a cedar tree, which I didn't know then but found out later when I came out because the boss said he was surprised the same thing hadn't happened to me. In the war I heard the boss made officer but got shot.

I tied one of the hooks with red feathers to the gut and tried to cast it into the pool. But it didn't weigh anything so it wouldn't go anywhere no matter how hard I flung it.

That whippy pole really pissed me off.

I tried all week, taking time off after work when I should have been sitting on the bench, resting, standing by the stream instead, trying to get that flimsy pole to toss the bait out into the pool. Once I tied a rock in the gut above the bait and tried to cast that way, but the pole felt like it was going to crack, the reel squawked like a rooster that got goosed, and the rock flew out of the knot. Fish squirted all over the pool when it splashed.

I took the reel apart to see if it had something stuck in it, or had any secret buttons that would let the spool spin free like it should. But there wasn't anything special about it except that it was made in England and it didn't work.

After a week of trying I got frustrated one day and whipped that bastard pole back and forth in the air as fast as I could. The bait got out there over the pool, which was a surprise to me, but the line cracked like a whip and snapped it right off its knot.

I watched it land in the water and drift, and a salmon tilted without moving any part of itself and rose from the bottom and took it. The bolt it made at the bait made me take a step back from the pool.

I tried whipping the pole back and forth with another bait and the same thing happened; it snapped off the gut and flew to the pool and salmon raced each other to get to it first.

I was so frustrated I put the damn pole away for a few days and didn't even look at it. I asked the mule guy when he came if he knew how to cast it, but he only knew that the guy that had owned it was made in England like the reel and was fine-tuned but not much good at what he did either.

I left it sit for another week while I puzzled about ways to use it. But nothing ever came to me, so I picked it up one Sunday again, tied on another feather bait, and whipped it like a sonofabitch back and forth through the air and smacked it onto the water before it could snap itself off the gut.

All the salmon squirted around the pool again.

That really pissed me off. There I finally got the bait out to them, and all it did was scare the hell out of them.

But I worked with that peckerhead fishing pole some more that day, and slowed down to where I could fling the line around and get the bait out there without snapping it off. I was glad nobody was around to see me do it, though, casting like that, the line flying back and forth through the air all wrong, first in front of me and then in back of me, when I'd seen catfishermen in Iowa make casts that shot the line far through the air in rainbow arcs, without the line ever going behind them like that at all.

It got to be September before me and that pole got along without quarrelling. Sometimes the bait would come down and catch the line in the air on its way out in front of me, and it would fall to the water all in a tangle. Other times everything would work and the bait would shoot out over the pool perfect, but my foot would be over the line and the bait would recoil back all the way to the bank. Lots of times the bait would hit me in the back and ricochet off or stick. One shirt wore one until I went out of the woods. I almost wore one myself, but I closed my eyes and jerked like hell and that's how it hurt when it came out, with a piece of me still stuck to it.

The way that pole and reel worked still pissed me off, but lots of times the bait would fly out and land on the water. I always practiced when the sun struck the pool because that's when I could look down into it and see what the salmon did when the bait swam over them. But when it landed they always did the same thing: swirled in a panic, then got as far away from it as they could in the pool, like they were in a cage and a bear had got in on one side and they crouched together on the other side, wondering which one the bear would get.

It didn't get any of them for a long time.

Then one day I woke up at dawn and it was raining—not hard, but I didn't want to go out in the wet brush that day. I'd been doing good work and knew that nobody was about to fire me, though it would have been all right with me if they did because some folks thought the war was getting closer, which was what the mule guy grunted when he brought my supplies—we wouldn't be there much longer doing that, he said some folks were saying, except it didn't take him so many words to say it.

I sat up in the sack scratching myself for a while that morning;

then I noticed the pole standing against the side of the lean-to. I got dressed and picked it up and went down to the pool with it.

The water looked different than when the sun struck down through it. I couldn't see into it at all. The surface was gray and roughed up by the drizzle, and it looked like it would be a waste of time to cast. I almost didn't. But I knew the salmon were down there and I didn't have anything else to do anyway except go out in the rain and cut more cedars, so I whipped the line back and forth until it was out and let the bait drop onto the pool, and a boil built up around it the instant it hit. I jerked it out of there and it flew over my shoulder.

After I'd got the line and bait all disentangled and caught some of my breath back, I cast it out again and the same thing happened. Only this time a salmon smashed the bait and the gut broke halfway back to the line.

My hands trembled when I tied the new bait on. I kept telling myself there was nothing to be afraid of, and I knew I wasn't afraid, but my hands shook. I didn't know what the hell I was feeling but it was the same feeling I'd had when a girl at school had hoisted...well, you wouldn't be interested in that.

My hands kept shaking but I got a new bait tied to that gut that was almost the size of the thick line itself, back where it broke.

I whipped the pole back and forth again and set the bait onto the water. The water welled up and the pole bucked down and tried to rip itself out of my hands, all at the same time. I held on and the salmon shot right up into the rain, all silver and slashing in front of me, and I can still see it hanging there in the rain if I close my eyes as an old one-armed man today.

It tore off through the riffle and I ran after it down the ladder of slippery stones, falling all over and catching myself with one hand and holding that whippy pole up in the air with the other hand so it wouldn't break.

That fish went down until it got into another pool like the one at camp, then it jumped into the air again, this time flapping back and forth looking like it was trying to fly and shake the bait out of its jaw all at the same time.

It didn't.

The salmon fell back and stayed in the pool, and I kept trying to draw it to shore but it kept surging out every time I led it over shallow water. But I could see it was getting tired; even though I never caught a fish on a pole before, I could tell it was getting near wore out because it didn't pull as hard, and because I knew how I'd get if somebody dragged me around the woods by a rope all that time and I was still trying to go where I couldn't.

Finally the fish wobbled on its side and I thought that was the time, so I backed up quick into the woods and the fish came up onto the rocks, flapping like it had in the air when it tried to shake the hook.

But this time it did.

I ran down onto the rocks, fell on my knees, grabbed the salmon, and lifted it against my chest with both arms wrapped around it. That's when I shouted into the woods above the stream, trying to remember it, "This is what it is!" But that's not what I said at all on my knees there, holding that salmon, but it's the best I could do once I quit the woods and got a piece of paper to write it to my friends back in Iowa.

It didn't mean anything to them. I must have wrote it wrong.

And so I got my arm shot off instead of my head. The right one, which was the wrong one, since I was right-handed then, though I'm not now, as you can understand.

I got sent back to the hospital in San Francisco. Another guy who had been in there for a long time was from back East, and he had a funny accent. He had liked to fish before he got hit, and was in a way thinking he would never be able to fish again, which I was too. But I had only fished the one time and didn't worry about it so much like he did.

He told me fishing stories all the time, the stories coming out of this body all wrapped up in bandages so I got the image of a white mummy walking along the stream banks whipping a pole back and forth and catching small trout, because as it turns out he was what he called a *fly fisherman*. When I got tired of listening to his stories I told him mine to fend off his, and lied to make the salmon bigger than it was to make his look smaller than what they were.

He told me that I had been fly-fishing and that I had done it right, though, as he said it, "Probably only approximately right."

He had a funny way of talking, and he made it sound like it was important to talk about fly-fishing right. For instance, he wouldn't let me call that bamboo peckerpole a pole, but kept saying it was a *rod*, and you never knew a word that short has so many syllables and took so long to say.

I got out of the hospital and signed up for college there in San Francisco because I figured it was okay to go ahead and stuff some things into my head that I might have use for, especially since with only one arm left—and that the wrong one—a guy better have some useful gear somewhere else. In college they told me I ought to be someplace else, if only I had more arms.

The Eastern fellow got better slowly and finally got out too. When he did, the first thing he wanted to do was go to this place he'd heard about called the Golden Gate Casting Club, which had been built by the CCC just before the war and was still new. We took a bus out there and the place was beautiful, big cement ponds surrounded by lawns and laurel and trees so that it was hidden in the middle of a park but open to the sun. Nobody was using it much then, because everybody was busy with what was still going on in the world that didn't concern me and my friend anymore.

Just one old fellow was there, about the age that I am now, so I didn't pay any attention to what he said, like people don't pay any attention to what I say now. He had a fly rod and a bait rod and was glad to share them with us. He wanted to talk but we wanted to cast.

I naturally got fascinated by the casting rod because just looking at the fly rod reminded me of the one I used in the woods, and it made my stump go into involuntary movements from memories that made it hurt. But my friend picked up the fly rod and found out that he could cast again, and got pretty excited by that fact. It seemed more important to him than when the doctors told him he's be able to use another part of his anatomy again, and the nurses were anxious to prove to him that the doctors were right. I laughed at him, he was so eager.

When we got done casting the old fellow asked us how the war was going, but we didn't want to tell war stories. So to keep from that my friend told him stories about his little trout from back East, and then I told him my story about the big salmon. The old man thought about it a while when I was done.

Then he said, "That wasn't a salmon. That was a summer steelhead you caught."

It didn't mean anything to me. I'd thought they were suckers and they weren't, so it didn't matter now that they got turned from salmon into steelhead. It wasn't going to change what had happened any, and what mattered to me was what had happened and where it happened, not what it had happened to. I didn't even know what a steelhead was.

"You say there were twenty of them in the pool where you camped?" That old man got awfully interested in those salmon once he'd promoted them to steelhead.

"There were thirty or forty of them," I told him.

"What was the name of that river?" he wanted to know.

"Just some river up in Washington," I said, which was all I knew; I'd never taken time to find out its name.

the championship of fly fishing

Randy Oldebuck

Author's note: I have appropriated the name Springhole Sippers from the trout of a famous pool on the New York Battenkill; they take insects with a delicate sip in the quiet backwaters. The Springhole was also the name of a tackle shop, on the banks of the pool, which was operated by Ralph DeMille, since deceased. It was more of an arcane social club than a business. Many of the characters in the following yarn are or were real people: Dave Male, Colby Hansen, Dud Soper, and some angling notables of past and present that you will probably recognize. None of the characterizations, attributes, or anecdotes here related are for real, nor are they meant to imply traits on the part of the persons named. This story is strictly satirical and euphemistic, and defamation is neither implied nor intended. It is offered purely for your entertainment, and it is hoped that all will appreciate the humor, and take no offense.

Dudley Soper was the captain and anchorman of the Springhole Sippers fly-fishing team, an honor he richly deserved. The other two members were Colby Hansen and David Male. Both cut their teeth on the inscrutable brown trout of the humbling Battenkill and were now anglers of international caliber. The Sippers had gone undefeated in the Battenkill League. They had then swept to a convincing victory in the New York State Championship and scored a nail-biting victory over their perennial nemeses, the Letort Hoppers, whose roster included such luminaries as Vince Marinaro, Charley Fox, and Ed Koch.

Now they were in New Zealand, competing in the World Championship. Miraculously, they had bested several of the greatest teams of North America. The previous evening they had defeated Michigan's highly touted Ausable Hackle Hustlers by a comfortable margin. Tonight, in the semifinals, they would compete against the formidable Labrador Retrievers, led by the redoubtable Joan Wulff. The winner would be matched in the finals against the renowned Test Ticklers of Great Britain, who had already won their penultimate match against an upstart team from Serbia, whose name translated to something approximately like the Happy Huchen Hookers.

"It won't be easy," observed Dud Soper as he surveyed the deceptive crosscurrents of the Matara River, the site of the championship. The evening was rather windy, which definitely favored the Labrador Retrievers. The Sippers' forte was precision, not distance. To make matters worse, their brilliant coach and spiritual leader, Ralph DeMille, was not feeling up to par. This was due to the unavailability of his beloved Fenswill Brown Label beer. The local beers, skillfully brewed from the purest waters and finest ingredients, didn't agree with the coach; his system was attuned to the funky taste and almost-chewy texture of Fenswill. It had seen him through many a tense match. Now only one six-pack remained of the single case customs had allowed to be imported. Coach DeMille had elected to save this for the finals, should the Sippers get that far.

The Labrador Retrievers arrived as a group, resplendent in their spawning-Arctic-char-colored jackets. The previous day they had narrowly defeated the Chesapeake Kreh-Fishers, despite a sensational performance by the team's namesake, Lefty Kreh.

Referee Harry Darbee and Field Judge Nick Lyons escorted the two teams on the traditional tour of the course. Each competitor was given a schematic describing the exact deployment of the fish he or she would be presenting to, plus information relative to rules and scoring. No charts of the deflections and nuances of the currents were provided; each angler would have to resort to his or her expertise in that regard.

Coach DeMille bravely displayed a cheery exterior, despite the dour condition of his digestive system, as he checked out his team in the warm-ups. "A little tighter loop on that backcast, Dave," he counseled. "Colby, you'd better check your leader; I think it's a bit too long for this wind. Way to go, Dud; you've got 'em shaking in their waders already." The coach watched in awe as his unorthodox and formidable anchorman dropped a size 18 Parachute precisely on the edge of a seam eighty feet distant.

Referee Darbee struck the gong, signaling the end of the warm-ups. Field Judge Lyons brought the team captains together and delivered the opening instructions.

"Good evening, anglers. This match will be conducted in accordance with the rules of ISFA, the International Salmonid Flyfishing Association. While I'm sure you are all familiar with them, I will reiterate, as mandated.

"Number one: Each competitor will be allowed to use three fly-fishing outfits at will. These must be presented to the tournament officials for inspection and registration. I believe you have all complied. No rod may be longer than ten feet or have an extension or fighting butt in excess of three inches. No fly line may be heavier than a weight nine. Reels must meet the specifications set forth in Section II of the regulations handbook. One hundred and fifty yards of backing is the maximum allowed.

"Number two: Scoring will be in accordance with the regular point-award system and there will be no bonus points for trick casts.

The predominant factor in scoring will be response; that is, the measurable effect a presentation has on a given fish, up to and including hooking, playing, and capture. Points are awarded for size and type of fish, hookups, and time played. Bonus points may be awarded for tactics that increase difficulty—such as size of fly, test of tippet, and distance from quarry—and also for landing a fish within the allotted time limit. Additional bonus points may be awarded based on combination factors; for example, difficulty imposed by the combination of outfit, leader, and fly used on a particular fish.

"Number three: Each competitor will select four stations from the twelve shown on the map. Five minutes per station is the maximum allowed for presentation. A competitor may make as many presentations as he or she wishes during the five minutes. Bonus points are awarded for raising and hooking fish with the fewest casts, and point deductions are assessed for 'alarming' or 'spooking' casts, as prescribed in Section III.

"Number four. When a fish is hooked, any unused portion of the five-minute period is supplemented by five more minutes for playing and landing, an additional benefit earned by early hooking. The time period is also extended by one minute per pound of fish weight in excess of five pounds. Early landing earns bonus points, as determined by the standard formula: five points for each fifty seconds of unexpired time. A landed fish automatically earns twenty points. Fish still on but not landed during the time allotment invoke the 'ten-point-must' rule, which automatically awards ten points for not losing the fish. A lesser number of points are awarded for lost fish, based on how long the fish was on.

"Number five: Larger fish being more difficult to lure, play, and land, a formula that awards points for size and characteristics of species is applied. Each station holds fish of different size and species, all salmonids. Each competitor may select any fish, and may angle for it with any legal outfit and fly. For example, suppose a competitor were to select the fifteen-pound Atlantic salmon at station eight, present to it with a size 10 wet fly, 2X tippet, and weight-six outfit, and bring it to net in nine minutes. After computing all basic points and points awarded for landing time and so forth, the size/species formula is applied. The result is added to the other points, and a total score for the station is thus obtained. All computations are done by the computer in our data-processing trailer, and are rechecked twice at the end of the match.

"Very well, competitors. Are there any questions? I see there are none. Fly fishers, man your rods—oops, I'm sorry, Joan. A traditional expression, no offense intended. Good luck to all."

At this point, the reader must be wondering how all the variables of water, fish's mood, and so forth can be balanced in order to validate the scoring system and ensure a fair match. It is done, to use a shopworn expression, through high-tech. Each fish has a microchip and electronic transceiver implanted in its brain. The reactions of the fish are controlled by the chip, which assures uniformity of response. Thus the fish never makes an inappropriate decision, such as ignoring a good presentation or responding to a poor one. As the competitor works the fish, the communications link transmits all data to the computer, where it is stored and then factored for scoring.

Back to the scene of the action: The Labrador Retrievers' leadoff man, Dave Brandt, selected a large Minipi-strain brook trout that was lying in a fairly easy spot, the strategy being to get some points on the board immediately. This he did with dispatch, raising the fish with his first cast, hooking it on his second, and landing it in a mere four minutes, twenty-seven seconds. The score, while good, was not outstanding because of the large fly and heavy tippet and the low difficulty rating of the brook trout. Nevertheless, it drew appreciative applause from the crowd.

The next angler was Colby Hansen of the Sippers. He chose a large brown trout in a rather difficult lie and opted for a size 12 nymph, a light rod, and fine tippet. At first it seemed an ill-advised gamble, for the trout completely ignored the first six casts. Colby came through with a superlative presentation, casting the nymph well upstream of the fish with a right-hand curve cast and a bit of slack. The fly came right down the feeding lane, drifting as though detached, and at just the right depth. The great trout undulated in the current and turned toward the fly as it neared. At precisely the proper moment, Colby raised the rod tip, swimming the nymph enticingly. His team members held their breath. The white mouth opened, the fly was sucked in, and the battle was joined. Seven minutes later the trout was thrashing in Colby's net, to the ringing cheers of the crowd. It scored almost twice what Brandt's brookie had registered, and the Springhole Sippers were off and running.

The match developed into an exciting one, as all competitors showed great form. Joan Wulff made up most of the deficit with a light-tackle conquest of a sizable rainbow, and Gardner Grant rang up several excellent scores on Atlantic salmon. In the end, however, the consistent brilliance of the Sippers swung the balance in their favor. Dud Soper sealed the victory with an unbelievable effort on his fourth beat, hooking the largest brown trout in the river on a tiny Trico and a seventy-foot cast. As the fish came to net, the crowd went wild and literally erupted from the stands. The Sippers had to be given a police escort back to their hotel.

Coach DeMille decided to sequester the team for security, and ordered dinner for all to be served in his suite. It had been a tough day for the coach, what with a close match and no Fenswill. New Zealand beer was too pristine for his system, and his stomach had become so queasy he hardly touched his meal. The temptation to break into his small stash of Fenswill was terribly strong, but the coach resisted. He knew the entire six-pack would be sorely needed the following day, when the Sippers would meet the Test Ticklers for the coveted crown.

While the Sippers spent a relaxed evening tying flies and talking in Ralph DeMille's suite, their usually unflappable opponents conferred nervously in their quarters nearby. They were watching a videotape of the match, and were duly impressed.

"Did you see that fellow Soper on that last fish?" said Jack Martin, the team captain. "I wouldn't 'ave wagered a bloody shilling on 'is chances of 'ooking the bugger, let alone landing it!"

"That chap Male's no slouch, either," commented Lord Blivet, the world-famous dry-fly specialist. "Taking that brute of a salmon on four-pound test; some feat, that!"

"That coach—what's 'is name, DeMille—'e makes a big difference. Terrific strategist and 'ighly inspirational. And I've 'eard 'e's not up to snuff, either. If 'e turns up 'ealthy tomorrow, it could be their day." So spoke Major Benbow, the third member of the Ticklers.

As the Brits fidgeted in their hotel, Coach Dermot Wilson paced the streets, trying to quell his nervousness. The score rung up that day by the Sippers *was* impressive, and it had been achieved with such apparent ease that he was certain they were capable of still greater accomplishments. His anglers, though tested veterans all, weren't getting any younger. Fatigued by a run of difficult matches in the fish-offs, the defending champions were showing signs of stress. Coach Wilson shuddered as he thought of the possibility of the cherished Halford Cup residing in the United States.

In yet another part of town, a sinister meeting was taking place. Sir Thomas Truffles, who had inherited an earl's title but had fallen on hard times financially, had slipped into New Zealand on a forged passport. He did not want it known that he was in the country, for his reputation as a high-stakes gambler would certainly alarm the officials in charge of the championships. A run of luck had put him many thousands of pounds ahead, and he had bet the entire bankroll on the Test Ticklers in the finals. He had watched the match that day, and had been walking about with a knot in his stomach ever since. His wager, he realized, was in dire jeopardy. If he won, he could return to England with enough money to live as an earl should, at least for a time. If he lost, he'd have to work his way home on a freighter. It was too much of a risk. Something had to be done.

The gambler had noticed one of the bellhops in his hotel; a shifty-eyed youth who looked the type to do anything for the right price. Truffles called the bell captain and had the man sent to his room.

"You rang, milord?"

"Yes—for you personally. I may require some rather—ah,

specialized services, and perhaps you can help me. But first, a few questions, if you don't mind."

The wily Truffles led the bellhop through an interrogation devised to reveal the youth's true character. Soon he had established that the young man was seriously short of money and hated his job with a passion.

"Then why stay with it?" asked Truffles.

"Only bloody job I can get," responded the bellhop sullenly.

"Why?"

"Well, I've 'ad a little problem. I used to be a jockey. Seems how a bunch of owners wanted certain 'orses to win at certain times, if you get what I mean. Got me and a few of the other boys involved. The owners got off scot-free; we got two years apiece. Served every damn day of it, I did. Rotten deal, that."

"Would you be interested in picking up a quick three hundred dollars?" inquired Truffles, in a guileless voice.

"Depends. What must I do for it?"

"Very little, actually. I want you to steal six cans of beer."

"That's all?"

"Well, not quite. It's rather special beer. It's locked up in this American bloke's 'otel room."

"Hotel! That's too risky. I'm known in every hotel in town. Which one?"

"The Astoria."

"Um. I got a pal workin' there. I'll need 'im for an accomplice. Cost you another couple of 'undred dollars; got to pay 'im, you know."

The gambler knew a rip-off when he saw one, but the stakes were too high to quibble. He sighed.

"Very well, m'boy, five 'undred it is. But you've got to move fast."

And so the unholy bargain was struck. Truffles hurriedly briefed him on the situation while the bellhop listened intently.

"I can't tell you exactly what room this DeMille chap is in," cautioned Truffles.

"Doesn't matter. That's the easy part."

"And 'ow do you plan to pinch the beer? It's kept in a refrigerator in the very room where 'e sleeps, I'm told."

"Leave that to me," said the bellhop, slyly. "Just gimme the money, and it'll be done."

" 'Alf now and 'alf when you deliver," replied Truffles, handing over $250 in crisp, new bills.

The bellhop scowled, but he took the money and set off to do the evil deed.

Stealing the six-pack of Fenswill was no great feat. The bellhop simply bribed his pal, who was a desk clerk at the Astoria, to get Coach DeMille down to the lobby on a fabricated excuse. The clerk also provided a room number and a master key. The bellhop took the elevator up, let himself in, grabbed the six-pack from the refrigerator, and left via the fire escape, which deposited him in an alley. Fifteen minutes later, he handed the beer over to Truffles and collected the balance of the money.

"And what will you be doin' with that five-'undred-dollar six-pack?" asked the bellhop.

"I'll be throwing it away," replied Truffles. "I don't drink such sheep-dip."

"I'd be pleased to dispose of it for ye, nice and foolproof," said the youth. "And that will be the end of it. For just another fifty."

Truffles sighed with resignation, seeing that he had met a true kindred spirit. He handed over the bag and a $50 bill, and the bellhop, grinning widely, departed.

The theft was discovered the following morning. Coach DeMille was making his final preparations for the title match, which included putting the indispensable Fenswill into an ice chest. Incredulous, he stood in front of the refrigerator for a long moment. Then the stark reality of the situation shocked him into action. He picked up the phone and dialed Captain Soper's room, asking him to come on the double. Quickly, he related the catastrophe to Dud.

"And what do I do now?" he pondered. "I can probably fake my way through the match, but when the lads see me without that brown can in my hand, they'll know. It'll surely dampen their morale. I figure we have to perform about ten percent better than we've ever done if we are to be a match for the Test Ticklers. Without me at my best, that could be a real problem."

"Not to worry, coach," consoled Dud. "You've carried us enough times. We owe you this one." Dud tried to exude optimism, but his heart wasn't in it, and the coach could feel it.

"Do you suspect foul play on the part of the Brits?" asked Dud.

"Out of the question," replied DeMille. "Crusty they may be, but honest to a fault, and the finest sportsmen you'll ever meet. No. I suspect a third party. A gambler, perhaps; I hear there's been some awfully heavy betting going on."

"Money!" snorted the captain. "Always the problem. Well, we're wasting precious time. Let's call the police and see what they can do."

"Hardly enough time for them to do anything," said the coach. "It's almost ten now, and the match starts at two. But let's give it a shot." He dialed the hotel operator and asked to be connected to the police.

In true New Zealand tradition, two detectives arrived so quickly that it seemed as though Ralph still had his hand on the telephone. The Americans felt rather foolish trying to impart a sense of urgency to the theft of six cans of beer, and were pleasantly surprised by the positive reaction of the policemen, who seemed to understand perfectly. Both of them, it seemed, were avid fly fishers and were extremely interested in the outcome of the championship. The thought of it being affected by skullduggery on their own turf appalled them. Waiting only long enough to get the details, they promptly phoned in a report to the precinct. A bulletin was radioed to all cars, describing the pilfered six-pack and urging vigilance.

"It had to be an inside job," said one of the officers. "Tell me, Coach DeMille: Did anything the least bit unusual happen last night? Did you leave your room for any reason?"

"No...wait a minute, yes! I got a call from the front desk about some problem with money, a technicality about signing for meals in the dining room. I went down to the lobby and got it straightened out with the desk clerk. But it couldn't have taken more than fifteen minutes, at the outside."

"That's got to be it!" said the second detective. "You were lured from the room, and an accomplice let himself in and pinched the brew. We'll get on it immediately."

"Thanks so much," said Dud, "but we won't be of much help. We're due at the river for warm-ups at noon and, Fenswill or no Fenswill, the match must go on."

"Of course—and the best of luck to you, Yank. Go along now and leave the rest to us."

After the detectives had left, Dud said, "Coach, are you sure you've tried all the local beers? Something down here must be close to Brown Label."

"Not a chance," Ralph replied. "It's the water; no pollution or sedimentation or anything. These New Zealand beers are just too damn good! Fenswill gets its water out of the mouth of the Charles River in Boston, you know. Gives it a certain pungency. Have you ever smelled your socks after taking off your waders on a really hot day? That's Fenswill! I guess it's a matter of what one is used to. Just the thought of that funky taste carries me back to the good old polluted US of A. Gives me a sense of security."

The two fell silent. Suddenly Dudley's face lit up with inspiration.

"Coach, I've got a plan. It may sound crazy, but hear me out. I've still got the six empty cans from the Fenswill you drank during the quarterfinals against the Ausable Hackle Hustlers. Sure, they've been opened, but if we're careful, I don't think anyone will notice. We can use them as decoys. I'll fill them with local beer and hand them to you. It may not fool your stomach, but it'll fool our guys, and the Brits too. But do you think your system will get you through it?"

"What in the name of God are you doing carrying around a bunch of empty beer cans?" asked the incredulous coach.

"No trash can at the river. I certainly couldn't just throw them on the ground, so I stowed them in my tackle bag and never got around to dumping them."

"I'm a son of a bitch!" said the coach. "It could work. By God, it will work! Let's do it! But be sure you buy the cheapest brand-X beer you can find; and you might wash your socks in it first."

Dud went to his room and collected his gear, including the Fenswill cans, and returned to DeMille's suite. The coach stood before the mirror, resplendent in his Harris-tweed jacket with leather elbow patches and matching hat. A handsome harness-leather belt encircled his ample girth.

"Ready, Coach?" inquired Dud.

"Almost. Normally, I wouldn't do this before a match, but today we have extenuating circumstances." With that, he produced a quart of Jameson's Irish whiskey, broke the seal, and took a long pull, then another. Replacing the cork, he turned to his captain with a wry grin.

"That ought to help me tolerate all that good beer," he said.

Part II
the fenswill is recovered but fate takes a cruel turn

While Ralph DeMille and the Springhole Sippers rode out to the Matara River for the pre-match ceremonies and warm-ups, the two detectives were working at a feverish pace. From the squad-car radio they transmitted a narrative of the circumstances surrounding the crime, insisting that the data be run through the computer immediately. In a matter of minutes the technician at Headquarters was reading back a list of hotel employees with criminal records. The cast of characters was large and hardly encouraging: winos, gamblers, petty thieves, small-time pimps, drug dealers, and the like. On a hunch, the detectives asked for a file sort by sports-related gambling offenses. Three names came up. Two were food-service employees at cheap hotels on the outskirts of town. The other was one Edward Tate, a former jockey convicted of throwing races, now employed as a bellhop at the Maori Princess, a hotel known for its night life and nefarious clientele.

Tate had been clean since his release from gaol several years earlier but had failed to show up for his last few appointments with the parole officer. A minor offense, perhaps, but it was the only lead that had any potential, and the pair jumped on it. A call to the hotel obtained the bellhop's home address and soon the detectives were knocking on the door of a dingy flat.

" 'Oo in 'ell's there?" came a bleary response.

"Police. Open up immediately, please."

"Wut for? Can't a bloke get 'is rest? I work nights, y'know."

"It's night work we want to talk to you about. Now open up that door, Tate, and don't make us break the lock, that's a good fellow."

Slowly the door creaked open, revealing a scrawny, unkempt young man, very obviously hungover. A half-empty bottle of Scotch sat on the table.

"Cardhu Reserve, as I live and breathe!" said the first detective. "I didn't figure bellhops at the Maori Princess could afford to drink $75 whiskey. Perhaps you've made yourself a little extra scratch lately, eh?"

"I ain't done nuthin'," he mumbled sullenly.

"Then you won't mind answering a few questions. A crime of international significance was committed last night, and all evidence points to a hotel employee. Can you account for your whereabouts between the hours of ten p.m. and six a.m.?"

"Bloody well can. That's me shift."

"And can you prove you were on duty all the time?" said the second detective.

"I don't see that I got to prove anyfing," slurred Tate.

"We'll be the judge of that. Get your clothes on right now. You're going back to the hotel with us, and we've no time for games."

"Show me a warrant, copper!"

The first detective sent Tate sprawling with a kick in the ass any

footballer would have admired. "Our warrant is those parole viola-
tions that are still hanging over you," he said. "Now get your damned
duds on before I lose my temper!"

"You can't do this to me!" whined the stunned bellhop. "I got
me rights."

"Your rights and a dollar'll get you a one-way bus ride to the
sheep-shearing pens," said the first detective. "Now move!"

Truculently, Tate complied. As he pulled up his trousers, the second
detective thought he saw him tuck something under his pillow with a
deft, furtive movement. Instantly the officer whipped away the pillow,
exposing a roll of fresh currency.

"The lad's got nearly four hundred dollars here; and on his
salary!" exclaimed the detective. "Looks like we've struck gold,
Jimmy." Without further ado, his partner collared the bellhop and
marched him out the door.

In the car, the two detectives decided to split up, one working
the Maori Princess, the other the Astoria. They called ahead and
instructed the respective managers to summon all night-shift employees, most of whom lived in the hotels. The officer named Jimmy
dropped Dan, his partner, at the Astoria and continued on to the
Maori Princess. By the time he arrived, the night crew was assembled,
disheveled and rather wary. The manager directed them to answer
the officer's questions promptly and truthfully, under penalty of dis-
missal. A similar scene was occurring at the Astoria.

The interrogations were time-consuming, tedious, and frustrating.
Most of the employees seemed cooperative enough but appeared to
have no relevant information. After a half-hour, the two detectives
spoke by phone.

"I've got nary a thing either," said a despondent Dan, in answer
to his partner's query. "You say Tate's story checks out?"

"The head bellhop swears Tate was on duty all the time," said Jimmy.
"I don't care for the man, but that doesn't make him a crook."

"I've got a slippery-looking bastard at this end too—the night
clerk. I don't like his explanation of why he called Coach DeMille to
the lobby. Technically, what he did was correct; DeMille had signed

an incorrect bill for one of the team's meals. But why bother him about it so late in the evening? It could have been straightened out in the morning. But that's no crime either."

Jimmy sighed. "All I can do is run this crew through the list again, and see if I can catch anyone in a contradiction. Beyond that, I'll have to let them disperse."

"Same here. I'll ring you again as soon as I'm through."

As Jimmy stepped out of the phone booth, he found himself confronting a rather frail, pretty girl: Janine, the night maid.

"I got to say this quick!" She was obviously frightened. "Phil—that's the head bellhop—oughtn't to be telling you that Eddie was on duty all the time, 'cause he can't be sure."

"Why not?" said Jimmy.

"Phil's my boyfriend, sort of; and he was in a vacant room for over an hour…with me. That would have been from about 10:30 to nearly midnight." The girl cast her eyes downward as she spoke.

"Why are you telling me this now?" asked the detective.

"Well, I'm—uh—he's got me in trouble. Last night. I told him. He said it's my problem; laughed out loud, too! But please don't let on I told you. Phil and Eddie—they're mean ones."

"Nothing will happen to you, Janine; you have my word," said Jimmy.

"One more thing," said the girl. "Eddie lied about not knowin' anyone at the Astoria. He's thick with the night clerk there; they drink at the same pub Phil takes me to. The bloke's name is supposed to be Cliff Stoddard—but sometimes Eddie calls him by a real odd name: Killy. It's a nickname, I guess. The fellow gets mad when Eddie calls him that."

A faint, yet distinct bell rang in Jimmy's brain: Killy. "Many thanks, girl; you've done the proper thing."

Jimmy called Dan and said, "A break, maybe," and related Janine's story. "Does that name Killy strike a note with you?"

"Saints, yes! Killy Kilfoyle! The Christchurch Downs scandal, where Eddie Tate got busted. There was a pari-mutuel window operator named Killy Kilfoyle that they thought was implicated—he was in all the papers—but they didn't have enough to indict him. A gay chappie, the papers said. Sounds like we need a quick ID check. I'll call it in."

When the detectives returned to their interrogations, things changed in a hurry. Jimmy took Phil and Eddie into a private room and closed the door. At the Astoria, Dan walked back in, smiled at the night clerk, and said amiably, "Hello, Killy."

In very short order, stories began to vary drastically. The police description of Ashley F. "Killy" Kilfoyle fit Cliff Stoddard perfectly, except for hair color. Kilfoyle was wanted for a number of sex offenses, including male prostitution. At first Stoddard denied all, but Dan pointed out that a fingerprint check would reveal the truth and the man broke.

"That bastard Eddie!" he hissed, tears running down his cheeks. "I only did it for him. And he cheated on me; I know he did—and with girls!"

At the Maori Princess, Jimmy told Phil he'd have to report the situation with Janine to the manager, and the man broke immediately. Eddie continued to smirk. "Don't matter what this jerk did with 'is bitch; you still got nuthin' on me." Then came the call from Dan at the Astoria: "We've nailed Killy and he's confessed!" Jimmy related the news to Eddie.

Eddie guffawed. "Some story! Who's gonna believe that dirty faggot? A jealous pansy, mad at a guy what prefers chicks."

"A jury will believe him, Tate, especially in light of your mutual backgrounds. Now, here's how it is: You can stonewall it, and we'll throw the book at you. Or you can cooperate, right now, and I'll get you as much leniency as the law allows. The choice is yours. You've got one minute before I call Headquarters."

Eddie's smugness disappeared and his face crumbled. Resigned, he said, "Awright, so I pinched the bloody brew. All this fuss over six tinnies, and the worst sheep piss a bloke ever poured down the inside of 'is neck at that!"

"How do you know that?" said Jimmy, sharply.

"Drank it, I did. The bloke what 'ired me gave me an extra twenty to get rid of the stuff. I figured the best way was to drink it. 'Orrible, it was!"

"The beer is gone? You drank it all?" asked Jimmy.

"Never! Two cans was plenty for me; all would 'ave done me in for certain. Gorry, wot a hangover!"

"Where's the rest? Answer me quick, boy!" said the officer.

"Pitched 'em where they belong—in the dumpster, in the alley besides the 'otel."

"When?"

"At six this mornin', when I left."

The detective handcuffed Eddie to a radiator and streaked for the manager's office. "When do they come for the dumpster?" he shouted.

"Two o'clock. It's five after now, but like as not they're late."

"Take me to the alley, on the double!"

The two men ran for the exit. As they entered the alley, a huge truck could be seen, its steel arms setting an empty dumpster onto its stand. For once the pickup was on time!

As Jimmy ran down the alley, the truck began to move off. "Halt! Halt! Police!" he shouted, but his words were drowned out. As the truck began to accelerate, Jimmy dropped to one knee, drew his revolver, and emptied it at the vehicle. Both rear tires went flat immediately.

"My word!" exclaimed the shaken manager. "All this over a few tins of beer?"

The driver of the garbage truck, scared to death, stammered from the cab, "I say, mates, what's goin' on?"

"Police!" shouted Jimmy. "Follow my instructions immediately. I want you to dump that load you just picked up!"

"You mean right here—in the street?"

"That's right. Ease it out as gently as possible."

The driver did as he was told, and in a moment a small mountain of rubbish lay in the alley.

"Oh God!" moaned the hotel manager.

"Get in here and help me search," said Jimmy to the manager. "We're looking for four cans—aluminium, brown with green lettering, name Fenswill."

Reluctantly the well-dressed manager approached the edge of the pile and with obvious distaste began rummaging. He was not to suffer long. In minutes Jimmy with a triumphant yell held up four cans, still joined by the plastic loops of the six-pack container.

"The purloined lager, I believe!" he chortled. Just at that moment, a squad car careened around the corner and screeched to a stop. Out jumped Dan. Seeing the beer, he emitted a wild "Hurrah!"

At this point, the manager made his contribution to expediting the mission. Upon seeing Jimmy with the beer, he had dashed into the kitchen. Now he returned with a large ice bucket. "Put them in here," he suggested.

Thanking him profusely, if hastily, Jimmy and Dan jumped into the squad car. Dan at the wheel, they streaked across town, lights ablaze and siren blaring. Jimmy called HQ and briefed them, giving instructions for picking up Tate. "Interrogate him immediately," he said. "We must find out who's behind this, before he makes more trouble. We're headed for the Matara full throttle. Perhaps we can save the day and make a big arrest all at once." If only it were to be that simple!

And now to the scene of the contest. The midpoint had been reached and the teams were at recess, with the Springhole Sippers holding a slim but significant lead. Coach DeMille, resolute man that he was, had pulled off the ruse convincingly and, so far as his team could tell, he was in fine form, relishing his usual stateside brew.

DeMille spent the fifteen-minute break issuing words of support to his anglers. "Boys, you're doing just great. I couldn't ask for better. The pressure's on them now; they'll have to play catch-up ball. They've all got tight jaws. Dermot Wilson's face is as long as one of those salmon rods the Scots use. But let's not be too conservative—that can cause a letdown. Go for the score, just as you've been doing. If we hold our own in the third round, it'll force them to take impossible chances in the fourth.

"Colby, you're the leadoff man. Have you checked over your tackle?"

"You bet, Coach. I changed my tippet and put a touch of grease on my reel spindle. That big rainbow at the second station really smoked it."

"You put on some show!" said DeMille, admiringly. "I never thought you'd land that fish on 6X."

"You can thank my days on the Henry's Fork for that," said Colby.

"I'd like to take a crack at that big salmon this session," said Dave Male. "How's that sound to you, Ralph?"

The coach reflected for a moment and said, "It's a bit riskier than I think we have to get at the moment. What sort of fly would you use?"

"I thought I'd feed him a dry—a Battenkill Bat-Catcher."

"Geez, Dave! To my knowledge, no one's ever caught a salmon on a Battenkill Bat-Catcher. I think it's a low-percentage move."

"Ralph, I'm positive he'll go for it. That's the fish Joan Wulff rose to a Bomber in three casts, and I think the Bat-Catcher's the better fly of the two."

"Maybe—but Joan Wulff is one of the greatest salmon fishers that ever lived. She knows exactly how to entice such a fish with a dry fly. The computer gave her a near-max score, man!"

"I'm sure I can do it," insisted Male.

"Perhaps. The way you guys have been going, I'm willing to believe just about anything. But it's still a high-risk play. We don't have to call the shot till you're up; let's wait and see how Colby comes out against Lord Blivet."

The voice of referee Harry Darbee came over the speaker, summoning the contestants back to the river. As they walked to their stations, Dud Soper got Coach DeMille's ear.

"How do you feel, Ralph?"

"Queasy as all hell, Dud, but I think I can make it."

"How many have you had?"

"Just two; I nursed 'em. Maybe I can get through the second half on one can, if the boys don't get suspicious."

"Hang in there, Coach, and don't make yourself sick on our account. I think we're going to win this thing, Brown Label or no."

"I'm not worried about you, Dud. But I'm afraid if one of the boys saw that I wasn't sipping away at a Brown One, it would unnerve them." The coach turned slightly greenish for a moment, then pulled himself together and by sheer willpower got his ruddy color back. As Colby Hansen stepped up to his station, DeMille lifted a brown can out of the cooler, beaming as though it were actually a genuine, funky Fenswill.

Colby took up where the Sippers had left off. He selected an eight-pound trout, plus a small Hornberg streamer on 4X. The tackle wasn't highly rated as a points multiple but he made up for that by moving the fish on his first cast, hooking it on his second, and bringing it to net in an incredible six minutes. The huge crowd went wild.

In moments the computer operator had transmitted the results to Field Judge Lyons, who intoned into the microphone, "Ninety-four points!" The crowd roared again, and the Sippers pounded Colby on the back.

Appearing slightly flustered, the usually intrepid Lord Blivet took his station. He selected a twenty-one-pound Atlantic salmon, casting for it with a tiny size 14 Blue Charm on six-pound-test. The fish took at the two-minute mark, but Blivet was unable to land it within the time allotment. Still, he had held it for the duration, surviving five leaps—a noteworthy performance.

"Eighty-three points," announced Lyons, and the crowd acknowledged the feat. Ralph DeMille beamed confidently at his team while struggling to hide a growing sickness.

"Forget the salmon, we don't really need it," he advised Dave Male. "What's your fallback?"

"The four-pound grayling on a size 24 and 7X," Dave replied.

"You do love to live dangerously. Okay, have at it, then."

The grayling proved to be more of a challenge than anticipated.

True to its kind, it rose willingly to the fly, but time and again the tiny hook failed to engage in the fish's mouth. The grayling was showing signs of alarm. At four minutes, Male used fifteen precious seconds to dry and manicure his fly.

"It's okay, Davy," called DeMille, "you've already scored well on rises, and we have a little cushion."

"Relax—I'll take him," called Male, confidently.

The next cast dropped the fly perfectly, and once again the gullible grayling obliged, taking with that picturesque head-dorsal-tail riseform. Dave tightened carefully, and this time the hook found its niche; scant minutes later it was struggling feebly in his net.

"Eighty points," announced Lyons. A few hisses came from the crowd and the Sippers shrugged in mild protest. Still, it was a good score, considering that the fish wasn't hooked until the eighteenth cast, just twenty seconds before the deadline.

Major Benbow was next, and he delivered his usual stellar performance on a huge sea trout, besting the powerful fish in less than nine minutes on rather light tackle.

"Eighty-seven points."

The match tightened up a bit. The Test Ticklers shook Benbow's hand warmly. Ralph DeMille registered no emotion, but inwardly his guts churned from tension—and the alien brew.

In the final pairing of the third round, Dud Soper and Jack Martin scored a draw, each with a fantastic performance. The Sipper's captain enticed a Pacific salmon—a sockeye—into taking a dry fly, a near-impossible feat. Captain Martin responded with an incredibly quick conquest of a grilse, using a size 16 low-water fly on three-pound test. Both were awarded 98 points.

Field Judge Lyons took the microphone: "The score at the end of the third station: Springhole Sippers 661, Test Ticklers 645. The fourth and final round begins in five minutes."

Coach DeMille spoke a few words of encouragement to his team, then excused himself for a trip to the comfort station.

"Is the coach okay?" asked Colby Hansen. "He doesn't seem quite right to me."

"I agree," said Dave Male. "Besides, I've never seen him have to pee on less than ten beers before, and he hasn't even finished his third."

Dud Soper spoke with feigned lack of concern. "Ralph's fine; as fine as can be expected, what with all the pressure."

"I can't figure the scoring on the last two pairs," remarked Colby, and Dave said, "Me neither. I was sure my grayling was worth a ninety, and Dud's sockeye should've topped Martin's grilse by a good eight points."

"I must admit I'm a bit mystified too, and so is Ralph," said Dud thoughtfully. "I think I'll do a little assistant coaching while he's in the head."

With that, Dud conferred briefly with Referee Darbee and the two disappeared into the data-processing trailer. Two minutes later they emerged and went their separate ways. As Dud rejoined his teammates, Coach DeMille emerged from the john, not looking particularly relieved.

"Ralph, I got ahold of Darbee and went in to review the scoring with the computer tech. All seems to be in order, but I still think the scores for the last two pairings were a bit odd. I suppose that's not possible; the system is foolproof; the program simply can't make an error."

But the system had made errors—man-caused errors! What Soper and Darbee had not seen during their visit to the trailer was the cold blue muzzle of a 9mm pistol peeking out of a closet door. Sir Thomas Truffles, who had nearly suffered a myocardial infarct when he saw DeMille with the Fenswill, had decided to affect the outcome of the match in a more direct manner. Disguised as a marshal, he had slipped unnoticed into the trailer just after halftime. Holding the computer operator and his girlfriend at gunpoint, he began to dictate subtle alterations in the computer scoring system.

"You'll never get away with this," said the tech. "The changes will be discovered when they run the diagnostic checks right after the match."

"Ah, but you're going to fix that as well!" said Truffles. "And to guarantee that you do, I'm going to take a hostage. I've a plane waiting to take me to a country that won't extradite me, and that pretty Kiwi girlfriend of yours is going with me. Cooperate, and she won't get hurt. Any tricks, and she steps on a cobra. Understand?"

The tech reluctantly nodded. "That's a very desperate plan."

"A chap can get damned desperate with 'alf a million quid at stake," said the gambler.

Part III

the heroic and enormously satisfying conclusion

And so the course of the match was altered, subtly but inexorably. The deviations were small enough that no formal complaint could be supported, yet they would be sufficient to accomplish the sinister earl's objectives. Thus, as the Springhole Sippers approached their stations for the final round, their defeat was being prescribed in the sophisticated, fail-safe floating-point operations of a computer.

Referee Darbee reminded everyone that the order of the teams reversed after each round, so the Test Ticklers would go first. Lord Blivet took position, opting for a most challenging fish: an enormous sea trout of Patagonian strain. The fish had proved hookable enough in previous matches, but was so powerful that no one had landed it, or even held it for the time limit. The Ticklers' backs were to the wall, however, and it was time to take some chances.

At first Lord Blivet had difficulty interesting the great trout in his Snipe-and-Yellow, but a teasing twitch turned the trick, and at the three-minute mark the battle was joined. Landing was Blivet's forte—he was considered the world's best at that aspect—and he proceeded to prove it. Incredibly, with thirty seconds to spare, the eighteen-pound hen lay gasping in the shallows. The Ticklers cheered their leadoff man with an uncharacteristic show of emotion, and the crowd gave the smiling peer a standing ovation.

Inside the trailer Truffles hissed, "Let that one be scored normally. No need to arouse suspicion unnecessarily." The technician did as he was bid.

"One hundred five points," came the announcement. The high score surprised no one.

As Colby Hansen stepped up to his station, Ralph DeMille started a fresh can of beer, his fourth. "Let's have your best, lad," he said with mock cheerfulness around the sour lump in his throat.

Relying on all the highly developed skills acquired during his long apprenticeship on the heartbreaking Battenkill, Colby decided to try for an eight-pound brown with a size 22 Blue-Wing Olive on 7X. DeMille wanted to object but didn't feel up to arguing with him, and Colby set about the formidable task. Reaching back in history to the legendary George LaBranche, he delivered a series of absolutely precise casts in rapid succession, creating an artificial hatch. The trout's programmed sensors responded and, with growing interest, the big brown tilted upwards. On the seventeenth drift, the trout sipped in the fly and turned down toward its holding spot.

"He's on!" exulted Dud Soper.

"But what of it?" groaned an olive-gray DeMille. "He won't hold that fish long enough on 7X to score sixty points; no one has yet."

But the coach underestimated his resourceful young lead man. For two agonizing minutes, Colby merely held the fish in the current, testing the strain against his terminal tackle. The trout spent precious energy maintaining its position against the gentle, yet relentless pressure.

At the six-minute mark, Colby began to back slowly downstream, leading the great fish out of its lair toward the slow pool below. Soon he had maneuvered the brute into a slow backwater. Crouching low to conceal himself, Colby gently worked the fish in smaller and smaller concentric circles, dazing the creature without actually alarming it. At last, with a deft pass that would have honored Manolete, he brought the fish over his net and lifted. The trout, only partially spent, threatened to tear the mesh apart, but to no avail. Colby had won! As the crowd roared, Truffles said icily, "Shave that one." Resigned, the technician keyed in a new factor.

"Ninety-nine points." intoned Field Judge Lyons.

The Sippers were appalled. Captain Soper again approached Referee Darbee, with DeMille following unsteadily, and lodged a complaint. Darbee listened courteously but replied, "Gentlemen, no expense has been spared to guarantee the accuracy of this system. Dud, you and I determined at recess that all was in order. You have the right to appeal after the match, in which case a full review will be done, which will include looking at the videotapes. Until then, the match must go forward."

Dud looked Darbee square in the eye and said, "Harry, off the record, is there any doubt in your mind over our last few scores?" Darbee looked beseechingly at Nick Lyons, who said, "Dud, they do seem a bit conservative; but we're only human, and human judgment is exactly what the system is designed to eliminate. It simply can't make a mistake—and even if it did, we'd pick it up in the post-match audit."

"I request an immediate recess and diagnostic run," said DeMille, weakly.

"I'm sorry, Ralph," replied Darbee, "you know the rules prohibit that. Say, are you all right? You look terrible."

"Yes, I'm all right—and I inform you herewith that this match is now being conducted under formal protest."

"That is your prerogative," said Darbee formally. The protest was announced over the speaker system, causing restlessness in the crowd.

It was Major Benbow's turn. Courageously, he selected a coho salmon and rendered his customary stellar performance. The reluctant fish was hooked inside two minutes and, while not landed, was held for the duration, despite much heavy thrashing.

Inside the trailer Truffles said, "Give him a little extra." In a moment, the announcement came: "Ninety-five points." The crowd applauded, but with a reserved air, somewhat surprised that an un-landed fish should score so high.

As Dave Male prepared to take his station, he turned to his coach and said, "Ralph, I want to know what's wrong with you. You're as green as pond scum and about as energetic. If you're as sick as you seem, let's get you to a doctor this minute. We'll carry on here."

One last time DeMille pulled himself together: "Now David, don't you be worrying about me; I've just got a case of coach's occupational disease. Look at Wilson over there; he doesn't look any better!" It was the truth. "So Davy, go out there and do your thing. What's your choice?"

"The salmon. We need it now."

Without a word DeMille patted Dave on the shoulder and turned away, forcing down a gulp of beer to reassure the young man.

David Male went on to demonstrate why he was a prime candidate for tournament MVP. With a ninety-foot Spey cast he placed a tiny Irresistible in just the right line of drift, riffling it slightly as it approached the salmon. The fly was true to its name and the salmon took. One cast! The crowd screamed approval, and in the trailer Truffles's hand grew clammy on his weapon.

Male played the fish like the true champion he was, and at the seven-minute mark it was obvious the salmon would soon be brought in. The rules allowed assisted netting on Atlantic salmon without deduction, but Dave waved the ghillie off. "I'm going to tail him," he announced. Very chancy, but with high potential for bonus points.

At this dramatic moment Ralph DeMille turned to his captain. A deathly pallor masked his face and droplets of cold sweat beaded his forehead. "Take over, Dud; I've had it," he gurgled, turning toward the comfort hut.

But he had delayed too long. Just as Male coaxed the exhausted fish within range of his grasp, DeMille's tortured guts registered their ultimate protest. With a thunderous *Yorrrrrech!* the coach regurgitated. Startled, Dave jerked his rod, the leader knot gave, and the silver giant drifted off, the tiny fly still visible in its massive kype.

Truffles smiled in grim satisfaction. "Score normally," he hissed. The technician operated the keys.

"Eighty points," came the announcement.

"That's too high!" said the alarmed gambler.

"Too late now," replied the tech. "A lot of bonus points for all the great things he did, you know."

"We'll make it up on the last pairing, won't we now." Truffles said menacingly. The chilling click of the pistol's cocking mechanism was distinctly audible over the soft whirring of the disk drives.

On the riverbank, a touching tableau had formed. Male's misfortune was put aside for the moment as the Sippers gathered about their fallen leader, applying cold towels to his forehead. DeMille sat on the cool, green bank, ashen but greatly relieved.

"I'll be all right, I'll be all right," he insisted.

"Request five-minute injury time-out, as prescribed by the rules," said Captain Soper to Harry Darbee.

"Granted, of course," replied the referee, and the announcement was made to the crowd. The Test Ticklers, in a display typical of their sportsmanship, helped minister to DeMille, and from somewhere produced a large umbrella to shade him from the afternoon sun.

"Damned shame, this. We'd gladly agree to a postponement, if the rules allowed," sympathized Dermot Wilson.

"But they don't," replied Dudley Soper. "Thank ye so much anyway, Dermot."

"Don't mention it," replied the Ticklers' coach. Jack Martin came over and seized Dud's hand firmly. "Best of luck to you, Yank!" he said sincerely. "And to you," replied Dud.

As the brief recess was about to expire, there sounded the shrill warble of a police siren. Into the arena hurtled a dusty squad car, knocking over several barriers and screeching to a halt before the judging stand. The doors flew open and out sprang two triumphant detectives, one with an ice bucket in hand.

"We've got it!" shouted Dan, "Or at least, most of it. The stolen brew, if you please. Four cans, all chilled and ready to drink. Hope we're not too late?" He held aloft a frosty brown can.

Ralph DeMille emerged from beneath the umbrella and strode toward the detective. He seemed to gain strength with each step, his back straightening, his shoulders squaring. He took the proffered can and as he popped it open, his face beamed like the sun after a cloudburst.

The coach raised the can in salute and said, "To the New Zealand police, to these two great teams, and to VICTORY!"

Closing his eyes, he blissfully chugalugged the brew.

Dave and Colby confronted Dud Soper and said in unison, "All right, you sly old bastard; what in hell's been going on here?"

Dud smiled. "No time to explain. I'll tell all as soon as the match is over. Hush now; it's time to start again, and we can't afford a delay penalty. Let's see what Martin does."

To no one's surprise, Martin did well—frighteningly well. He enticed an enormous steelhead into taking a small Green-Butt Skunk on his second cast and brought the fish to net in a scant eight minutes, pressuring the fragile leader to its limit.

Inside the trailer the tension had reached a new level. "Jack it up," ordered Truffles unsteadily. The announcement came: "One hundred seven points." High, but not beyond credibility for such a feat.

A rejuvenated Ralph DeMille gathered his team for a hasty assessment. "Before Martin's fish, we were down five points," he said. "His score certainly puts a lot of pressure on Dud. We need 112 points to tie, 113 to win. That rules out a trout.

"Dud, it'll have to be a salmon, and a whopper at that. In fact, I'd guess you'll have to take him on a dry. There's a twenty-nine-pounder at this station. I calculate that if you can hook him within a few casts with a size 16 on six-pound and land him in under eight minutes, we might just sneak by."

"Do you know what you're asking?" said Dave Male. "That would surpass any record in the books. No one's even come close to whipping a fish like that on six-pound in eight minutes!"

"It's that or second place," replied the coach. "If anyone can do it, Dud can." The coach and the two younger Sippers looked to their captain anxiously.

Dud Soper spoke with reassuring calm. "There's another way, perfectly legitimate. It's seldom used—in fact, never in a championship round—but at this point I'm willing to have it out one-on-one with any fish in this earth's waters.

"I'm going to call for the Wild-Trout Option."

Male and Hansen gasped but DeMille said, "Okay, Dud, it's your ball game. I'll inform Lyons and Darbee."

Upon hearing of Dud's decision, the two officials registered shocked surprise. Nick Lyons said, "Very well. Let me review the Wild-Trout Option over the sound system so that everyone understands.

"Gentlemen and ladies. The rules of international competition provide that in a final pairing, one or both contestants may elect to have the electronic programming in the brain of his or her chosen fish defeated. This simply means that the fish is normalized and will behave according to its nature. It may choose to ignore a perfect presentation or foolishly respond to a poor one. In either case, the result is a low score. The fish might even flee the station, in which case the score is zero.

"In recognition of such high risk, the rules provide for super-bonus scoring, based on the type of fish selected. For example, a typical Yellowstone cutthroat has a five percent multiple, a large brown trout, twenty percent.

"Coach DeMille, if you are committed to this course of action, I'll instruct the computer operator. Have you chosen a fish?"

Dud Soper responded, "There's a seven-pound wild brown at this station. I'm going for it with a size 20 Gangly-Legs and 7X."

A word about the Gangly-Legs: This bizarre fly had been designed by Dud to match the craneflies on the Battenkill. The tiny body and sprawling, grossly oversize hackle made it resemble a tiny, feathery Alaskan king crab. Its improbable appearance, along with the small hook, would ensure a high scoring factor.

Nick Lyons shook his head and relayed the news to the hushed crowd. The computer tech acknowledged from the trailer that he understood.

"What sort of bumpf is this?" asked the suspicious Truffles.

"As you heard, the fish is deprogrammed. Everything's the same except that the trout is on his own. A foolhardy gamble, I'd say."

"That's what I like to hear. Let it ride," said the gambler. With that, the technician transmitted the program-defeat message to the chip in the fish's brain, and the stage was set.

It was late afternoon. No breeze rippled the treacherous cross-currents of the slow pool. As Dud Soper approached the station, the crowd held its breath and nothing stirred. Even the birds sat motionless on their perches, as though aware of the unfolding drama.

In six feet of gin-clear water and fully seventy-five feet out lay twenty-seven inches of cerebral German brown trout. Dud could not see the fish but he knew exactly where it was—or at least where it was supposed to be by the schematic. But now the trout was deprogrammed and could have chosen to move. He could only cast, and hope.

Dud took a few seconds for one final evaluation and turned toward his coach. For a moment, the two old friends held each other in a warm gaze. DeMille smiled and took a long drag of Fenswill.

Dud turned back to the pool, took a deep breath, and began false-casting. He knew the delivery had to be perfect—perhaps even that wouldn't be enough. The old Garrison rod cut the air in purposeful swishes, the pale green line forming tight, smooth loops. With a subtle double-haul Dud added a bit more line speed and released the cast. For an instant the line seemed to stop and hover, fully extended, over the water. Then, as if by magic, a small morsel of fur, feathers, and steel appeared on the very edge of the seam, like ghostly thistledown.

What trout could resist? The brown rose slowly, majestically, drifting beneath the fly. Its newly restored senses registered hunger. As the fish neared the surface, Dud's pulse pounded. Easy, easy, easy! With a magnificent swirl, the trout took. Dud tightened, the minuscule point sank home. In unison the spectators inhaled, but not another sound could be heard.

The fish immediately went to the bottom, seeking to rub the nettling thing in its jaw against the streambed. Dud kept the rod high and moved downstream, staying below the trout, trying to make it work against the current. Despite hooking the fish so early on, Dud knew that he had only about eleven minutes, and landing this fish was a must. With a surgeon's touch he applied pressure. Enraged, the brown trout leaped uncharacteristically, which nearly caused a dozen coronaries. Dud instantly gave slack and the connection held.

To the crowd, the ensuing duel was tense and electrifying. To the small group of master anglers on the bank, it was a doctoral thesis in angling. Dud coerced the trout into one mistake after another, the fish expending its energy in futile thrusts like a brave Miura bull, never suspecting the ridiculous ease with which it could instantly defeat its adversary. Soon—amazingly soon—it was foundering in the shallows. Three times Dud readied the net but the trout shied back into the current. The fourth time, it came in on its side. A skillful scoop and it was a captive. The field clock, unofficial but always accurate, read eight minutes, twenty seconds.

For a moment all remained still. Then an avalanche of sound boomed from the grandstands, rolling across the valley, rising to a pitch more suited to the Super Bowl or World Cup soccer. But inside the data-processing trailer, utter tension and quiet prevailed. Turning to the gambler, the technician spoke.

"All due respect to your gun, mister, but if that score gets pared down enough that the Sippers lose, this place will be teeming with police and officials within fifteen seconds—and probably half the crowd in the bargain."

"I don't care," snarled the desperate earl. "I'm not backing down now. Give 'im 110. Do as I say." The gun hand was shaking now.

Outside, spectators, officials, and contestants awaited the results in suspenseful anticipation. Shortly Field Judge Lyons was heard to say, "Would you repeat that, please?"

"May I please have everyone's attention. Mr. Soper's score is 110 points."

An angry roar erupted. "Wait! Quiet please, I'm not through. To that score, we add twenty percent, or twenty-two points, for the Wild-Trout Option. That brings Mr. Soper's total to 132 points, a new world's record. The final score of the match is, Test Ticklers 952, Springhole Sippers, 972.

"I give you the new world's champion fly fishers, the Springhole Sippers!"

A s pandemonium reigned outside, mortal danger prevailed in the trailer.

"So you've tricked me!" snarled the gambler. "You didn't tell me they added the percentage later."

"I didn't know—I never did Wild-Trout before!" the tech lied artfully.

"Well, you'll pay for your ignorance. I can still escape, with you two as hostages. Now just walk as though you 'adn't a care—out the door, across the lawn. You'll see a black limousine. Get in, with no fuss. You might just live to tell about it."

The threesome emerged and began to stroll off with apparent nonchalance, Truffles, hand in pocket, in the rear. Amidst the tumult they were unobserved—except by two keen-eyed detectives, who knew their job wasn't yet finished.

"Look there!" said Jimmy. "That's the bloke that runs the computer. Why would he be sneaking off, before the scoring is checked and all?"

"And look at that fellow behind him, with his hand in his pocket," said Dan. "He fits the description we got from Tate of the villain. Let's move in on them."

"Carefully, now," said Jimmy. "This looks dangerous."

It was no simple task to sneak up on the criminal, and Truffles spotted the detectives while they were still yards away. In a flash, the Parabellum leaped from his pocket. Seizing the tech's girlfriend by her blonde ponytail, he pressed the muzzle against the base of her neck.

"That'll be far enough," he warned. "I'm leavin' with the lady, unless you'd like to see 'er 'ead blown off. Keep your hands up where I can see 'em and walk off toward the far exit. Do like I say and no one gets blasted."

At this moment another person noticed the scene. It was none other than the hero of the moment, Dudley Soper. Surrounded by admirers, he still had his fly rod in hand. The retreating detectives and the black pistol against the girl's head registered instantly. This was the ultimate culprit, the master criminal, making his escape!

Reacting instinctively, Dud did that which he did best. Shoving people aside, he whipped the rod into action. One, two, three false-casts, building line speed. Then, when he could aerialize no more line, a perfect double-haul. The cast shot across 120 feet of lawn directly on target, and the Gangly-Legs struck Truffles's gun hand. Dud jerked sharply and the gambler screamed. The leader snapped but the pistol flew from the villain's grasp. In an instant the computer technician pounced on it and turned it on Truffles. Jimmy and Dan followed in at once and snapped handcuffs onto the despairing criminal. And with this last bit of heroics, the deadly game ended.

In the wee hours, long after the signing of statements at the police station, long after the official cocktail party, the awards ceremony, the banquet, the speeches and celebrities and the wonderful dance in the Astoria ballroom, a select group sipped nightcaps in Ralph DeMille's suite. In addition to Coach DeMille and the Springhole Sippers, there were the Test Ticklers, Coach Dermot Wilson, Harry Darbee, Nick Lyons, the computer tech and his girl, and two off-duty cops named Jimmy and Dan.

The events of the day, which would soon be broadcast throughout the world, were discussed and re-discussed. Few ever experience such real-life drama, excitement, and danger, and none present would ever forget the slightest detail. Children not yet born would listen to reverent accounts of the heroic deeds of the men who rose to such heights on that day, in the cause of justice and sport.

At last the Test Ticklers rose to leave. Dermot Wilson, slightly flushed but dignified as always, grasped DeMille's hand warmly and said, "I'll say it once again. Losing to fellows like you is only slightly less of a pleasure than winning. You are truly World Champions. And this man Soper! Pulling it off with the Wild-Trout Option, indeed—and with a fly that looked like a blooming unsanforized tarantula! And then the cast heard 'round the world, that brought a scoundrel to justice and perhaps saved a life! What can one say to that, eh, Ralph?"

Coach DeMille smiled as he hadn't smiled since he'd sat on his bench beside the Battenkill's hallowed spring hole.

"Class will tell," he said simply.

Love Story of the Trout

old masters

Rob Brown

The glowing red letters on the digital clock said 6:15. Harold had seen a lot of changes in his eighty-one years, and this was a good one. He didn't need the tick of an old alarm clock to mark the passage of time. There were more pleasant reminders: the change of colors in the Kispiox Valley was one, the return of the steelhead another.

He pulled the chain on the lamp. Yellow light flooded the table, illuminating his well-chewed briar, his glasses, and a box of flies.

The temperature had fallen again, his joints told him. Gingerly he pushed himself up.

In the first seasons of his twenty-three on the river, he cursed the fall rains and the inevitable cold snap following them, but now he welcomed both, though they made his days along the river more difficult.

The growing scarcity of wild steelhead had brought more and more fishermen to the valley each year—able young fishermen with dirt bikes, drift boats, rubber rafts, and the latest innovations in fishing gear. Quickly they found the Lower Patch, the Dundas, and the Root Cellar, and the fish holding in them.

Forced from the best reaches, Harold started fishing lesser lies, but the youngsters discovered them too. Finally, even the edge given him by his intimate knowledge of the river was not enough. For the last two seasons he hadn't wet a line in September; this year he'd already passed up most of October.

The rains and the spate following them were his salvation. A week of high water had the kids leaving in droves. The skies cleared, the temperature fell, and with it the river. The fish would be older and slower now, but so was he, and at least he would have a chance at them.

His clothes were only an arm's length away. He'd put them there in anticipation of the stiffness he was feeling now.

Wool pants, flannel shirt, wool shirt, one suspender then the other, all pulled on with awkward deliberation; thin socks, wool socks, and finally—with a dull ache in the lower back—the damn boots; then a rest before lacing them up.

Harold looked at the clock: 6:25. He sat on the bed to recover some strength and let the throbbing in his back subside. One brandy and coffee too many the night before, and the excitement of seeing the river clean in the morning, had crippled his sleep.

Harold pushed himself up, tested his feet, and shuffled out the door. The air stung his face. The cottonwoods were black geometric shapes. Harold could hear the rush of the river behind them.

Thankfully there were only three steps from the porch to the ground. He navigated them carefully, then set out across the path to the lodge and stopped at the stairway leading up to it. Six steps this time, six steps on a steeper incline.

Stairways, he thought as he clasped the cold wooden handrail, *are designed and built by younger men.*

PLEASE LEAVE WADERS OUTSIDE. Harold always found that sign slightly offensive. The bell jangled as he walked in. He shuffled to his table and lit his pipe.

"Morning, Harold," chirped the waitress. "Two eggs over easy and some toast?"

Harold nodded.

"Going fishing today?" She always asked that.

"Going to try," said Harold, punctuating the sentence with a wisp of blue smoke.

The waitress turned toward the kitchen. "Marty was in yesterday. He said the river was clear," she called over her shoulder.

"Good," said Harold as he picked up a copy of the local newspaper somebody had left on the counter.

When he left the lodge, Harold could make out the mailboxes along the road. The sky had a bluish cast.

He walked to the car as quickly as he could and climbed in. The engine wouldn't fire. He turned the key again. A rasping metallic sound came from somewhere under his feet before the engine turned over. *Arthritis,* thought Harold as he looked into the backseat to take inventory: waders, vest, flies, rod. The energy to go back for some forgotten piece of tackle was more than he could afford today. Satisfied everything was with him, he turned onto the road.

He passed the rodeo grounds. The yellow of the cottonwoods, their tops still shrouded in fog, was barely visible. He looked down as he crossed the Bailey Bridge. The walls of the canyon were wet and cold, the river below was black. He turned toward the fishing camps and pulled over at the run named for the cottonwoods.

Pulling on the waders, getting the rod and staff from the backseat, and putting on his vest seemed to take ages. When he was finally finished, there was enough light to see the river.

With the welcome support of the staff, he crept down the rocky path to the water. Here and there a gnarled and toothy dog salmon carcass, turned to leather and partly buried in the sand, stared at him through empty sockets.

Harold scanned the familiar contours of the run: the fast riffle at the head spilling over a piece of ledgerock; the two swirls at the top of the slot where, ten years earlier, he found a twenty-eight-pound buck; the quick, flat tail where he'd never done well.

A fish rolled.

Harold was sure it was a steelhead, perhaps one of the few bright winter fish. The boil was a large one. The dog and spring salmon were finished ages ago. It had to be a steelhead.

Another fish rolled, a different one, closer to the far bank and nearer the tailout. *Rolling like a bunch of sea lions,* Harold thought.

He shook his head. He simply couldn't believe it. He'd seen Morice fish chasing mayflies, and once he'd watched steelhead rolling on the surface like pink salmon in the riffle just above the Walcott Walk Bridge; but never in his many Kispiox autumns had he seen one of its fish move to the surface.

He waited a moment, hoping that a third fish might show itself, then he shuffled to the head of the run, wishing he could jog.

He stripped off a length of line and began to false-cast.

A sharp pain shot through his arm, and in one horrible moment he realized he wouldn't be able to fish. Even if he weren't shackled to his arthritic arm, the small labor of putting on his waders and the short walk to the river had drained him completely.

A wave of anger and despair swept over him. All that time spent looking down on the Lower Patch from the high cutbank while others fished over the steelhead suspended in the river below; all the hours spent in the coffee shop overhearing the youngsters talk of their fishing. And now that his turn had finally come—now that he had active fish before him—he was unable to fish them.

Painfully he reeled in the line and placed the fly in the keeper. He looked across at the cottonwoods and leaned on his staff.

The idea came to him suddenly—*Ira.*

Someone had to fish these fish, and who better than Ira? Ira, who had fished this run almost exclusively for the past fifteen seasons and knew its nuances better than anyone. If anyone on the planet could hook these fish, it was Ira.

Harold made his way back to the car and rattled over the road to Olga's camp. He parked beside a silvery trailer. The brittle leaves crackled under his boots as he moved across the field. More stairs— Harold climbed them to the wooden porch. He pounded on the screen door.

Ira's raspy voice came from inside. "It's open."

Ira was sitting at the table smoking a crudely built cigarette and gazing out the window over the icy fields into the yellowed distances.

"You're not fishing," Harold said, relieved.

"No hurry in the cold mornings. Water needs to warm up some."

"Not today it doesn't," said Harold, surprised he still had the energy to get excited. "The Cottonwoods is full of steelhead and they're frisky."

"Frisky?"

"They're rolling on the top like a bunch of seals."

Ira looked away from the window and straight at Harold for the first time. He brushed the ash that had fallen onto his lap to the floor.

"Rolling?"

"That's right, rolling. I've never seen anything like it."

"Why didn't you cover them?"

"Joints," replied Harold.

Ira understood immediately. He scratched the stubble on his grizzled chin and stubbed the cigarette in an empty sockeye-salmon tin.

"We'd better go fish then, before somebody else does," he said at last.

Harold sensed an excited edge to Ira's voice.

"Yeah, we'd better," he agreed.

Over the years Ira had reduced his equipment to the minimum, and, like Harold's, it was always at hand. In moments he'd pulled on his waders and buttoned the solitary strap holding them up. Together they walked back across the field to the car, sharing a quiet, growing excitement.

The inexpensive digital wristwatch Harold kept pinned to the inside of his fishing vest said 9:03:58 when they got out of the car. Harold was surprised there was still nobody else on the river.

He found a rock large enough to make a comfortable seat and give him a view of the proceedings. Ira was already at the head of the run. He yelled something that was lost in the sound of the river. Harold strained but could not hear him. But waved and nodded as if he had.

Ira hunched over, his rod resting against his shoulder, and searched through his leather fly wallet. He found the appropriate pattern, knotted it to his leader, and sent it out across the water with the economy of motion only men who have made thousands and thousands of casts over thousands of fish are capable of.

The fly landed with a force that would have made a trout fisherman shudder, but Harold knew it was a function of Ira's craft: a technique designed to carry compact flies to the cold places where late-returning steelhead lie.

Ira guided his fly through its first drift as Harold watched intently, anticipating a pull—fishing with him from a distance.

Nothing.

Another cast, another drift, again nothing. Ira took a few short steps downstream and repeated the motions exactly. The line hesitated. Ira struck, Harold's arm twitched in painful sympathy. Ira pulled again and once more, to free the fly from the bottom.

Harold breathed out. "At least he's near the stones," he said out loud.

Ira checked the hook, gave it a cursory stroke with the file, then picked up the rhythm again. As Ira repeated the motions, Harold noticed there were almost imperceptible changes to the routine each time: Sometimes the mends were smaller, sometimes a little later in the drift; sometimes a little line was held back on the forward stroke and later fed into the flow at different junctures in the swing. Periodically Ira would give the rod tip a twitch so fast Harold would have missed it had he not been following the performance with such care. The more closely he watched the more convinced Harold became of the deliberation and design in Ira's craft. Every movement was precise and rooted in necessity. Thin and bent and accurate, Ira looked like a giant wading bird prowling the margin of the stream.

Harold had fished beside Ira many times before, but never so close to him as he was now. From his rock he could appreciate a performance so fine that he couldn't help but become a part of it.

Ira lifted his arm. The rod bent deeply. Seconds later there was a boil at line's end.

Harold saw a large tail. He whooped and jumped up, but Ira said nothing. His concentration shifted from the drift of the line to the fighting fish.

The fish did not jump. Instead it ran hard and deep. Ira palmed the reel and shifted his left hand up the rod. He began to work the fish—again deliberately and with practiced accuracy. The fish responded with a purposefulness of its own.

"I'll bet it's a big buck," Harold called out as Ira, who hadn't heard him, pulled the large male ashore and unhooked it.

After pausing for a moment, Ira resumed the hunt where he had left off—exactly where he had left off.

Harold was just getting caught up in Ira's art again when the rod was over once more. This fish mirrored the first, but though it was smaller, Harold noted Ira took longer to bring it to shore. After they released it—Ira up close, Harold from afar—Harold breathed more quickly; the cold air showed Ira did too.

"Take a break," said Harold. "Take a break, you old coot."

A pickup rumbled past—Harold could tell by the rattle of the box against the frame. He looked toward the road, then back upstream to Ira who was playing the third fish of the morning. *My God, another one,* he thought. *Unbelievable fishing for so late in the year.*

This fish was best of the trio. It ran far down into the run, where it threatened to bolt into the fast water below. Ira held his ground.

Right, thought Harold, *dead right. If you chase him he's sure to go out and downriver.*

Ira pumped the rod; the fish came back, only to turn and run downstream again. Three times the fish ran, each run shorter than the last. After what seemed a very long time, Ira wrestled it to shore. Harold noticed him stumble as he unhooked the fish. He was within earshot now.

"Three's more than you can expect from this pool this late in the season," Harold barked.

Ira smiled. He was still breathing hard. He stumbled again, steadied himself, and sent out another cast.

Harold had forgotten his aches, but as he continued fishing with Ira, they returned.

"You can stop now," he yelled.

"No, I can't," said Ira.

"You're only a few years younger than me, pal. You've got to stop."

There was another slap and splash. The rod bent again.

"They won't let me," Ira called back, his words punctuated with the short raspy breaths.

Harold was no longer enjoying the fishing. As Ira struggled with the latest fish, slipping uneasily and awkwardly over the stones, barely keeping his footing, morbid scenes began playing out in Harold's mind. In one he saw his old friend freeze abruptly; he saw the rod, then the fisherman drop into the river. In another, Ira grabbed his chest and collapsed. Harold saw himself hobbling over the rocks to the aid of his old friend, and he imagined the pain in his limbs and an overwhelming desperation as he tried to lift his stricken partner but could not.

Break him off, old man, he mumbled to himself. *For God's sake, break him off.*

The line went slack. The fish had come unstuck. Harold felt relief. He watched Ira with anticipation. The old angler stood stock-still for the longest time. *He's had a heart attack after all,* thought Harold.

Ira moved his rod arm. "Don't make another cast," said Harold under his breath.

Ira began reeling in. He anchored the fly to a guide and turned slowly around to face Harold. He leaned on the staff. Harold could see he was still breathing heavily. Ira waited. Harold rose and waved him to come back. Still Ira waited. Then slowly he made his way over the uneven beach, relying heavily on his staff. When at last they were standing face-to-face, Ira fixed Harold with his pale gray eyes.

"Maybe we should rest the pool," he said, still breathing hard.

Harold nodded. He put his arm around Ira's shoulders and led him up the path to the car like a trainer leading his fighter from the ring after a split decision.

The sun had burned the mist away. It started to warm them as they put away the gear.

A car pulled up. Harold saw it was full of young fishermen. With agile movements they leaped out and began extricating gear. Their vests were clean and their rods sparkled in the sun.

"Any luck?" one called as he bounded by.

"No luck," said Harold, shaking his head. "No luck at all." He folded himself into the car and looked at Ira.

"Just skill," he said. "Just a hell of a lot of skill."

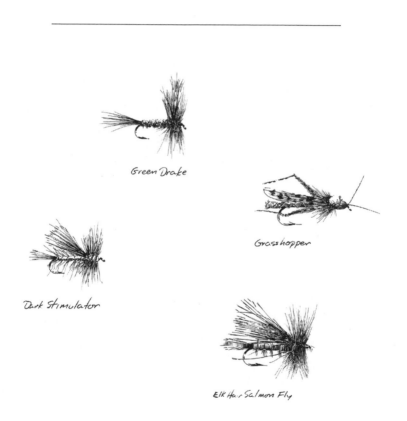

Green Drake

Grasshopper

Dark Stimulator

Elk Hair Salmon Fly

Love Story of the Trout

michaud's fine rods & flies

J. H. Hall

The first fall after we met, I moved into Jack's dilapidated farmhouse outside Augusta, Maine. While Jack tied flies and built rods, I fixed up the place, a small gray Cape connected to a barn that didn't have a right angle in it. That's my profession, interior design. No office, no overhead, just a business card (ANNA'S INTERIORS), a mailbox, and an answering machine. I deal in concepts. You could say I'm an artist and my canvas is other people's homes. Nice concept, huh? Then winter came.

There's a brutality to Maine winters that isn't conveyed by calendar art. It's not all ice formations on lobster boats. It's air so dry you have to add water before it's fit to breathe. Days shorten and the world shrinks: the inside of your house, your car, your place of work, the inside of your head.

By mid-January I was feeling lost at sea with no land in sight— spring and fall beyond the horizons of my memory and imagination. One subzero evening I was particularly restless. Deep cold does that. It's intimidating. Trees and timbers pop; pipes seize; pressure builds in people, same as in the plumbing.

Jack was tying flies, as usual. I could hardly remember how he looked standing in the river with the wind in his hair and a rod in his hand, which is how he looked when we met, on the upper Kennebec. He was guiding my father and me for landlocked salmon. His waders were cut like overalls and, with straw-colored hair swirling around his head, he looked like a big farm boy. Now he looked about as romantic as an accountant. He didn't smell the same either.

"We *could* go to Florida, you know," I said apropos of nothing except that every winter my dentist-father fished the Florida Keys.

Jack didn't even look up. "And spend more in one week than I make in a month of guiding?"

"I didn't mean for a week," I said, speaking slowly as if my thoughts were just that moment forming. "I meant for the whole winter."

I went over and knelt on the floor beside him. "What I mean is, you could guide down there. In the Keys. People do it all the time. I've read about it in magazines. These guides work in Alaska or Montana in the summer and fall, and then in the winter go somewhere warm. Jack, I've seen this type of fishing. You'd love it. It's nothing to learn. Just tides and about two new flies. With your talent, you'd learn it in a week."

"I've got enough around here to keep me busy."

"What—tying flies and building rods? You can do that down there. Heck, with the money you'd make guiding, you wouldn't need to tie flies."

"Not just that. Patrick and I have some things going on the river." He and Patrick were trying to reopen the Kennebec to migratory fish, a commendable goal.

"The river! Jack, wake up! There is no river now—just a block of ice. It's trying to tell you something. You can write your angry letters from Florida."

Jack put his fly-tying tools down and looked at me. "Anna," he said, "you should have figured out by now, I'm not some migratory-type person. I'm a Mainer. This is where I belong. If you want to take big expensive trips, you should marry a dentist, someone like that. With money."

"Jack, darling, I don't want to be rich. I just want to be warm."

"Oh, why didn't you say so?" He reached over with his foot and opened the damper to the woodstove. The fire that had been smoldering roared.

"That's really funny," I said. "You bastard." I screwed the damper shut, started pacing back and forth across the room—four paces. "You know who you're starting to remind me of?" I said "My mother, really. Not my father, my mother."

"She seemed nice enough to me."

"Right. You know what I think? I think you're afraid to go down there. I think you're afraid you couldn't make it down there with the big boys. You'd rather stay up here and be a big fish in a little pond. Pound that one stretch of river over and over again, day after day."

"I can find fish anywhere," Jack said matter-of-factly. "Anywhere there's water."

I plopped down on the old worn sofa and looked up at the ceiling. The problem is, to have a violent scene you need violent people, and Jack, for all his crude habits, had the heart of a poet. I talk big, but when push comes to shove I'm most likely to plop down on the sofa and stare at the ceiling.

The first year my father fished the Keys, he returned tanned and refreshed and full of fish stories, full of himself. I had never seen him so invigorated, so handsome as when he first burst through the door. "I have seen the future," he announced, "and it works. But it doesn't overwork."

I laughed and hugged him. That sort of comment was so unlike him.

My mother, a native Mainer and non-fisherman, was not impressed. "No bettah than a summer person," she said.

"I never once said I was," he replied.

It was such a sensible answer, I wanted to applaud, to shout, "Bravo, brave father," but I knew better. So I did the next best thing. I took up fishing.

I bought magazines, catalogs, checked books out from the library—the classics: Bergman, Brooks, Haig-Brown; the modern masters too: Kreh, Sosin, Whitlock, Apte. I became fluent in the language. I knew the names of flies and their histories. I knew the tensile strength and Modulus of all commercially available graphite, though naturally in freshwater I preferred Tonkin cane. I learned my knots too: Turle, Bimini, clinch, improved, and unimproved; blood, nail, Duncan loop—if it was in print, I could tie it.

One night my father "caught" me practicing my Bimini Twist on the back of his rocking chair. He stood silently and spellbound as I spun my magic, deftly twisting, wrapping, hitching, and re-hitching. This was no harder for me than Cat's Cradle or Jacob's Ladder. And of course this wasn't really practice. Practice had been earlier in private. This was my audition.

When I was done, he sat down in the chair with his *Wall Street Journal*. "If you really want to go that badly," he said, "next year, you may."

I almost wept. The poor man, the poor son-less man, so alone and outnumbered in that house.

Patrick reminded me of a rabbi—dark clothes, dark hair, dark beard, intense gray eyes—but he was actually an artist and fishing guide and fly tier. He painted and sculpted fish. Not scenes of people fishing, not trees and mountains and rivers. That would have compromised his principles. He painted fish, period. And I'll say this: He could make a fish look as fierce and regal as a Bengal tiger or as graceful and majestic as an eagle. Because that was how he saw them, how he believed them to be. Jack said Patrick was the best painter of fish in America—maybe the world. Maybe so, but he was the worst friend Jack could have had. They were too much alike; even had the same religion. It shared a symbol with Christianity, but they didn't worship Christ. They worshipped the symbol, the fish. They were heathens, nuts. Their conversations worried me.

No matter where they started, they ended up on fish, then the river, then the Augusta dam, which they were determined to eliminate. They would talk of congressmen and coalitions; as the evening would wear on, the talk would inevitably turn to dynamite. Dynamite was direct and didn't require the complicity of politicians. And once the dam was breached, once people saw the river flowing free through their city, they would not allow it to be rebuilt and the upriver dams would fall like dominoes! So what if Jack and Patrick got caught? It would be worth it.

"Not to me it wouldn't be," I said. "I'd rather have you free than an open river. What good's an open river to a lonely woman?"

They looked at me like I was a heretic. "I'm sorry," I said. "I just don't want you to lose sight of what's at stake here. The human perspective, I mean."

They thanked me for my input and resumed their conversation. Detonators, that was tonight's topic. Sometimes a woman has to take matters into her own hands. Men like Jack and Patrick, they need taking care of.

If there's been one rap on me as a woman, it hasn't been my looks or brains. It's been that I manipulate. So what? It's human nature to manipulate. (Look what we've done to our environment.) Not only that, it's my profession. Really, doing a life is not that different from doing a large living room. The same principles apply: First you get to know your subject inside and out, his wants, needs, desires, dreams and doomed visions. From those fragments emerges a theme. In Jack's case the theme was, of course, fishing. Fine, I could work with that. I'd need help, however—Patrick's help. And he needed mine, though naturally he didn't know it at the time.

One day I called him up and said, "Patrick, I've been thinking about you a lot lately, about your work, your career. Jack says you're the best painter of fish in America, maybe in the world."

"Because I told him that."

"Let's say it's true. The question is, why aren't you rich and famous? Why aren't your paintings hanging in all the finest homes in Maine, in America?"

"For one thing, I don't have enough to go around."

"Exposure, Patrick. For an artist, exposure is the name of the game. You have got to get your work before the public."

"I'm listening."

"Suppose it could be arranged that your works—and your works *only*—could be displayed in a proper setting. Not just a setting, a context: a fly-fishing shop and art gallery all in one. I'm thinking of elegance: fine art, fine merchandise."

"What do you want from me, Anna?"

"Fifteen percent of all sales of your work, a free sign, and maybe some weekend coverage."

"A sign?"

"It'll give you something to do with your evenings. If you'll pardon me for saying so, Patrick, you boys need a better project than blowing up dams."

Have I mentioned that I once redid my father's office? Formica and vinyl make a statement, I told him, and it's not the sort of thing I'd like said about me. I went with dark hardwood, what I call my Merrill Lynch look. He almost died when he got the bill, but he paid up, and—here's the point—never looked back. "Best investment I ever made." he said. Lovely man.

For Jack's sign, hardwood was out. It's hard to carve and it weighs a ton. We went with stained basswood instead. The top half was a huge brook trout in bas-relief, carved in meticulous detail, painted in full spawning colors. Below the trout, in block letters: MICHAUD'S FINE RODS & FLIES.

Late one evening Patrick helped me lug it in and lean it against the sofa. Then, giggling and whispering, we snuck into the kitchen and shared a beer. "Blood brothers," I said. I tried to talk him into staying till morning so we could share the moment of Jack's discovery, but he said no way. We were both a little scared.

After Patrick left, I couldn't sleep, so I just sat up and waited until sunrise. I'd forgotten how far south of us the sun rose in winter. Probably straight up over Florida, struck Maine a glancing blow at best. Sort of made you feel neglected. When Jack came staggering out in his skivvies, half awake, he almost tripped over the sign. "What the hell is this?" he asked.

"Looks to me like the sign fairy has been here," I said.

He went into the bathroom, then came back out. "What have you done, Anna?" So serious.

"Read the card."

In a tasteless moment in the wee hours, I had taped a little red bow to the top of the trout's head like a cap (thereby violating a cardinal rule: Never get cute with fish!). Jack tore the bow off, tossed it in the trash, then read the card.

"My birthday's not for weeks."

"Then call it late Christmas, okay? Let's not split hairs."

I grabbed him from behind, held him tightly, told him everything. "I know it's pushy of me, but I've found the perfect place, in Hallowell, on Water Street—can you believe that?—right beside the river. *Your* river, Jack."

"I just can't believe that Patrick was in on this. The son of a bitch."

"He's not a son of a bitch. He's your friend—and partner, if you let him be."

Jack unlocked my arms and knelt down to get closer to the sign. The sign was as wide as his arm span. I dressed and went out for a walk. When I left, Jack had his eyes shut and was examining the trout with his fingers like a blind man.

There were beaks of ice along the road, marking a sort of miniature glacial retreat. I broke the fragile edges with my boots. We have to do what we can to help things along. Around here spring is always a difficult delivery. When I got back, Jack was still kneeling, half naked, before his sign.

I had leased an interesting space, long, deep, and narrow, not unlike an aquarium. I scattered Patrick's fish throughout the space, hung them unevenly along the walls, dangled carved pieces from the ceiling; I even cut a skylight through the roof and hung a brown trout under it, looking up as if through its own watery window. Very aquatic concept, if I do say so myself.

Fly-tying materials were arranged according to colors on a freestanding, powered rack rotating just fast enough to make the furs and feathers undulate as if in a light current. When the sun hit that display, it was like a piece of living coral. The rods were racked, assembled and strung, along one wall. Want to try one? No problem. I'd run a walkway across the back parking lot to a casting platform at the river's edge. You could try your rod over fish. How many shops offer that?

When it was done, even Jack was impressed. "I had no idea you had so much talent," he said.

"You think anyone who can't cast a hundred feet is retarded."

"That's not true; but this, this is really something."

He walked around timidly, like a visitor. "Don't be afraid to touch," I said. "After all, it is your shop."

"Must be," he said. "It's got my name on the sign."

"You'll get used to it. Now shut your eyes." I escorted him past a partition to the unfinished rear of the shop: concrete floor with one small rug, woodstove, a straight-back chair, and a plain workbench for tying flies and building rods.

"You can open them now." I handed him an EMPLOYEES ONLY sign with a ribbon on it. "Your space," I said. "No customers allowed— not even girlfriends if you don't want them."

Tears welled up in his eyes. He turned away, then turned back to me and put his arms around me. "Anna," he said. "You had me worried."

"You had me worried too," I said.

Soon spring arrived upcountry and summoned Jack back to his beloved river, or at least to the stretch from the East Outlet of Moosehead Lake to Indian Pond. This was the last section of free-flowing Kennebec, four miles of rapids, riffles, deep slots, wide pools, and landlocked salmon, Jack's favorite fish. Favorite except for one thing: He didn't like the word *landlocked*. His goal in life was to unlock them.

Jack's summer camp was a wall tent atop a wooded bluff over a deep run known locally as the Colorado Canyon. When the morning sun hit the run at a certain angle, the boulders near the bottom glowed like enormous emeralds. We had a fire pit and a crude bench where Jack and I would sit in the evenings, listening to the river, protected from the bugs by swirls of wood smoke. Later we would fall asleep to the same sounds with the aroma of smoke still in our hair.

When you live so close to running water it becomes part of your circulation. The river's flow rate affected my metabolism. When the canyon roared with water released from Moosehead, I felt restless. Its more-normal, languorous rate was an invitation to sleep in. At least for me. Jack, in fishing season, was an early riser regardless of what the river was doing. He liked me up early too, when I was around. Not to make his breakfast—he was a better camp cook than I—but to hurry down and reserve good water for his clients. On weekends there was competition for the better pools. I thought using me to hold water was unethical, but Jack said, "Zane Grey did it," and that settled that. He knew I had great respect for fishing history.

So at first light I would quickly eat and, coffee in hand, wander down to my assigned pool, at the head of which I was supposed to stand and fiddle with my tackle or cast a flyless line. But under no circumstances was I to disturb the fish, which were reserved for Jack's clients. Well, maybe that's how it was done in ZG's day, but times change. I had splendid fishing, though I would have enjoyed it more if I could have told Jack—the beauty of the silver fish swirling in the green water or leaping high into the air, or glistening on the wet grass before being released. Not that he hadn't seen it all before, but it was still fun to watch Jack's face light up in the way that a fish story and *only* a fish story could ignite it.

Although I felt deprived, I didn't dare tell. Jack would have felt betrayed and he would have pouted—though eventually, of course, he would have forgiven me, because he understood, as I did, that a fisherman's or fisherwoman's first loyalty is always to the fishing. So that wasn't why I didn't tell. I didn't tell because he would have beaten me to the best water. I certainly didn't drive all that distance every weekend for the sex.

As a matter of fact, in July, when the fishing slowed, I quit visiting so often. It wasn't just the slow fishing. Business at the fly shop was picking up, and Patrick was growing weary of weekend call. Also he was finding it stressful having his work critiqued in his presence by people who, in his opinion, didn't know what they were talking about. Patrick had a tendency to argue, to try to educate his critics. It wasn't good for sales. He needed a break, more time to paint and sculpt and, naturally, to fish.

"Of course, you need a break. Take all the time you want," I would say, quite generous now that I had clandestinely helped myself to the choicest part of the fishing season.

I think if we had charged admission to the shop, we might have shown a profit. Many people simply came to look, to touch, to wiggle rods and talk fishing. Fine. We wanted people to be comfortable. We were working to create an ambiance, like an art gallery, but friendlier. Sell the ambiance, the fishing tackle will take care of itself. I believe it would have too, if only Jack hadn't returned that fall so full of fire and brimstone.

To some extent I blame myself. I left the man alone too long on his river. It affected his mind. He left his hair long; he grew a beard and a crazy glint in his eye. He looked like Moses and talked like Martin Luther King. He'd had a dream: Maybe it wasn't possible to remove the Augusta dam through politics; and dynamite, he'd finally realized, was impractical—so why not have the dam declared a public nuisance by referendum? Let the *people* decide. "Free the Kennebec 150" was his rallying cry, the phrase he put atop his petitions, "150" being the approximate mileage between Moosehead Lake and Merrymeeting Bay.

I tried to be supportive. I said, "Fine, we'll leave a petition by the cash register and one over by the coffeepot. That way they can hardly be missed." Jack looked extremely skeptical, but pressure, for a signature or a sale, was exactly opposite to everything I'd been working for.

"All right," he said. "We'll try it your way first."

The first week we got three signatures—mine, Patrick's, and one customer's. "You know how many signatures it takes to bring an issue to referendum?" Jack asked me.

"More than three?"

"I'm glad you think it's funny."

"Do you have to take everything so seriously? Try and relax. Give it time. You've been away."

But he couldn't relax, and he became increasingly restless and found it harder and harder to stay in his work area. No matter that I delicately suggested that until he readjusted to being around people and until he got his hair and beard trimmed, in his work area was exactly where he ought to remain. For my part, I promised to try to be more aggressive with his precious petition. "And here's another item you might be interested in...," I would say to the customer, always after the sale.

Jack did not consider this approach aggressive enough. One day he cut his hair, shaved his beard (his eyes were wild as ever), and started mingling with the customers, always with petition in hand. At first he'd wait until after the sale to make his pitch, but gradually he swung over to ambushing them at the door on the way in. One day he chased a man down the street, waving the petition and accusing him of moral cowardice.

"Jack," I said, as calmly as possible when he returned, "that man was on the verge of buying a rod. I've been working with him for several weeks."

"Anybody that wishy-washy, we don't need their business."

"We need everybody's business."

"That's all you care about anymore, isn't it? Goddamn bottom line, the almighty dollar. You don't really care about the river, do you?"

"You guide for free now, do you?"

"You're just like the rest of them. You're like the power company."

"You're right, Jack. You're absolutely right. No one cares about the river except you. You're the river's only friend. I hope you two are very happy together. Would you mind watching the shop for a few minutes? Thank you."

I grabbed my favorite 8-weight Sage and marched out across the catwalk to the casting platform. The river is tidal and quite wide in Hallowell. The far shore was a blur of grays and browns. The water was high, slow, and dotted with clumps of foam from the mills. I used the clumps as casting targets, cried, and asked myself, *Why can't we protect our men from themselves? Why must they resist? What makes them more afraid of our efforts to help than of death itself?* I demand an answer.

That winter the living room wasn't nearly big enough, so I enlarged it. I knocked out the wall to the kitchen. Still wasn't large enough; I knocked out another wall. "One more wall, you'll be outside," Jack said.

"That's a thought," I said, sledgehammer in hand.

But Jack's and my life together did not end in violence of that sort; it ended with an act of God. It ended with a flood, the Flood of '87, the Hundred Year Flood of the Kennebec. They marked the high water with a plaque on the back of our shop. I thought they should have put our names on it, along with the dates of our life together:

Jack Michaud

Anna Cameron

6/3/85–4/1/87

Otherwise, how would anyone know?

Let's get one thing straight: I ended it. He never said "Leave." I don't think he ever would have. But he would have been tugging at me all the time, taking line, while I kept trying to bring him closer. We would have fought to the point of exhaustion. The only ethical thing to do in that situation is break it off, let him go.

The night before the river crested, we stayed up late watching TV footage of the rising water. Jack edged closer and closer to the set until he was sitting on the floor a few feet away. This natural disaster, as it was called, this catastrophe that carried off trees, houses, and casting platforms, moved Jack to tears—joyous tears! His beloved river was taking revenge on all those who had tried to throttle it—or, I suppose, throttle him. As the helicopter swept low over the river, you could see and feel the power of the water, brown waves the size of wall tents moving like a huge encampment out to sea.

The Augusta dam was under several feet of water. When the water receded, the dam would still be standing, but for the moment it was damming nothing. Jack cheered and clenched his fists. His dream was finally realized, if only for a few hours—which, if you think about it, is probably above average.

Then the sports came on. Against everybody's better judgement, the Red Sox were about to start another season. Jack turned the TV off. He sat a while on the floor. I was on the sofa behind him. It was dark except for the light over the kitchen sink, now the living-room sink. "Anna," Jack said, after we had sat there for a while in silence, "I'm sorry, but I'm just not cut out to be a businessman."

"I know," I said. "And I wasn't really trying to turn you into one. I hope you believe that."

"I do. I know you wanted what was best. But I'm just a fishing guide. And rod builder and fly tier. I'll never be more than that. Or less."

"I don't know. You'd make a hell of a preacher."

"Ha, I'm no politician either. I finally figured that out." He turned and looked at me. "I've thought about it a lot lately. The best thing I can do—probably the *only* thing I can do—for that river is take people fishing on it. Let 'em see for themselves what it's like. Let them imagine what it could be. If they can't see it for themselves, nothing I say will make any difference. In the end, people will get the river they deserve."

I didn't say anything to that. It sounded like something he might have read in a magazine. Or maybe it was the beginning of wisdom. Either way, it sounded like good-bye.

"You want me to help clean out the shop in the morning?" I said. It was getting harder to talk.

"Patrick and I can manage. Thank you, though."

"You're welcome. I think I'll toodle off to bed now, if you don't mind."

"Anna..."

Jack was up at first light, whistling as he left the house. "What's he so happy about?" I asked the ceiling. "It's not *all* insured."

I got up, fixed a cup of coffee, ripped a page off the calendar, and realized why he was whistling. It was April first, April Fool's Day, and so the flood would be labeled. In our family, though, April first wasn't April Fool's Day. It was the opening day of fishing. My father always went fishing opening day, never mind that in Maine it was still winter and most waters were frozen. He'd find a little patch open somewhere or, failing that, he'd make one. Then he'd wet his line, his feet, freeze his hands, and come home shivering and jubilant, ready finally to drill a few teeth for the home team. It's a disease, this fishing, but it's not the afflicted that suffer. It's the next of kin.

So I may have been the only person in the state of Maine neither surprised nor particularly amused when, later that morning, the TV cameras caught Jack and Patrick paddling out of the flooded shop in their float tubes and waders, their rods strung and ready. They took opposite sides of our street and started working slowly downstream, casting to "structure"—in this case, storefronts and submerged cars.

"Any luck?" the newsman called when Jack passed their boat.

"Just started," Jack said, without taking his eyes off his fly.

"What're you fishing for, antiques?" There was a reaction shot of the newsman laughing at his own joke, the joke being that Hallowell was the antiques district.

"Brown trout," Jack said seriously.

"You're kidding!"

"No, I'm not. There are a lot of browns in the Kennebec. Hard to find 'em in this high water, but they're in here."

I had to laugh. To Jack, the Flood of the Century was "high water," memorable because it made the fish hard to find.

"People don't realize what a great river this is," Jack was saying. He stopped casting for a minute and looked straight into the camera. "Or it could be, if it was treated right. People around here think it's part of the sewer system. They don't realize it carries fish, and it could carry a whole lot more if people started taking care of it. It could be the best fishing anywhere."

There was another reaction shot of the interviewer, this time bemused, not quite sure how to take all this.

"Look down there," Jack said. "See how the water swirls around the corner of the building? See the slick water in the center? That's good holding water for trout." He began laying out more line, one lovely false-cast after another—tight loop, no wasted motion, beautiful to watch. The fly landed in the center of the slick. The cameraman panned to the reporter. He had a strange, expectant look on his face. Either he was a much better actor than I thought or Jack had him believing that a large brown trout was about to rise at the corner of Water Street and Elm.

love story of the trout

Dave Hughes

Not a lot of big fish were left in the basin. Once in a rare while a five-pound brown still got caught. When one did, it found itself hung on the lodge wall with a look of surprise, the dry fly, streamer, or rubber-leg nymph that fooled it still stuck in its jaw, the tippet curving around behind the fish as if heading off in the direction of the client who had hooked the trout, been coaxed to kill it, been talked into taking it to the taxidermist and then been conned into leaving it at the lodge to impress future clients.

"I want one like that," the current client said, looking up at the row of trout on the lodge wall. He was not yet forty, had his hair carefully combed over a spot where it had started to thin, had his right hand open on the hip of the younger woman with him, like the hip was a football and he was about to cock it into the air behind his balding head and drill a spiral with it. It was a big, powerful hand. It might have done that with footballs once, in high school or in college, maybe even in the pros. He had the shove and confidence of the ex-jock who's been revered. He strutted while standing there.

What he looked at, and what he wanted one like, was the mount of a brown trout that, according to the plaque beneath it, weighed six pounds, made its mistake on an Olive Woolly Bugger in Santee Pond, and had only recently found itself surprised on the paneled lodge wall.

"There aren't many that big left," the lodge owner said. He was short, thin, restless with wanting to tell this client that he was going to catch lots of big ones. But knowing how seldom that happened anymore, and how often it backfired when promises of big ones fizzled into bushels of small to medium ones, he didn't dare it. What he wanted to dangle before the client was not the promise of a trophy, rather the hope of one. "There's a few," he finished with a gesture toward the mounted trout, "and this last guy got one."

"Stubby'll get one," the woman said. She turned away from the wall, which removed her handsome hip from the possibility of being thrown for a touchdown. She surveyed the massive, polished pine-work of the lodge, the peeled log beam that held up the high ceiling: elk heads, deer heads, antelope heads, all big ones, peered at her. "You ought to come here hunting, Stubby," she said to the far-from-stubby man who still stared at the trout on the wall.

He turned with her, scanned the heads, smiled, and said, "Maybe I will. Let's see how things go this time." It was the kind of comment that goosed the lodge owner into further nervousness; said to him, *You're on trial.* It was no accident.

The poor fellow danced a bit, then said, "Let's go meet your guide."

The guide was eating dinner. He stood up when his clients entered the dining room propelled by his boss. He was half a foot taller than the prime client, had wide but thin shoulders and the tapered body that would have made him right at home on a horse, riding with the Cossacks, riding with Custer.

"Stubby Link and Linda," the lodge owner said, "this is John."

John put out his slender hand and got it crushed.

It was a small campaign that rode up to Santee Pond. John led, rocking happily in the saddle, setting a pace that made it no easier on his clients than necessary. Once in a while he switched the reins to his left hand, looked at his right, shook it, then kicked his horse to urge the pace toward greater discomfort.

His clients, male and female in that order, bounced awkwardly in his wake. Their horses lazed, nibbled at lush grass, dropped behind, suddenly trotted to catch up. Stubby and Linda got lifted off their saddles, dashed against them, lifted again, smacked again. Their horses caught up to John's, but quickly lagged and the punishment repeated itself.

A young man of less than medium height hung a hundred yards back. He rolled a cigarette, lit it with a kitchen match ignited on his thumbnail. He twirled the match out, pinched the head between his calloused thumb and forefinger to make sure it was dead, tossed it off the trail. He took a deep drag on the cigarette, blew smoke over his horse's ears, glanced at the packs on the three mules he towed, then gazed at the difficult scenery unfolding all around him. *Ah, Montana,* he thought, but didn't try to work words around a concept that only the mountains and meadows and forests and what lived in them could complete.

This was Ron—Roncito he was sometimes called, because the affectionate fit him and because he spent the off-season guiding fishermen in Chile. But in Montana he was what he came to call the *least guide.* He wrangled the horses, set up the tents, cooked the meals, dug the latrines, smiled at clients. If the boss ran out of guides, Roncito became one.

Santee Pond stood on a bench beneath a horned peak, the mountain sharpened to a point by glaciers, the pond formed when a landslide slumped off the mountain and blocked a small stream that had been full of small cutthroat trout. The stupid cutts had been caught out a generation earlier. Somebody had brought browns up there to replace them. The pond was less than five acres. The blocked stream didn't provide much spawning gravel upstream, so the few troutlings that escaped the egg and then the gravel and then the mink and birds and bigger browns could drop down to the pond and enjoy its richness in a relative lack of company and competition. They grew fat fast.

They were rare, which is why the lodge owner held out the hope but was careful to avoid the promise. Other tarns had got caught on benches and in basins of the uplifting and downslumping mountains around Santee; lots of streams held trout. They were all great places to fish, surrounded by an alarming beauty, but most held the medium to small trout that quickly tired folks like Stubby Link. Beauty alone didn't do much for him. Santee was the only place the lodge owner had left to send a client like him. John was the right guy to send him with because John loved big fish, hated the clients who caught them, and was such a good fisherman himself that the contest could become electric if the client urged him to fish too. And John always managed to get the client to urge him to fish. John also always managed to direct the final discharge of electricity, the lightning, correctly, when it struck.

The expedition reached the pond. John jumped down, strode to the water, watched it intently while his horse drank. Stubby stumbled off his horse, caught himself just short of falling, stood stiffly and holding the reins tight, as if unwilling to move until his legs caught themselves up and he could do it with dignity. He watched the pond too. He didn't look at the woman, who sat sore in the saddle but made no attempt to dismount.

Ron the wrangler caught up, tied his horse and the lead mule to a bottle-brush spruce, helped the woman off her horse with a hand under her arm and another on her hip. He steadied her for a moment. "Thanks," she said. "I'm all right."

Ron gathered the reins of all the horses, tied them up, began taking saddles off, smiling. "Lunch," he said, "as soon as I've got the packs off those mules."

By the time the cook hollered "Lunch!" John was pursuing Stubby across the pond, both in float tubes, one casting a black Woolly Bugger and the other an olive. They probed fallen trees, tumbles of rock, drop-offs near steep banks. They'd already seen a few rises, always big fish, always out of reach. Things looked good. Fish were moving. Stubby could cast. John saw it was only a matter of patience, waiting until a cruising fish and a retrieved fly intercepted each other. They had three days for that to happen.

He left his line out, the fly in the water behind the tube, as he paddled to shore and the promise of lunch. Nothing hit. He noted that Stubby let his fly dangle too, still fishing for him. That was good.

John emerged from the water, shed his tube and his waders, then asked the woman, "How you feeling?" She sat in the grass, rubbing her legs.

"Sore," she said. She had changed jeans for shorts. They fit her well.

Stubby said, "Fishin's a pain in the ass, isn't it, hon?" He laughed. John laughed.

As quick as lunch was over the two men went behind bushes, then wadered up and launched again. Half an hour later John had a hit. He hit back hard, with an involuntary shout. Stubby turned to him. John felt the size of the fish and felt it coming up at the same time, so he spun the tube to increase his leverage against the trout and broke it off. It all happened in an instant.

Stubby said, "What happened?" It hadn't seemed right to him.

"It got slack and got a run at it and broke off," John lied.

"Looked like a nice fish."

"Was."

They went back to fishing in silence. The hit and the depth of the bend in John's rod and the something wrong about what happened afterward spurred Stubby into a quiet flurry of casting. He flippered his tube farther from John, flung the fly with more brutality, fished his retrieves more intently. But too high in the water and too fast.

John eased up on his fishing. Strikes weren't going to come fast, and they'd come easy just as well as they'd come hard, so long as the fly was in the water. He'd already jabbed his client's ribs. He fished idly and watched the man and his anxiety for half an hour, enjoying the discomfort he'd caused. Then he caught up and said, "Give your fly some time to sink. Don't fish it so fast."

He saw his client choke down *Don't tell me what to do!* and say instead, "All right."

After a while John said, "Your wife's a fine-looking woman."

"She's not my wife," Stubby said.

"Why not?"

"What do you mean, why not?"

"I mean, she's a beautiful woman."

"I know that."

"Sorry. None of my business." John *was* sorry. He didn't mind pissing off clients about fishing; there was a reason for that. It spurred them into nailing fish up on the lodge wall and forced them to come back to defend them. Who they fished with was his business; who they slept with was not.

But she was a fine-looking woman. He kept on fishing, thinking about her.

"Fish it deeper," he called. "Slow it down."

Ron got the mules picketed, the horses hobbled, the clients' tent pitched, the cook tent pitched. He unrolled the tent he and John would sleep in and noticed the woman sitting and watching the men fishing.

"Want to go fishing?" he asked.

"*They're* not catching anything." she said.

"We wouldn't go here," Ron said. "This is where guys who want just big ones fish. If we went, we'd go to where there's more."

"How far? We have to ride? I'm not riding again today."

"Me neither. There's another pond close. An easy walk. We can get some trout for dinner."

"All right. Trout sounds good."

"I'll tell Stubby and John we're going."

"Don't bother. I don't think they'll care."

She gathered her gear. She went into the tent and put long pants back on because a cloud had come up and rested against the back of the mountain, threatening to spill over and bring some rain. Then they walked through a meadow of tall grass and summer flowers— blue lupine, red Indian paintbrush, yellow mule's ears. Because there was no trail and the ground was open and even, they walked not in single file but alongside each other.

Linda asked questions like clients do of guides, trying to find what it was like to live out there, what kind of person liked that kind of life. He was used to it, knew what the curiosity was about, knew it was a way for clients to gauge not the guide's life but the client's life, compared to it. So he told her stories about Chile that didn't have any clients in them. Most of them didn't have any fish in them, or fishing either. Then he told her about being the least guide. He smiled.

She laughed and hit him on the shoulder. They reached the other pond. It was shallow and had a meadow right down to its edge. Trout rose all over it.

The woman wasn't a very good caster, but she had exactly the right equipment. Stubby had bought it for her. It didn't take Ron long to show her how to get the fly out onto the water. The fish were cruising not very far out, and they weren't even remotely fussy about how the fly got there or what it looked like; they came up and smacked it. Linda lifted the rod, made the trout dance, brought them up onto the grass still thrashing. They were all rainbows. Ron sent them swiftly on with brisk thwacks from the handle of his knife, then flipped it in the air, caught it by the handle, and sliced them cleanly: one, two, three, and four, zip, zip, zip, and zip.

"That's enough for dinner," he said.

"What now, then? Do we quit already?"

"Let me pinch down that barb," he said. "Then you keep fishing, release them." He pulled the pliers from his vest.

"Don't you want to fish?" she asked.

"Oh, yeah. But I didn't bring a rod."

"Use mine."

"I got this," Ron said, and he fished a paperback out of his vest. "You go on and fish."

She went on and fished, shouting when she hooked one, working down the shore. Ron sprawled in the grass and read, looked up and smiled when she shouted, went back to his book. The cloud kept its distance. The sun felt good. He read himself to sleep.

When he woke up the woman was still fishing, on the opposite side of the pond. She was still shouting to him whenever she hooked a fish. Her voice carried across faintly. He wondered why a man would want to catch a big fish more than he'd want to catch the delight that was lighting up this woman like a struck match.

Ignition of any kind makes heat. When she quit fishing and came around the pond she was excited. Ron was the one who was there. She told him, "I didn't know fishing could be fun!"

They walked back to Santee Pond slowly and Ron and she both noticed that they were the same height. He cooked the fish while Stubby bragged that she was the only one who had caught any. She sat with her man and he touched her, listened to her about the fishing, was no more possessive of her than a man is possessive of his back yard when he's trimming the grass. She was part of the territory.

During the conversation under the stars that emerged above the cookfire, Stubby told John that his territory came from being a football player with good hands, which caused him to develop good friends who had money. Football didn't develop into a career for him, but his friends with money *did* develop into a career. It was called real estate. It was easy for him, and it meant he could fish where he wanted and wait for the big one if he wanted to, like he waited for the big sale.

The man talked to his guide and his guide listened. The man's hand was on his woman as he talked about the big sale and the big fish as if they might be the big moment. The stars came lower toward the fire. The man's woman watched Ron washing the dishes.

Time got by, a whole second morning of it, one-sixth of the trip to Santee Pond, in which no big fish were caught. John asked Stubby if he wanted to try one of the ponds or streams nearby.

"What's in them?" Stubby asked.

"Lots of fish," John told him.

"What kind of fish?"

"Mostly rainbows."

"What size?"

"Not so bad."

"Which is to say not so big?" Stubby asked.

"That would be right."

"Let's stay here." That was that. The flies stayed in the water where big trout swam. No fish hit.

The least guide, reading, offered to take the woman fishing. "I know a stream near here; it's pretty," he said.

She smiled at him. "Pretty, eh?" she said. It was kidding but somehow caustic.

Ron sat up, set the book aside. "Sorry. I mean it's a nice place. Clean water, lots of colored pebbles, aspen trees, flowers." This was clumsy. He didn't know why what she'd said, or how she'd said it, made him try to backpedal from pretty. Then he caught it, leaned back on his elbows, looked at her and grinned.

"It *is* pretty," he said, and the woman blushed. He'd transferred the discomfort back to her. She'd said it the way she did not because she wasn't interested in pretty places, but because she wasn't used to hearing men use that word. He gave the discomfort back to her by being comfortable using it.

It's too bad, Ron thought. *A restricted world to live in.* He looked out across the pond at the two men, still in float tubes, still flippering around and around the cincture of the shore, still casting, letting their flies sink, retrieving with short strips, long strips, fast strips, slow strips—all the ways of doing it that might fool a fish.

She watched them too. Then she said, "It's pretty *here*."

"Let's stay here then." Ron leaned back with his book.

Linda was silent awhile, then said. "What about that mountain?" The mountain above the bench suddenly became the biggest thing around to talk about.

"You mean, is it pretty up there?"

"No; I mean, can we go up there?"

The mountain looked close but Ron knew it was farther than it looked, and dangerous. He'd gone up there once. It took a full day, up and back, and he'd nearly lost his grip and gone skidding down in one place before reaching the top.

"It would take all day," he told her, "and we don't have all day left."

"What about tomorrow?"

"You can't go alone. I'll be packing camp; they'll be fishing."

She hadn't had any interest in the mountain until it was denied to her. Then she wanted to go. "So the mountain's right there in front of me but I can't climb it?"

"Well, if we came here to climb the mountain, we could go climb it. That's what we'd be here for. But we came here geared up to go fishing, and that's what we've spent our time doing. Now we're running out of time, and the fishing isn't over. So we can't climb the mountain." He knew that was all the sense he could make out of the situation, her suddenly deciding she wanted to climb the mountain and him sitting there telling her she couldn't do something. That was Stubby's job, not his.

"So why can't we come up here, see what's here, then decide what we want to do when we get here? I didn't know that mountain was going to be here when we left."

"You're missing the point," Ron said. "What you do up here is between you and Stubby, not you and me. I got nothing to do with it. I want you to climb that mountain. I want all of us to climb it. But there's no trout up there."

"You're right about trout. You're right about Stubby. You're right about what we came here to do. Stubby's doing what he came here to do, isn't he?"

"I think you got it now."

"How did you get it so quick?"

"I been watching you."

"And watching Stubby?"

"Nope," Ron said.

John set it up the final day. He had to break off another trout, but that time he did not shout and did not let Stubby see it happen. Finally he hooked the right one.

"Fish on!" he shouted. He let it come up and they were both watching when it jumped. It was a brown, beautiful, well over four pounds. When he had subdued it, John held it half in and half out of the water alongside his tube while Stubby paddled over for a closer look. Then John let it slide out of his hands, tip down, disappear. Stubby moved off without a word.

The sun got hot. Insects began to move: dragonfly nymphs, damsel nymphs, mayflies, midges, all restless in the warmth. They prompted the trout into movement. Sometimes fish swirled on the surface. They got easier to find.

Two hours later one boiled forty feet from Stubby's tube. He lofted his fly into the air and extended his backcast. He put the fly into the subsiding boil. The trout came back, took the fly, set the hook itself, ran with it.

It was the lightning quietly striking; it was John setting the hook into another client he'd learned to hate.

Stubby quelled the fish quickly, got it in fast, gauged its size against John's, against the one on the wall in his mind. It was bigger than both. He killed it, turned it carefully into the folds of his net, let it trail in the water as he flippered toward shore.

"This one's going on the wall," he said to John.

When he got to shore he shouted, "Linda! Linda! Come look at this trout!"

He got no answer. He looked around. "Where's women," he asked John, "when you got something important to show them?"

Where his woman was, was lying next to the least guide, on her belly on a grassy bank above that pretty stream, a mile from the camp that was already packed. The two of them watched a pod of small trout hovering over the bottom in a run of clear water just inches deep.

"They're establishing territories," Ron told her. He whispered, "See how they hold three or four inches apart?"

"I can't see them very well." she whispered.

"Here, take mine," he said offering his polarized glasses.

The bottom open out to her. "That makes a lot of difference," she said. "I can see them now."

"Watch those two," he told her. "One's coming too close. The other will run him off." He pointed and made his shoulder touch hers. It was no accident, and no accident either that her shoulder was not withdrawn after she'd seen the two tiny trout take off in surprisingly swift and violent battle. Only one trout returned, but she couldn't tell which one it was.

"It was the one that was there first," Ron said.

"How can you know?"

"Because that's the way it happens with trout."

"With trout?" she said.

"Other animals too," Ron said.

"All of them?"

He looked at her, trying to figure out if she was translating this into what it sounded like. He figured she was. "Not all of them," he said.

She asked, "How do these trout happen?"

"What do you mean?"

"How do they get here?"

"The big ones come up out of the pond and spawn."

"How do they do that?"

He told her the love story of the trout: How the female digs her redd, a dish in the gravel, how the dominant male moves in next to her, how they quiver together and turn on their sides and how the eggs are spilled and fertilized and later covered with gravel.

"That's it?" she said.

"Not *it*," he answered.

"What's the rest?"

He laughed. "I shouldn't tell you."

"Why not?"

"It might involve you and me?"

"There is no you and me," she said. "What have we got to do with trout?"

"When the big male moves in next to the female," Ron told her, "he doesn't have his mind on her; there's always other males around. Some the same size, some precocious little guys half his size. That's who he's thinking about. Not her."

"What happens?"

"Lots of times, just when the female begins to quiver, another big male moves in. The first male stops quivering and takes off after him. Drives him out."

"And...?"

"And one of those little males darts in, quivers at the right moment, and it's all over by the time the big male gets back."

"Somebody else is paying attention while the big guys fight?"

"That's right."

The sun was warm and the rest was equally easy for both of them. When it was over and about to begin again, the woman nestled against the least guide and said, "My Roncito trout?"

"Yes?"

"What's it like in Chile?"

"There are lots of mountains you can climb," he said, "if you decide climbing mountains is what you want to do when you get there."

the key to all mythologies

Jim McDermott

For most of the past decade, anyone who fished Huckleberry Run near Remington, where I live, was used to seeing a tiny man settled on a hill overlooking the stream, avidly scanning the water with binoculars and smoking a freakishly large-bowled pipe. This man would appear to have on his face a condescending look of scientific high-purpose, as though he were posing for an enshrining bust or portrait. To his watch over the valley he brought a precision better fitted to midges or to nail knots than to the aimless appreciation of pretty country, and he would pause, at intervals, to write feverishly in big, wine-colored ledgers, now and then licking the tip of his pen with a deftness that reminded you of a cat. In that his shadow literally darkened the little worlds of those who dared to address the vertiginous bank beneath his perch, it was hard not to sense his presence and not to be spooked by it. You would tread lightly and cast poorly. You would want to apologize for something you hadn't done. The Huck Run regulars used to call this man "The Mayor." I happen to know that his name is Joe Gould.

A number of years ago Joe Gould stopped fishing, for the most part, in order to collect observations for an extraordinarily long book he was writing about every aspect of fly-fishing. When I first met him, he had already drafted an 800-page exegesis solely about fly-casting; on the bluff at Huck Run, working both from erudition and immediate observation, he went on compiling a massive resource of notes for the masterwork he liked to call, without the sense of irony that would have given one comfort, *The Key to All Mythologies*, after the ever-unfinished, ever-metastasizing opus of Casaubon, the Faustian scholar from George Eliot's *Middlemarch*. In the main, Gould's proliferating archive contained a narrative of fly-fishing history that memorialized legendary fly fishermen and streams and canonical fly-fishing literature; a review of pertinent research in entomology, ichthyology, hydrodynamics, and riparian botany; browbeating, almost threatening commandments about reading the water and presenting the fly; a consideration of fly-tying as a separate art; an eccentric survey of useful gear, with both a historical and advisory perspective; a treatise on river management; a salty, autobiographical *bildungsroman* about a young fly fisherman coming of age; and, in the largest, most interesting section, at least to my mind, a discourse on ethics. Here Gould presented a wide-ranging philosophical tract nourished by most of the great metaphysical and ontological texts of Western civilization. More so than the other sections, it made clear the tremendous reach of Gould's autodidacticism, the dizzying crookedness of the lines of influence that informed his oeuvre. The entire work was sufficiently bizarre and original to merit the singular name "Gouldian."

Up close, Joe Gould remains an unkempt-looking person. He has short, stiff, brilliantly white hair that is grained a dozen different ways; a flat, crooked nose; and prominent tea-colored front teeth. Aside from an overall theme of disorder, not one of Gould's features fits; imagine an undead collage of spare parts. At fifteen feet and in, he and his clothes smell strongly—though not unpleasantly—of tobacco, and for this reason you begin to notice, when you're talking with him, the vagaries of the wind. His facial skin is red and craggy and liver-spotted most everywhere, but it is shiny and relatively clear and smooth on his forehead. This island of inviolacy he attributes to years of wearing hats with shallow brims. There's a toppling look to him when he walks, a consequence of having a head so large for so slight a frame. He has in speaking the quality of a political pundit about to be cut off; he half-finishes some words, runs others together and generally tries to talk faster than his mouth can move.

Gould might dress in his other life as do men of affairs, but I have hardly ever seen him in anything other than full fly-fishing battle gear. He wears patched, re-patched, and otherwise jury-rigged rubber chest waders over a dingy, pilled cotton sweatshirt, a filthy porkpie hat—brownish-gray with the brim turned up in back—and a bulging vest misshapen by boxes and spools and bottles and tangled from pocket to pocket with nests of unruly tippet material. Since there are no free ends anywhere in this riot of monofilament, you sense that to try to organize it would be to unravel the vest itself. Once I heard him refer to someone else as a "tangled person," but he himself is tangled too.

For one thing, he merely shrugged his shoulders when it happened; he never longed for what was lost, once it was gone forever, and he never cursed his luck. I find that strange, and still I wonder what would have happened if anyone other than Joe and I had gotten to read the *Key*. Would Gould have been celebrated within and without the fly-fishing community and his name made synonymous with brilliance and craft, if others could have read what he wrote?

One May evening a few years ago I turned up for the last phase of the Huck Hun Sulphur hatch, in these parts traditionally a nearly sacred occasion, for the season begins in earnest when the bigger, yellower, more fluttery duns appear. These are known locally as "Harbingers." Though I'd anticipated fishing well into the night, the crowds monopolizing the water that evening persuaded me to quit early. After catching two rather anemic, dull-colored browns, I wandered around and studied the scene.

Beneath the poplars leading to the high-water bridge, where a kind of narrow canopy encloses the stream, there were fly fishers gathered in great, loud gangs. Apparently a crowd had become a party, as I guess always happens when a shared interest makes strangers into friends. No one was fishing anymore, not that I could see, though all were staring up and down the stream, the surface of which was dimpling all over, as if rained on. Here was a kind of intelligent herd, neither altogether savage nor entirely civil, gaping dumbly at a chance to catch trout in the best possible way, and preventing me from catching them instead, or from trying to.

Upstream of the canopy, along a seemingly endless stretch of snaking water, I did have to watch for ambitiously long backcasts, but more often had to walk around lounging shadows. I saw one fly fisher hook and land a good trout, but most of the anglers were not even trying to be tricked; they were hiding behind sociability, so I felt, on the whole, depressed. Perhaps it was this mood that caused me to seek out Joe Gould for the first time. I suppose I imagined we were two Huck Run regulars of like mind about the deteriorating character of our old neighborhood.

It was good and dark when I neared the towering bank over which Gould then presided, so dark I wasn't sure at first that he was still there. As I got closer, though, by the beam of the flashlight Gould was using, I could see his pen in motion, and I could see the bit of page over which it slowly moved, but I couldn't see the ledger itself. Thus the pen seemed to inscribe shadows in a luminous white circle that hovered in the air, until the page was turned and a new circle materialized in its place. Soon I could make out Gould and his chair, and the ledgers stacked beside him. It was at this point that I stopped and wondered whether I should go on. In doing this, however, in hesitating, I must have made a spectacle of cowardice too pitiful to ignore. For Gould called out in a ragged voice, a voice with the quality of a mountain-climber's boot dislodging pebbles. What he appeared to say was that I had a "diseased casting motion." He cleared his throat apologetically.

"You could cast better, is what I meant," he said.

At this he held up the notebook and either waved me over with the flashlight or abused me by dancing the beam around my eyes and face—I'm still not sure, though Gould has never joked, kidded, or cut up that I have seen. I said calmly, but with what must have been a revealing defensiveness, that I wasn't very pleased with my casting either, though I usually caught fish at Huck Run. My casting was good enough for the trout if it wasn't good enough for him. Feeling a bit regretful, for my words seemed angrier against the ensuing silence than I had intended them to be, I advanced the rest of the way up the hill.

"Everyone catches fish at Huckleberry Run," Gould said, peering at me. "They stock the hell out of it every fall and spring, the fish are all stupid. I write letters about it, letters, letters, and more letters, but no one deigns to answer them."

On the second "letters" Gould's voice quieted; from then on he seemed to be talking to himself, more repeating a litany for his own comfort than communicating with me.

"From this very spot," he said in the same tone, "I could hook a nice hatchery-trough brood sow, God, it's a piece of cake. Trout thirty-two, catch her again, the umpteenth time? If you had a reason to fish, you could."

"What's wrong with my casting?" I interrupted.

"A number of things," he said flatly. "Hold on."

While Gould finished some notations or diagrams or whatever they were, I stood beside him in perfect silence, looking on a constellation of taillights flaring red in the parking lot, where a mass exodus appeared to be in progress. Looking the other way, I could just see the steeple of the church behind which Huck Run engenders itself from nothing, beneath neat privets of elodea, at the Mt. Solon Spring. We seemed to be the only people in the entire valley still outdoors. Gould pointed the flashlight at the ledger and pushed it up to me with one hand. This was a waiterly gesture; the tiny man seemed solicitous and a little timid. I have since learned that this was the first time he had shown anyone his pioneering work on fly-casting. I saw a page nearly black with heavily edited casting diagrams. While I studied it, I turned my head from side to side as traditionalists do at abstract art exhibits.

Gould said eagerly, "See what I mean? For starters, you stop your backcast too far gone in the arc and too softly, an almost ladylike delicacy there, as though you're afraid of hurting the rod. That's idiotic, and you know it." He shot me a shyly stern look and continued. "On top of that, you have abysmally bad timing, what I call 'neuromuscular facility.' "

"You mean, 'hand-eye coordination?' " I shot back.

Gould seemed to be confused, or he was pretending to be shocked. It was hard to tell in the dark, but he did have a disgusted look on his face. He shook his head quickly, as if to lose a bee, and went on, "A wrongly furled line has a dearth of good energy—maybe you can't see it; a footnote will explain in subsequent drafts."

Satisfied with this rehearsed-sounding declaration, Gould turned away and began rummaging violently through some loose papers. He leaned out of the chair to retrieve sheets that fluttered off, al the while murmuring to himself in a rebuking tone. I got the impression that he wished to protect what was on the escaped papers—they must have been doubly secret—so I made a show of being lost in the ledger I held in my hands.

"What's this?" I asked him, pointing to a crude likeness of a human being.

He peered at the page.

"Oh, right, it's you," Gould responded, falling back. "That fedora you wear and the glasses, those are nifty glasses, from a study I was making of your casting performance, beginning season 'alpha,' "—he said "alpha" very distinctly, as if he still doubted the decision to use Greek—"which was seven years ago, up until this evening when I saw you and your wrist put down half a pool of small fry."

"I don't remember that."

"Very well," he said, in a tone that would go well with eye-rolling. "I made a note of it there."

He pointed to a lot of smudges on the opposite page. Gould went on: "You would benefit further from slight wrist pronation, not to say flexure, following the forward initiative, a more wide-open here-I-am stance, more body English like a shot-putter, and a less three-quarters (think George Blanda) more wholly up-and-down (think Sammy Baugh) rod position. You lack torque, I would say, but also structure."

I suppose I must have looked a little peeved to hear this litany of flaws, because Gould jumped nimbly out of the chair, drew himself up, and said with formality, "You're better than most, Mr. Fedora! Ever since three years ago I've seen practically only people who've never held a fly rod before, and it's beginning to make me sick, very sick."

That evening Gould proceeded to give me a three-hour casting lesson that improved quite a bit all the components of my delivery. Whenever I approached his lair in the succeeding months, he would drop his notes and look attentive, and he would train the binoculars on my casting motion. If I was able to hear the ragged command voice in my mind's ear and able to do what it advised, my audience would dispense applause or a few feeble whoops. This made me feel strangely virtuous and happy; I would hurt myself trying not to grin. My bad casts were simply ignored; Gould would pick up his notes and appear to forget I was there and I would slink away shamefaced. Even on other streams I began to hold myself to his high standards; if I was lazy or plainly clumsy, I felt I had let my mentor down.

I visited Gould often on the hill, getting to look piece by piece at the various sections of the masterwork—which he would bring along in fat portfolios—and just as slowly learning about his personal history. He said he used to live with his grandson and granddaughter-in-law about thirty miles south of Remington, but that the couple's children became too distracting in time.

"I was molding them," he told me, "doing my part to raise them, and pretty soon they were het up to go fly-fishing all the time. It got so all I did was give casting lessons in the morning, then again around noon, when the kids, the twin boys and the little girl, came home for lunch, and then spend all afternoon fishing and all evening again casting, sometimes until they fell asleep in the yard. Joe the third, he's my grandson, was getting on me: His kids were losing interest in life. Naturally they were excellent casters, especially little Katherine, and they could fish rings around most people, but they were unable to read, tie their shoes, or play hopScotch, so I decided to take an apartment for a while and it worked out fine. I just visit them when I can. I still live in the apartment, what I call my 'hovel,' which is a little efficiency just big enough to hold the papers—as you might imagine. I've got boxes and boxes of papers—the rods and the bed. It's not ten minutes from the stream, and that's walking time."

"You walk down in your waders—you carry all your stuff on your person, the rods, the ledgers?"

Gould shrugged his shoulders. "I'm not allowed to drive anymore." he said. "I'm too old."

Gould never invited me to pick through his filing cabinets when that was still possible, and to this day he has never asked me for a ride nor invited me to have a beer with him at the Speckled Setter Tavern—nor have I ever offered or asked. And while I sneak in questions about his private life from time to time, because I'm forever trying to make sense of this odd person, he has never asked about mine. We have a friendship that is all business, somewhat like those between coworkers who never see one another outside the office.

I know from reading the *bildungsroman* portion of the *Key* that Gould worked for railroad companies out West as a young man, and that he would periodically quit his job in order to be a fly-fishing hobo for months at a time. I managed to pry out of him that he has taught physics at a liberal arts college in Maine, worked for a high-technology weapons firm, and published a book about aerospace engineering. And I learned that he was married for a long time to a woman now deceased, whose name he seems afraid of saying out loud, apparently because it saddens him that she is gone. That's about it.

Gould seemed most human when timidly exhibiting a passage from the *Key*, but, all in all, his writing methods also smacked of the supernatural. Without fidgeting, he could write, draw, and take notes for sixteen hours a day. And he could do this while holding—with occasional breakdowns—fairly lucid conversations, which themselves nourished the text. This frantic writing and recording invariably covered Gould in ink; he would have smudges on his cheeks, lines on his neck, and globs on his fingers, always in black.

At first it was disconcerting to know that my every move was being represented on the page—some of our conversations he took down verbatim, in shorthand—but eventually I came to accept that

Gould was a man who liked to observe and record every sensation that appeared before him. But I wondered what besides immutable nature motivated the creation of the masterwork. Did Gould hope to do some good through it; did he really plan to publish it and thus give up his only passion? The closest I came to getting an answer was when Gould volunteered his worries about the decay of Huck Run, as he does to this day. He makes it plain that he hates the sheer numbers of people trooping in and out, and that he hates the obviously lackadaisical attitudes of the fly fishers. He seems to resent that they appear to be after a little fun and nothing more. It is only a guess, but I suspect that Gould hoped to save fly-fishing by making a sort of arcane textual museum about the sport. I do know that if *The Key to All Mythologies* had become the foundational textbook of fly-fishing, very few people would fly-fish; there would have been a weeding out of dilettantes. And those few who did fly-fish would have done it well, as well as Joe Gould does when he can bring himself to wet a line.

Another of my concerns had been to get Gould to fish, or at least to comprehend his self-denial, and to these ends I began to harass him mercilessly about how foolish it was to remain on the hill when there were trout to be caught. I was sure that my efforts would never work—sure until the murky, humid, gloomy August evening I happened to find Gould out of his chair and fishing about a mile downstream from his perch. I came upon his unmistakably tangled figure standing to the waist in the middle of Huck Run, playing what appeared to be a huge fish. Gould held his severely taxed and tormented rod straining high above his head, in a fair imitation of a referee announcing a safety. His face was, nonetheless, impassive; he puffed his pipe in a slow, regular cadence and seemed to be more interested in some new theory than in the struggle. Before coming any closer, I waited for Gould to land the fish, the largest I had ever seen at Huck Run, easily more than twenty-five inches of hook-jawed, golden-bellied brown, release it skillfully, on autopilot, and climb the bank while forceps, flex-lights, and clippers swung wildly from a constellation of mini reels newly appended to the overstuffed vest.

"Trout will take gliding water striders," he announced evenly. "Those hordes that skate leg-deep through the meniscuses of trout streams?"

I didn't know about this.

"Deer hair, eight legs, nothing fancy, though the rearmost appendages are tricky. I caught twenty-seven other browns and brookies—to be precise, twenty-two browns and five brookies, only smaller."

"All today," I said.

"All this evening," he responded, without a trace of arrogance, and hustled past me. I probably imagined it, but Gould seemed uneasy to have been surprised like this. There was a sort of panic in his movements. I tried to sound casual as I said to his back, "Not to be nosy...."

"You can't help it, can you?"

"I suppose not," I said. "I am curious: Why are you fishing today?"

"Short version," he said. "I couldn't dope it out from pure hermetic contemplation."

I followed Gould to a log that had rolled to the base of the hill, and we sat together as the sun set. Once the portfolio was open and a ledger was resting on his knee, he calmed down, ceased to say things like, "If you'll excuse me," and began to describe the problem he had just solved.

"I hypothesized that their noses knocked the striders away just as a blade of grass in a great-grandchild's bath water evades the grasp of fingers," he said. "And this was so. But what some of the trout do is drink the meniscus pod on which the strider rests. They vacuum the entire square inch or so of water down their throats. This causes a tiny whirlpool that is almost invisible to the naked eye. The whirlpool either carries the strider down the gullet or paralyzes it long enough for the trout to crush the legs. About that part, I'm not sure."

He drew tiny whirlpools on the paper and put open trout-mouths beneath them, and shaded in wonderfully detailed but still rather crude bodies. Some of the trout were big and some were small. Most had hookish jaws, soulful eyes, and fat cheeks. All had finely delineated dorsals that looked like Japanese fans.

"When I think I know all there is to know about fly-fishing," he said, "and have pondered these truths again and again—you've seen me do this, and, friend of mine, you know me better than anyone—I find I have to leave that chair, nice as it is, and wade in deep."

I don't know that Joe Gould has ever blamed me for what happened about a month later, but, in the sense that one event leads to another, I do hold myself partly responsible. Had I never ascended the hill that May evening, I feel certain that Gould's masterwork would be with us today. Maybe you would be reading it right now, and maybe it would be changing you already, just as it changed me. But I'm the one who parted the curtains, who interfered with and interrupted and destroyed Joe Gould's contemplative paradise, because, in the end, I couldn't help myself. At first I was overwhelmed by a selfish desire to find out why he sat on the hill and watched us all but never descended to fish among us. Perhaps I also resented what I perceived to be his arrogance, but what was really only purpose. And at last I was undone by a perverse need to make him leave that book alone; I felt that I knew better, and I bothered him until he did what he swore he would never do, which was to fish again. That was the jinx, I suppose—that, and his admission that he couldn't do without a rod, a fly, and a fish if his masterwork was to be truly masterly.

It was long after midnight, late in September, when he fell asleep with the pipe, freshly stoked in advance of further work on the waterstriders section, stuck loosely in his mouth. At some point it fell, spilled its generous bowl onto a floor carpeted with pages and pages of the *Key*, and started a hot, fast fire that soon consumed not only the hovel and its contents, but also the entire building in which Joe Gould lived.

Having heard on the radio about the fire, I was at the scene not long after it had died out, helping Gould salvage what he could.

"My clothes were on fire," he told me, wonder in his voice. "I was burning, and the boxes were burning and falling over, and all these pages were floating toward the ceiling: bright orange it was. They flew upward, they were dematerializing in the air, and the leavings of them were rushing dead-on into my eyes. The damn things were blinding me, but when I jumped out the window to save my hide, or what was left of it—I landed on an azalea bush—I managed to roll around until nothing was afire anymore."

I noticed that Gould wasn't wearing waders, that he had no hat on, that his sweatshirt was gone, too. He wore the kind of clothes other people wear, though these were tattered and black. His face and arms were covered with soot, and he coughed as he spoke.

"What was destroyed?" I asked.

"The rods in cases are fine." Gould said, and, though he did not exactly smile, he looked to be quite happy about the surviving rods. He continued, "My waders and such were on the line out back. I have quite a few hooks left. The fire department swamped the deer hide and drowned the hackle necks, but they'll dry out; they'll be good for something, perhaps saddle at the very least."

I turned from Gould and looked at the smoking rubble that used to be his home.

"What about the *Key*?" I asked in that same direction, away from that great book's author, trying not to sound as desperate as I felt.

"Oh." Gould coughed. "It's just as well," he said calmly. "It's just as well."

I turned around and stared at Joe Gould's face, which was now neither happy nor unhappy.

"I'll help you," I said quietly, again looking off, "and we'll piece it together; it'll be just like it...."

"I don't follow you," said Gould sharply, and he appeared to be honestly confused. "Even you," he said, "are too old to start something like that now. You'd be dead, you know. You'd be dead before you'd even begun."

Later that day Gould moved the remnants of his former existence back to his grandson's house south of Remington, and he lives there now. I encounter him often at Huck Run, but he is usually quite busy fishing with his great-grandchildren (there are now five of them), and we never get the chance to sit and talk about *The Key to All Mythologies*.

I see him watching, though. I see the wheels turning.

labor day

Gary J. Whitehead

"You coming tomorrow?" I asked, and he didn't look up from the magazine, only shrugged. The fish tank gurgled on his bureau. In one of Linda's china dessert dishes a June bug spun on its back, kicking at nothing. "That a yes?"

And it must have been. Morning and he's up before me, standing there in his skivvies, tying a black fly in my Griffin vise clamped to the counter. He scoops a spoon into his Cheerios. Same dessert dish as the June bug and I wonder if it died from the effort. I can relate.

I'm in the garage packing gear into the truck when I hear him on the cordless with his buddy Skyler. Something about the river, the rain, the old man. That would be me. He comes out carrying the sleeping bags, sour-pussed, and almost trips over the Lawn Boy.

"You know, you don't have to come if you don't want to," I tell him.

"Who said I don't wanna go?" He stuffs the bags behind the seat, turns his baseball cap backward, and walks back toward the door with a hitch in his step. "Sky might come looking for us later on tonight, though. If it stops raining."

I open the garage door harder than I mean to and it bounces back halfway down.

The river is four miles away and at the spot I have in mind the water curves out of a busy downhill over some rocks and then widens into a pool. You can get there by hiking down the sandstone bluffs or by circling a farm and crossing to the west side over a log footbridge. It's muddy after three days of rain and the river is high. Could tell that much when we crossed it on the highway a mile back. Either way I know it'll be a mess.

The truck bumps over the potholes and frost heaves. It's drizzling enough that I leave the wipers on intermittent. When we turn onto it, the gravel road is nearly washed out. Deep gorges where streams run their jagged way toward the ditch make it a bumpier ride than the county highway. Will smokes in quiet with the window halfway down. Since the day we buried Linda, in May, he's been smoking in front of me. The wisest time to start, since it was the least of my worries. Now he seems embarrassed, nearly sticking his head out the window just to exhale. When he's done, he folds the butt in the ashtray and closes it, then lifts the leather buckle on the creel wedged between us.

"What's this?"

"Ham sandwiches."

He closes the lid. "I don't eat pork," he says. Before Linda died they watched a documentary together on the hog industry in Iowa. She was already a vegetarian, had been for fifteen years. If this is Will's way of remembering her, I know he'll soon forget. The kid loves ham, and the imported stuff was on sale at the Fareway.

"Cook what you catch, then," I tell him.

He rubs his upper lip where for almost a week sparse, dark hairs have been sprouting, scoters in a line around the mouth of a river. "Won't make no fire in this rain," he mumbles.

It's so muddy, we circle the farm in our waders. Along the fence lumbering Angus cows pause their cropping to look at us. Then they go on chewing. From inside a round brick barn a horn beeps five pigeons into the rain. Will checks the guides on his rod as we walk through the mud.

"Watch it you don't snap the tip," I tell him.

He lifts the rod higher. "Why you sweatin' me? Have I ever snapped a tip?"

I stop to cinch the pack on my back a little tighter and Will walks on ahead, flexing the rod. He's only fifteen and he's probably twice the angler I am. "Got the smell," Derry would have said, and I remember him saying it about me.

A place called the Sextons, east of the Kennebec, and I was close to Will's age. Late in the year, probably October because we climbed a fire tower on the drive back, and why else but for Derry to see the foliage? All morning he'd been watching a pool out of aviator sunglasses, the same ones he'd worn on bombing runs over Germany and kept unscratched as long as I knew him. Maybe I could see my father upriver, knee-deep in the water, throwing wind knots. I know Derry hadn't made a single cast.

Derry pulled me close. "Know why the biggest fish in the river is the biggest fish in the river?" he asked. He laughed up a bit of phlegm and shot it into the foam. "Because she's smart enough to hide. The sun comes out, she don't let it trick her out. Learned that from a Spaniard, 10,000 feet over Leipzig. You listen to me now, boy. Might learn a thing." I could see my face in both lenses of his glasses.

At the end of a natural stone jetty there was a dark cove where white birch shadows scratched their dark fingers into the lap of small waves. "Try there," I said, and he did, and that's when I saw the mother-of-all-rainbows leap full out of the water. A pink, honeyed arc, dazzling a white spray. Of course, she missed Derry's fly, and neither one of us saw her again, except in our own slow-motion replays whenever she swam into mind. I thought the old man was going to fall in the river, he was so excited.

Maybe he'd flown over Dresden, not Leipzig. Maybe my father was there with us when Derry made the cast. My selective memory more often than not has him off somewhere drinking. Juice of the sour grapes I can't stop chewing. That October afternoon Derry was right to wait, but I was right to tell him where to cast, and, walking back to his jeep, the open-eyed catch flopping along his back on a knotted hemp string, I heard him tell my father I had the smell.

Not long after that we left Maine and moved to Minnesota. My father had lost his job as a press operator and my mother wanted to be close to her mother, who'd recently been made a widow by a lumber mill accident. I never did get the full story, but I imagined it involved some monstrous circular saw and my grandfather losing limbs. Derry wrote, but I never saw him again. He went to Korea. He was my first teacher and the last thing he sent me was the split-willow creel I now see Will fishing through for a ham sandwich as he labors on ahead of me in his green waders.

Something about a river as you approach it makes you lose yourself momentarily in its ever-changing language so that you almost understand what it's saying. Then you're just yourself again. And after a while, you stop hearing it altogether.

The river is high, full of flotsam, but there's a good feeling in the urgency of it. I'm surprised that Will stays close. Even with a cigarette in his mouth, he makes tight loops that I envy. The sky's only spitting now; far to the south there's a band of promising pink light. Linda maybe, up there doing her best to make our day. God knows we need it. By eleven all I've caught is a walleye that slipped out of my hands before I had a chance to show it to Will. He's gotten two small brown trout. Nothing worth keeping. When the sun retreats into the bruise of gray, I leave Will to fish alone while I set up the tent, a four-pole blue geodesic dome that I bought us for Christmas and haven't yet used. It's easier to set up than I thought it would be. Ten minutes and it's standing. I unzip the door and throw our sleeping bags inside. It smells like new rubber. High in the trees a woodpecker taps a hungry Morse code.

When I find him, Will is crotch-high in the current, popping the sunken tip of his line out of a pool.

"Get any?"

"One rainbow. With an Elkhair Caddis." He works the line all the way in, inspects the tippet.

I wade out to him. "I set up camp. Just need to find some dry wood. The tent looks good."

"You dig a trench?" He's got a smoke tucked above his ear. A regular James Dean.

The sky is a white wall that rings me in when I turn. "Nah. It's gonna clear, I can smell it."

Back on shore, I catch a whiff of a cigarette.

I scout for dry wood along the overhanging bluffs. High up in the pines there are dead, barkless branches that look dry, at least on their undersides. I half-hitch a tent stake to the green nylon cord, swing it like a lasso, and loft it onto the nearest dead branch. When it's taut, I buckle my knees. A crack, and the branch falls beside me; the piece left sticking out of the tree wags like a diving board just sprung. When I've made a big-enough pile, I untie the stake and stick it in my pocket, loop the cord around the wood, and hoist the load onto my shoulder.

It's a place we used to camp when Will was younger and Linda wasn't sick. All along the mossy sandstone ridge the chiseled initials and names tell a story older than mine. Love's labor lost. After I drop the wood, I go back to look for the heart I carved, the letters I printed into that ancient sandstone. It's a difficult climb; the rock is wet and crumbly as pumice, the ledges narrow and unreliable. I'm blinded for a second by the sun and then it's swallowed by another cloud. Nearby, I hear the flap of a small sail filled with wind, a kite someone is flying in a pasture the other side of the river. I think about lightning, and Will swinging his graphite rod high in the air. But it would hit the kite first, wouldn't it? If it's some boy thinking he's Ben Franklin, it's an experiment in stupidity, and I think about hiking across the river to tell him so. But the water's so high, I could never cross it. Ten feet up the ledge, I catch a glimpse of Will, thigh-deep in the river, intent on a small lee and the protruding V of a black, sunken branch. He's looping a fly over the shadows. *She don't let it trick her out.* My boy, and he's got the smell. A born fisherman.

Will came flopping into this world with an argument. Ten hours of labor before it was finally over. He came out breached and cyanotic and the doctors whisked him away from us. When I saw him later, his skin was pink and his shiny eyes black as a bass's. Now they're somewhere between hazel and green, and he's fifteen, motherless, and on weekends I hear him banging around the kitchen, drunk. In July I woke one night to the smell of a roast cooking, two in the morning, Will sprawled asleep before the muted TV. I worry about him. Especially since it runs in the family—my father, who died a drunk; my sister, a graduate of Hazelden, sober now nine years. Somehow it skipped over me. A lucky chromosome. Or sheer willpower.

Will. It's a name without irony. Fifteen, and his first year of high school was more like a prison bid, the truant officer calling me a half-dozen times at the college so I could worry through my lectures on Homer and Dante. Detention so many times Will started calling it a class. School starts back in less than a week, and I'm thinking it's just what he needs. Just what I need. He'll be a sophomore; maybe if I can get him to quit smoking he'll join the cross-country team. Teaching again, maybe I'll let go of the image of Linda the last time I saw her.

My fingers are aching, my boot-tips inching out of the small crevices. The black-and-red kite, high above the trees, starts to spiral downward. I reach upward, searching for the heart I carved on a golden day, and it's like a dream I can't go back to because something woke me. Tired of climbing and looking, I decide it must have been washed away by rain and wind and twenty years of time.

The sun finally comes out just as it's falling into the trees, some hope for tomorrow. I'm blowing on the fire when Will comes walking up the path holding the rod in one hand, patting the creel with the other. "Dinner," he says.

I point, grinning with shame. "The fire."

"Looks more like the smoke," he says. He hands me the dripping wicker basket. "I'll make you a deal. You clean, I'll get the fire going."

As much as I hate to clean, I take the two trout and the knife and walk down to the river.

When I get back, the fire doesn't look much better, but Will's made a small pit of coals and he's slicing butter into the iron skillet. Soon the whole camp smells like the fish fries we have at the firehouse every Sunday of the summer, the ten of us who volunteer to fight the one or two brush fires we might be called to all season. For me it's an excuse to get out of the house, to wear a black beeper and a red T-shirt and to feel like a good citizen. It's also an excuse for all of us to get together once a week for fish and beer. This summer I've gone religiously. And not so much just for the beer, especially since the night of Linda's funeral, when I almost swallowed too many pills with a bottle of wine. I go now just to hear people laughing.

Will and I sit on the cold stones I rolled into camp, eating the fish and baked potatoes off aluminum foil with our fingers because we forgot utensils. Hanging from a tree, the lantern wheezes a pulsing light, winking where there's a hole in the mantle. Will's got the yellow plugs of a Walkman in his ears and I take that to mean he's not in a talking mood. I walk off to pee into the black woods.

It's a Saturday night, and the stock cars are racing in town. The drone of their looping intrudes into the peace of our camp. Will pulls the earphones down onto his neck like a stethoscope. "So I might go to St. Paul next week. Our last weekend before school really gets going. Sky's brother's band is playing at an all-ages club." He breaks a branch over his knee, adds the two halves to the fire. "So can I go?"

"I'll think about it," I say, and he nods. Skyler doesn't top my list of Will's friends and they both know it. He's a year older than Will, but in the same grade since he repeated a year. In the seventh grade they were both kicked off the bus for swearing. It's my hunch that it's Skyler who started Will smoking and now drinking. He's a preppy kid, the all-American, but he's a sneak who takes his father's Lincoln out without permission. "How do you plan on getting there?" I say.

"Sky's gonna borrow his dad's car."

I gird myself for some shouting. "Is he planning on asking first?"

"Nah, Pop, he knows better. He already asked."

I want to say no, but I was fifteen once. The endings of all those teenage summers, the thrill of a night away from home. And when Linda died, Skyler was there for Will. Hell, the two of them were up all night playing cards, crying between hands of hi-lo-jack.

"Let me just think about it, Will, okay? I'd like some peace of mind, at least for tonight, while we're here." I stand up to get more wood because my hands are shaking.

"Fair enough," he says, putting the headphones on as if to listen to his own heart.

When I unzip the tent and crawl out, the camp is half-lit with fog. Will's sleeping bag is empty in the tent and he's gone. The fire is cold. Across the river a crow is cawing. I'm stiff from a damp sleep, groggy and thinking of coffee. Could Skyler have come in the middle of the night? I'm sure they would have woken me had he come. I kick at the ashes, the last branches from the pile of wood. Everything is soaked from the fog. I think about walking back to the truck and driving to Casey's for a coffee, but hell, I came here to fish. I yell Will's name and it blows out of me, a visible mist. Cold for early September. I crawl back in the tent for my toothbrush.

Will's rod is gone; so is the creel. All around the camp tiny fronds of fiddlehead ferns have uncoiled overnight. When I pull the waders on over my shorts they're as cool and clammy against my legs as a bull-frog. I take my rod and box of flies toward the gurgle of the river.

She don't let it trick her out. But isn't that just what Linda did? Gave in to it finally because it was easier than fighting it? I lean on a tree to catch my breath. I can see the river now, impelled by its own nature, a brown continuum bent on its ending. Some place far to the south it must just branch off into a hundred tributaries, a thousand creeks that themselves divide until they're dry. It's the nature of things to go with the flow, and it's what I'm trying to do. Go with it. Like the nights I weep until I'm dry. Grieve and go on angling by increments until I feel the pull of something else.

The tip of my rod catches on a root in the path and before I feel it bend, it snaps. I blow the mud out of the guide and stuff it in my shirt pocket. Should have brought the tubes, should have held the tip up, but I never practice what I preach. The worst thing a teacher can do. Or a father.

Twenty yards upriver I see him, knee-deep in the current, hat turned backward, casting where a fallen tree has made a shallow pool. No sign of Skyler. I skip from rock to rock until I'm behind him. Then I just sit and watch. He works the pool from right to left, skipping the fly across the swirls. The yellow line arcs and collapses, arcs and collapses, and he makes it look effortless.

Just above the treeline to the east, the sun is conjuring its way through. Now and then I can see the perfect circle of its edges behind the white veil of fog.

Finally, Will turns around. "Hey. How long you been up?" he asks.

"Oh, a little while. Catch any?"

"Not yet." He tugs at the line.

I pull down the straps of my waders, step out of them. "I'm going into town for coffee. Need anything? A juice?" I ask him.

"No, I'm all set," he says, jumping to my rock. "Don't you wanna fish?"

I take the tip-top out of my pocket and hand it to him. His eyes go wide and he grins, and then he gestures as if to button his lips. He's lost some weight this summer. His arms are bony and tanned. His mustache is far from full, but from my angle he looks for a second just like a man. "I'll be right back," I say.

hobard's gate

Seth Norman

We strolled along the embankment watching great rainbows sip midges. It's absurd to see such trout rise to creatures that tiny; also aggravating, since on size 22 hooks and 7X tippet they're nearly impossible to land. A chance to try is one of the ranch's attractions.

Calvin nodded at the smutters and smiled. Host here, he's usually smiling, as suits somebody who's found his place in the world. Also, Calvin has a secret: He favors the fish.

"So you hooked a couple," he said, his Tennessee accent drawing out words and smoothing edges. "Little Brassie?" I shook my head, grinned back. We've been here before.

He looked at me hard. "Landed 'em, didn't you? Damn. Don't tell me…You did some wild thing again, am I right?"

I squinted into the low sunlight and kept my hand firmly wrapped around the fly keeper. "I beg your pardon," I said, softly, with mock indignation. "I observe the natural order and fish accordingly. In any case, it's your fault."

"Mine?"

"As it happens. Remember what you told me to listen for last summer? The frogs? I listened again last night; this year, I came prepared."

Calvin made a variety of displeased noises. "You know I tried to bet Helen you would do something like that, but the lady would not take odds at eight to one. Now then, sir, you let me see."

I slipped the fly from the wire, held it out for his inspection. Calvin enforces a size 8 maximum hook rule; this one was about 5X long, a light-wire Aberdeen without even a bump where the barb had been. I'd packed it with dyed green deer hair, then added feather legs wrapped to heavy mono kickers. Badly bent now, it had kept three fish.

Calvin sighed as he turned it over. Then, shaking his head, he strolled off to study some construction behind the dam. He would be back. I knew that, just as certainly as I knew that while the fish had rushed a big meal at dawn, dorsals breaking water as they attacked, they'd do no such thing in the better light of this hour. They didn't, as I leisurely cast my way down the bank. Fifteen minutes later I'd reached Hobard's gate.

There's the lake and a stream on the ranch. The former holds those giant rainbow smutters, fish stocked over years. The latter keeps wild fish, both rainbows and browns. Anglers can move from lake to stream by walking several hundred yards along a pasture fence, hiking downhill at the corner, then fishing back along the river below the lower fence line. This detour avoids the domain of the only animal that justifies "ranch" in the lodge's name: Hobard is a Charolais bull the size of a Studebaker. A young stud when I first came here, edgy and active, he had also aged, and lately faded toward idle. His lassitude prompted a few old-timers like me to flaunt a posted rule, and even to take a childish pleasure in daring the warning sign nailed to the rail: GO AROUND.

I stopped just in front of it, to let Calvin catch up with me again. He pretended to still be stewing about frogs.

"I take it that you will not mention this to anyone, ever. And that we will talk about something else at breakfast?"

It was neatly done—a clever segue. Breakfast was what Calvin had come out here to address, never mind what I'd caught or the dam work. He knew I wasn't coming to meals this morning, or noon—not even tonight, when I'd drive into town. He also knew the reason: that among the half-dozen guests now at the ranch was one with whom I would not share a meal—break bread, if you want—not on a prayer.

Calvin had come out here to tell me he felt bad about that.

"My regrets to Helen," I said evenly, "but I'll skip breakfast. I'm down to the stream right now."

"Uh-huh." He turned his head to the side, distracted for a moment. "You're not going through this gate, though. Not with me standing so close I can't pretend I don't see you?"

I shook my head. "Of course not," I said solemnly. "I'm going to wait till you go in to breakfast."

Calvin started to object, then slowly turned to look toward the lodge. After a moment he swung his gaze around to stare at the mountains in the east. It was the day after Halloween, and the slopes flamed with autumn. "I want you to know I am sorry," he said in a voice suddenly soft. "I really am. Wilson booked him, like he'd book anybody with a credit card. I wouldn't have."

"Not on my account, I hope."

He shrugged. "He'll kill a couple fish, just to get pictures and because he doesn't much care. And I don't like the way he talks to Helen."

The man I would not sit with went by "J.R.," just like the villain on the old TV series. This real-life version was the industry's leading predator in small companies like mine. On a personal level, nobody ever said he was charming.

"He better watch out for Helen," I said.

Calvin nodded. "Yes." A long pause. Then, "He knew you were coming, didn't he? That you're always here this week of the season. That's why he chose now to come, and to bring all his brown-nose pals."

I said nothing.

What Calvin said next seemed to come out of nowhere, words spoken with more Tennessee in his voice than usual, and with an edge I felt on my skin. "I am told…that he will drive you under pretty soon."

I blinked. I was somewhat shocked that he'd say it, or that he'd say it that way. Friends though we were, the subject seemed beyond the pale of our usual conversations. And protocol—manners—is important to Calvin.

It took me a moment to think out my answer. "Let's say…this is my last year up here. For a while, anyway."

"It is, is it?"

"Yeah. So maybe Wilson is smart to bring in another big spender."

Calvin said nothing.

"Now then…those October caddis are coming off in Helen's Pool?"

He nodded. I thought that would be the end of it, but he spoke again, now with a kind of low vehemence. "Interesting, isn't it? I mean, to have anything in the world today, even just a sport, that's so knit into ideas about honor. And practiced mostly by people committed to decent behavior—who'll stand by a word and a handshake." He shook his head, smiling. "And they're the same ones who haven't a clue that all they are is a market for some of the folks behind those fine ads—"

"Calvin."

"—pandering sons of bitches—"

"Calvin."

"—pretending—"

"Calvin!"

"What?"

We stood looking at each other. It felt like a long time and I knew there was probably as much color in my face as in his. "Leave it alone, please," I said, speaking softly, though that wasn't my intent. "I can guess how you feel, and I don't want to talk about it or even see you angry. Not now, maybe not ever—not on caddis time, for damn sure. It's done. It's water under a bridge where I'd like to be fishing."

"Is that right?"

"It is. I have no patent. You know that."

"Simpson had one."

Another friend in the business: He had a patent, but not a spare $50,000 to defend it. That's why most of us don't bother. Patents are weapons for corporate armies, not for small companies pushed into battle.

Or maybe it isn't so simple.

I sighed. "Then I guess that's just how it goes."

"Is that right?"

"I'm afraid so."

"No. Is that *right?*"

Like many men who laugh a lot, Calvin can get cranky about issues he thinks important. He tends toward absolute stands: Helen says that since the *Valdez* spill he would hike before stopping the truck at an Exxon pump.

"Never mind," I said to Calvin. "Will you go to breakfast, please? About now, while we're young? Fish are biting and I want to get past Hobard before he gets hungry."

Calvin raised his arms, let them fall, chewed on something. "All right," he said, and looked again toward the lodge, where he had to return and entertain. He calmed a little. "But I'll tell you something. J.R. is the reason for fifty-dollar contracts." It took me a moment to get that, then I laughed. I laughed harder, I suppose, out of gratitude for the sentiment, and for the lightning touch. Calvin smiled as he watched me. "Speaking of which," he said amiably, "I'll talk to you later about buying some of your frogs."

"Sure you will," I said. Like hell: Calvin could tie them better blindfolded. But his flattery made me feel good, and it wasn't the first time he'd managed to do that.

I waited until Calvin got to the lodge's back door. When I did slip the gate old Hobard eyed me so closely I thought he was hungry indeed. So were the browns, and I raised half a dozen in an hour on a big orange Sofa Pillow, landing one as long as my forearm.

Not a bad morning. When I was sure everybody else had finished breakfast, I hiked in for coffee.

Helen was cleaning up when I double-wiped my feet on the doormat. She stopped when she saw me, stood silent before the wall of windows with both hands full of dishes. "I saved you something. Calvin's gone out to feed Hobard a treat. Sit. Eat."

It was a cardinal rule of the lodge that if you missed a meal you didn't ask for food later. I hadn't asked.

"Yes, ma'am."

Helen and I go way back. She'd been one of my wife's nurses, the last of those years. Some time later, when she went to work at the VA hospital, Helen rang me up to ask if I might have jobs for patients. Among the best of some good referrals was her fiancé, not as an employee this time, but as a guide. Calvin was so good at that game that when I told a few friends about him, I was really doing them the favor.

Seven or eight years later, when Helen and Calvin came up to manage the lodge, I was one of their first customers. We still joked about how I arrived for the weekend with a letter typed up to their boss, testifying to the fine time I'd had with his hosts.

It had been the truth then and all the years since. Now Helen put a plate of eggs, potatoes, and bacon in front of me, next to a cup of coffee already swirling with one level sugar and cream. She sat down across the huge table and lighted a cigarette, knowing I didn't mind. Her gaze seemed a little pinched.

That's unusual. If Calvin's mostly a happy man, then Helen is one reason why: bright as late-morning light, acerbic, laugh-out-loud funny when she wants to be.

This morning, though, she wasn't in the mood.

"Somebody broke a rule," she said flatly. "Sure as hell, somebody walked right through Hobard's house, in front of God and man and five breakfast guests."

I looked out toward the gate where I'd taken leave of Calvin. The view had always been better screened. No wonder Calvin had stared.

"We chopped some willows," she said, "for the beginner classes."

"Sorry about that. I should have noticed."

She took a long drag on her skinny cigarette. When she smiled, that also looked thin. "I don't mind any more than Hobard does. But Calvin's already upset, you know, what with having that abbreviated bastard around."

J.R.: Abbreviated bastard—that's what I mean about Helen.

"So am I," she continued. "Upset. I was in the shop in town last week…You'd think he'd at least have the grace to change the color of products he steals. At least the color."

That would have suggested shame. "Not you too," I said wearily.

"Me too," she snapped.

I put down my fork. "Judas, Helen. Am I going to enjoy this breakfast or not?"

She exhaled. "Eat. Enjoy."

I started to, which, as I'd expected, didn't slow her a beat. "You know, last night in bed Cal and I were talking about the differences in people. The way they treat one another. Calvin was remembering how it was growing up outside Brownsville. The expectations folks had there and maybe still do. 'Do unto others, or else,' that sort of thing. He was talking about the consequences people faced if they didn't behave. You know how he gets."

I did. Calvin had once laid out a theory that Southerners were polite to each other from respect for a violence they knew was right under the skin, hard as bone. "People are naturally dangerous," he'd said. "That's why we have Law, to remind us that we don't need to bloody our hands to put a wrong right." Of course, like everything else Calvin spent time considering, this idea ultimately connected to fly-fishing. "We like to hunt living things down. Fly-fishing, the way it is now, makes us follow some silly rules to do that, so that we can work out the lust and still feel civilized. It works pretty good that way too; I'm always surprised."

Remembering that, or the feel of Calvin saying those sorts of things, I had a sudden insight into his outburst at the gate. That glimmer was followed by apprehension. "Helen? Calvin's not going to do anything foolish with J.R.? He's not going to…antagonize him?"

She hesitated. "As in punch him in the nose? Or push him in the pond?"

"Anything. Because that wouldn't be—" My turn to pause. Was I really going to say "right" again? "Wise," I finished.

"Oh. No, it wouldn't be."

From relief I allowed myself a chuckle. "Not that I wouldn't like to see it. Eating your home fries and watching Calvin throw J.R. to the fish…that would be a breakfast to remember. We're talking big tip here, sweetheart, count on it."

Helen laughed shortly. "Uh-huh. Uh-huh." Then, "Calvin would never do anything like that."

I didn't buy that. If J.R. or the President ever put a hand on Helen's backside….

Maybe I arched an eyebrow at her.

"He wouldn't. Believe me."

"If you say so."

"I do. And I'll tell you why." She leaned forward. "You remember when Calvin was a patient at VA. Did you ever find out what was wrong?"

"Sure. A respiratory problem. That stuff on his skin, too."

She nodded. "Right. Right. But there was another diagnosis, if you want to call it that, that was about something else. Calvin was one of those Special Forces guys who did things. The sort of things some of them had a hard time getting past." She leaned back again. "I wanted to tell you that before the first time he took you out, but he would have known if I did by the way you treated him. You didn't know, did you?"

"No."

"You're not mad now, are you?"

"No. I don't think so."

"I hope not. I mean…you just can't guess how important it was to him then, to come back to fly-fishing and have it work out for him. He was such a mess and…he'd fly-fished a lot with his grandfather as a boy, for bream and bass. And he started thinking about that time again when we gave those tying classes in the wards."

She gazed out the bank of windows, remembering. "I'm fairly certain," she said slowly, "that another reason he dove in so deep was that he decided fly-fishing was its own world. That it included a world view. Tradition and whatnot. Things his grandfather believed, and that he had before." She smiled. "He imagines it's about honor, you know. Respect. Natural laws and, God, you just can't imagine how important that was to him, to have a sanctuary like that." She inhaled deeply, then spoke while still holding her breath. "Even now."

I was still nodding when I saw her expression change, as if she'd thought about something unpleasant. She was squinting as she sighed out smoke. "Even now. The truth is, he's just as passionate today. So, people like J.R., they bother him a lot. A whole lot...But believe me, he would never punch anybody out or throw them in a lake." She laughed. "Special Forces types just don't do a lot of that."

I nodded again, a little too quickly. I was getting uncomfortable. I murmured something vague, asked for more coffee. She poured, looked at me closely, smiling a little. "He thinks a lot of you, by the way. Friendship is another one of those important things."

"I'm proud to be his," I said, speaking the truth before I was even aware I'd framed the thought.

She looked surprised too; we stared at each other, pleased. At last she reached over and tapped my coffee cup with her fingernail. "A toast: To honor and friends," she whispered.

I lifted the cup.

"Yes," she said, then she rose and went to the window.

I was comfortable again. We stayed quiet a little while. I supposed she was also watching the bruiser fish midging on the lake, those slow, head-to-tail rises. Then, with a rush, I was enormously sad that I might not soon get a chance to sit like this and feel this way again.

"To friendship," she said again at last, softly, almost in a monotone. "And to people who live what they believe."

I nodded, sipped coffee, looked past her again and snapped forward in my chair.

"Helen?"

She turned and looked at me with an expression that seemed to inquire and almost to warn. I felt hair prickling on the back of my neck.

Beyond her, at the fence line 200 yards away, a man was approaching Hobard's gate. I saw him turn to look at the lodge window.

I recognized him.

"Calvin told him not to," Helen said softly. "Warned him specifically, after the foul bastard saw you do it and said he was going to. Calvin told him. But he's one of those: No rules apply. Not even the most common courtesy—that's why he's here right now, isn't it? To show you how it is, put your face right down in it. Isn't that right?"

"Helen. What's—"

"I guess that works for him in business, not even changing colors. But sometimes nature's a different story. And you know what? So are men who honor the nature of men, and have rules."

I stood up.

Helen never paused. "One rule is that you never can be sure what a bull will do—did you know that? Especially a bull that will eat anything you put under his nose."

"Helen."

I went to the window, stood beside her. J.R. had turned away and was pulling at something. I realized after a moment that the gate was locked. Calvin never locked that gate; today he had. "Christ," 'I breathed. "I thought...."

J.R. was a heavy man, and he swung heavily over the rail. I heard the back door open and I turned to see Calvin. He nodded and was out again—snap, like that.

When I looked back Hobard was already at J.R. On him. I was certain I could hear the moist sound of flesh giving way to horn, hooves thudding into softness.

It just didn't stop.

Calvin trotted by the window toward the gate. There were shouts from somewhere out of sight.

Helen took my hand with one hand and turned my face toward hers with the other. "Calvin," she said firmly, evenly, as if to steady

me. "Calvin said something...about some flies he wanted from you."
She pursed her lips. "He didn't say how many, exactly, but it should
be fifty dollars'worth. I think he wants you to bring them with you,
when you come back next year."

Love Story of the Trout

greenwell's glory

Thomas McIntyre

It was a late-May evening, and Oklahoma light-sweet-crude and natural-gas magnate "Buck" (né Evelyn) Buckram stood on the bank of one of the seventeen trout-fishing ponds he had fashioned for himself on his 100,000-acre Far West Ranch retreat and, with a pair of rusty needle-nose pliers, tore a barbed treble hook from deep within the mouth of a three-pound rainbow. The sound was fully audible to "Shanks" (né Horatio) Greenwell, ranch foreman and—during Buckram's twice-yearly three-day sojourns (spring for fishing, fall for hunting)—chief guide and majordomo, from where he stood some ten yards away, a Panther Martin lure swinging lazily at the tip of his seven-foot spinning rod. Greenwell never flinched, having heard it all before.

"I been thinking."

"Sir?" Greenwell asked, aborting a cast. And so it all began.

Buckram raised the dazzling, gaping trout and let the light play on its silvered sides.

"I been thinking that this is just too much natural beauty for one man rightly to keep all to himself," he said. "You know, there ought to be a way we can share some of it with other folks." He deftly cracked the neck of the trout, and slipped it into the wicker creel slung across his chest.

Greenwell glanced at the pudgy, red-faced little man with a dimple in the middle of the first of his chins, an Ecuadorian Panama tilted low against the sinking sun, a Cuban double corona smoldering against the mosquitoes, and a University of Texas MBA on the wall of his Houston office, and knew all too well what Buckram meant. Greenwell had been going over the books just last night before presenting them to Buckram after lunch today; the annual numbers on the ponds—from maintenance and repairs to stocking fingerlings, to keeping those fingerlings well fed with freshwater shrimp and crawfish, to varmint control on various wild bandits, to the night patrols to keep human-type bandits at bay—had spoken for themselves.

Admittedly, Buckram could write off a percentage of the pond expenses by entertaining clients and employees every summer on the ranch; but it was nothing like what he'd done under the tax laws in effect when he'd first thought to call up the dozers, the plastic lining, the bentonite and the aerators and decreed all these fabulous fishing holes. Now he found himself having to maintain a large-scale catch-and-gut operation that saw several tons of iced trout going out every year with little or nothing coming back in. Even with enough oil under his control to founder a fleet of supertankers and one gas well alone capable of meeting the total heating needs of greater Milwaukee, a high five figures (particularly red ones) was still a high five figures.

"I been thinking," Buckram said again, casting his Mepps and setting it hard almost immediately, "that maybe we ought to look into seeing if there aren't some other good folks out there who'd enjoy this wonderful experience as much as we do." As he cranked in another thick rainbow, he added, as if in afterthought, "And possibly pay a little something in return for the privilege."

Greenwell nodded as nighthawks swirled in the leaden sky overhead. "'That's certainly an idea worth exploring, Mr. Buckram," he said, wondering what he was getting himself into this time.

Buckram was dragging the trout across the dirt and rocks of the pond edge, the rainbow making wet slapping sounds as it thrashed. Pinching the lure, he lifted the fish and admired it in the sunset. Greenwell wasn't sure Buckram had heard him, and was going to repeat his measured response when Buckram, his eyes on the trout, said simply, "See to it, then."

Before departing two days later, Buckram told Greenwell that he remembered some of the boys down at the Petroleum Club talking about how they'd first publicized the sporting potential of their ranches by giving away free trips to outdoor writers. That seemed like a sharp idea to Buckram, and he'd authorized Greenwell to invite as many outdoor writers as he saw fit, as long as the number did not exceed three. Greenwell didn't have a clue where to begin looking for an outdoor writer, or exactly what one was, except for a magazine Buckram left behind in the bathroom of the main ranch cabin, *Multi-National Fisherman,* a publication apparently dedicated to extolling the increased offshore-fishing opportunities created by the erection of oil platforms.

Greenwell phoned the editor of *Multi-National Fisherman* the morning after Buckram left, and by noon he had arranged to pay the way out and provide a free fishing trip for one of the magazine's freelance contributing editors; he also obtained the names and numbers of five or six other actual outdoor writers. Greenwell finally located his other two at a northeastern Missouri daily with ties to the religious right and French-language weekly tabloid in southern Louisiana.

The three writers came out together in June; Greenwell, with nothing else to judge it by, rated the affair as at least a qualified success. After he loaded them all into the Suburban for the eighty-mile run from the airport to the ranch, the two newspapermen immediately wanted to know where the beers were, while *Multi-National Fisherman*'s contributing editor asked for coffee, and if anyone minded if he smoked. As it turned out, the contributing editor was good for some thirty cups of scalding coffee a day. He would glare in seemingly irreconcilable indignation at the two newspapermen (who consumed the better part of a case of Budweiser en route to the ranch, and would grab a fresh bottle of brandy and one of sour mash each morning on their way out to the fishing ponds to augment the beer supply) every time they took yet another drink. He glared in even higher dudgeon after his cigarettes ran out on the second day and he could find no one on the ranch willing to make the 160-mile round trip to buy him more smokes.

All of the writers, however, seemed to take genuine delight in jerking dimwitted trout from the ponds all day long (and all night, if Greenwell had been amenable) and stacking them in the freezer to be turned into blocks of ice for the trip home. After some brandy and more than a few beers on the final afternoon, the journalist from the Cajun weekly even plunged, bearlike and fully clothed, into a pond to wrestle a five-pound cutthroat that had slipped from his grasp, then staggered dripping up to Greenwell, hugging the trout to his chest, and inquired, "They any way to eat *and* mount one of these?"

The newspaper articles appeared as promised in July, while *Multi-National Fisherman* went into receivership a week after the fishing trip, and the contributing editor wound up doing public relations work for a nationwide chain of drug-and-alcohol rehabilitation centers. Greenwell's first telephone call came, on the day the first article ran, from some town down along the Gulf Coast that was familiar to him only from news accounts of the preceding season's hurricanes. A man with three young-boy's names ("Billy Bob Jimmy") and an accent like someone with a mouthful of undercooked hominy wanted to know what they-all charged for a day of fishing. Greenwell told him $450, three-day minimum. No license, no limit.

"You sure proud of your trout," said Billy Bob Jimmy after a moment's pause. "Believe I'll stick to catfish." And with that he hung up.

More men with strange-sounding names (a disconcerting number of which ended in "-vis") from faraway places called, and upon learning the price said much the same thing: Catfish was what they, as well, all believed they'd stick to.

July was turning into August and Greenwell had yet to book a single fisherman. As someone who had grown up on ranches, fishing stock tanks and seasonal creeks, eating whatever he caught (and more than once having to catch something in order to eat), he was beginning to sense a profound flaw in his marketing strategy. It began to become clear to him that fishing on the ranch meant traveling too long a way and spending too much money just for meat. No matter how many trout he let a fisherman take home, it was never going to be enough. Yet what did he have to offer them except trout?

To make matters worse, Mr. Buckram had taken to phoning Greenwell nightly, asking him casually but nevertheless pointedly when he'd be booking those fishermen for the ranch. Greenwell found himself mouthing phrases like "several promising inquiries," "things looking up," and "any day now," the sort of verbal soft-shoe he hated only slightly less than having to come right out with the truth.

"I know you can do it," Buckram would end his calls, in that same admixed tone of wheedlery, seduction, and veiled threat he'd perfected years ago while selling bulk quantities of frozen foods door-to-door. After Buckram hung up, Greenwell would sit in his Naugahyde lounger with the duct tape on the arms and muse, *I could have stayed in the navy.*

Then in early August Greenwell had his epiphany. Its first stage came when he opened the newspaper one morning and read a letter to the editor from a local fly fisher complaining about all the scarred trout he was pulling from the nearby Sandbur River. About all the ripped lips and deformed mandibles, and how this was entirely the fault of the troglodytic spin fisherman and their vicious treble hooks, and how the only sensible solution was to make the river totally zero-limit, barbless-fly-fishing-only. It was, to be sure, one of the most astounding examples of asininity Greenwell had ever run across (if he knew one thing, it was that spin fishermen never threw back a legal trout, and so—unlike fly fishers—left no unsightly fish in the river). But what really caught Greenwell's fancy was the way the writer had signed his letter, with those three little consonants that meant so much following his name: DDS. Because if there were two things that Greenwell knew, the second was that when it came to money, members of the dental profession were nothing less than the dodoes of the human race—large-breasted, meaty, and too easily caught and plucked for their own good. And here was a dentist proclaiming himself a blathering fly fisher for all the whole wide world to see.

It was then that Greenwell understood that it was not fishermen he should be looking for at all. It was fishers. He had never picked up a fly rod in his life, but something told him that if it was the way to dentists' thoroughly overstuffed wallets, then he would need to be picking one up very soon.

That afternoon found Greenwell cruising the streets of town in his battered, dusty ranch pickup, hunting for something he somehow recalled once as having been there. He finally located it nested between a car-stereo outlet and a tattoo parlor: Dame Juliana's Shoppe of the Angle, the only real fly-fishing shop within a 200-mile radius (of course, the town was also the only real town within a 200-mile radius).

Greenwell felt uneasy as soon as he walked in and saw the owner. He'd seen lady anglers before, but this one, with forearms like a certain one-eyed sailor's and hands as ample as fielders' mitts, not to mention a bluish penumbra along the line of her jaw and her fishing wear of many ripe-berry colors, was unlike any of his acquaintance. Luckily, she was engaged at the counter with another customer in an animated conversation about, it seemed, hackle, permitting Greenwell to duck his head and move directly to the book and magazine section in the back without having to exchange a word.

Greenwell stared at the book racks for some time, wondering where all the books on fly-fishing were. All he was looking for was basic fly-fishing pedagogy; yet all the titles before him seemed to be more about dysfunction, emotional crises, and recovery than fishing with an angle—twelve-step programs with rivers running through them. They reminded Greenwell of nothing so much as all those truly terrifying Venus-and-Mars books his wife was forever lugging home and staring over at him in enigmatic silence. It took him a good quarter-hour of browsing before he was able to discover three books that appeared to be solely about the catching of trout on a fly; as he was turning toward the counter to pay for them, he noted a magazine—*Float: Journal of the Artificial*—and picked up a copy of it, too.

Long after midnight, having skimmed through the three books and having read *Float* from cover to cover, Greenwell experienced the ultimate stage of his epiphany, understanding perfectly, if paradoxically, exactly what he'd been doing wrong. Fly fishers (certainly a large-enough number of them to keep things interesting, anyway) wanted never, ever to kill a trout. They were, apparently, even quite willing to pay exorbitantly for the privilege of not doing so. The less they had to show, in fact, for the most amount of money spent on their fishing, the better. The secret Greenwell had been struggling to find now lay open before him: Don't give them all the trout they want; on the contrary, guarantee you'll give them none at all.

The next morning, Greenwell wrote an ad to run in the classified pages of *Float* and sent it to the magazine along with a ranch check. The morning after that, he drove back into town and walked into Dame Juliana's and up to the owner.

"Teach me fly-fishing," he croaked nervously.

Three days later (after hours of the owner's bruising hand wrapped completely around both his wrist and the cork grip of the rod, the eternally repeated mantra "One o'clock, eleven o'clock" seared into his consciousness as his arm was worked back and forth like a pump handle), Greenwell could lay out a creditable seventy feet of weight-forward floating fly line and was the proud owner of some $1,200 of brand-new fly-fishing equipment, including a fishing shirt of vibrant cranberry.

The ad appeared in the September issue of *Float*, and Greenwell was able to book one group of fishers on the basis of it. It was to be a party of four from a town that sounded like "Fennel-on-Leek," in Connecticut. The man Greenwell spoke with said he was the head of the local chapter of a fly-fishing and trout-preservation society, as well as a member of the organization's national board. He questioned Greenwell closely about the nature of what he insisted on referring to as the "fishery"; Greenwell, due to his intense study of the fly-fishing books, and especially *Float,* could answer the questions competently, and was always sure to stress certain key phrases like "classic Western hospitality," "classic stillwater fly-fishing," and "classic catch-and-release," *classic* being a word, Greenwell had learned, that could not be used too much or too often within the hearing of fishers.

The man, whose name was Wrench, seemed more than satisfied, and they closed the deal during their first telephone conversation. At the end of the call Mr. Wrench let slip the fact that he was in actuality Dr. Wrench.

Greenwell felt his hand holding the receiver begin to tremble as he asked, "Oh, what kind of doctor?"

"Oral surgeon," said Dr. Wrench.

Greenwell didn't know if he dare ask the next question, but he somehow managed to find the courage.

And the other three? What did they...do?

Two orthodontists and a specialist in the field of periodontia.

Greenwell suddenly found it hard to swallow. The trip was booked for October 1, which was as late as Greenwell felt he could comfortably accommodate the group. It was also the start of Mr. Buckram's hunting holiday. Buckram, when he learned that Greenwell had at last booked some paying anglers, was only too happy to forgo his services as guide and gave over the entire main cabin to Greenwell and his clients, moving into the bunkhouse a goodly way out back with his third wife, Tawny (née Margaret). In the excitement, Buckram never asked Greenwell what kind of anglers were coming to the ranch, and it simply never occurred to Greenwell to mention that they would be fly fishers, having nearly forgotten that any other kind of anglers existed.

On the last day of September Greenwell picked up his fishers at the airport and was just able to get all their gear into the back of the Suburban. All four wore oiled dusters and identical Australian Snowy River hats. Nobody asked for a beer. Or a light. As they drove in, even their conversation seemed barbless.

Greenwell had spent the previous two weeks poring over wine

guides and cookbooks, working with the ranch cook on the menu—including the picnic hampers for lunch—to get everything just right. Even so, as dinner was being served Greenwell had a moment of intense panic as he suddenly wondered if he should have asked if any of them was vegetarian. They all seemed to tuck into the barbecued rib eyes enthusiastically enough, though, and after a flaming dessert and approving remarks about the rustic decor of the cabin, including the antique fishing gear (by which they meant Mr. Buckram's wicker creel that he'd left on the granite mantelpiece last spring), all were asleep by ten o'clock, while Greenwell lay awake until nearly three, too pleased, yet also still too anxious, to close his eyes.

The next day brought a perfect autumn morning, crisp but not cold, sunny with no wind. Greenwell had already decided to take his fishers (he had to admit he liked the sound of "his fishers") to the upper end of the ranch, where the fall colors would be most vivid and where they would be out of range of Mr. and Mrs. Buckram's hunt. The Buckrams would be looking for pronghorn and mule deer; one of the hands, Julio, would go along to help with any heavy lifting.

After a breakfast of *pain perdu*, fresh-squeezed Valencia orange juice, and cups of Kenyan coffee, Greenwell's fishers assembled beside the Suburban, two of them carrying custom-built split-cane rods and the other two state-of-the-art graphite ones. Greenwell, in brand-new neoprene stocking-foot waders and felt-sole wading boots, looked over all their signature-model tackle and was relieved to find that his own held up rather favorably in comparison.

Greenwell ran them just shy of ragged that day. If a pond did not pay off after a half-dozen casts, then it was on to another. If a hatch came on while they were fishing a Woolly Bugger, Greenwell was right there to tie on an Adams. He was launching them in float tubes, netting their fish before a trout could get so much as a grain of sand on it, snapping grip-and-grin portraits (both verticals and horizontals), swiftly measuring trophy dimensions, and taking more photos to pass along to the taxidermist so he could produce absolutely lifelike replicas. With each and every fish, Greenwell knelt down or waded out with it to move the water oh-so-gently through its gills and let it regain its equilibrium, one of his fishers often kneeling right beside him, sometimes actually bidding the trout *adieu*, before releasing the fish back into the green depths of the pond.

At noon Greenwell laid out the picnic lunch (looking just like a photo spread he'd seen in *Float,* right down to the linen napkins and carved walnut napkin rings) beneath the shade of a cottonwood; and as he uncorked a bottle of chilled white wine, he began to think that he might be able to get quite used to this—a stemmed glass of Chateau Grillet Viognier instead of a can of Bud, the odd tournedos with béarnaise in place of chicken-fried steak and white gravy. Maybe even an armchair of actual leather. And no slimy trout to gut at night.

By the end of the day his fishers were talking about this trip in terms they had previously reserved for Venezuelan bone-fishing or stays at five-star Alaskan salmon lodges. As they headed down to the cabin in the evening, their rods secured in magnetic holders attached to the hood and roof of the Suburban—not one single trout to show for their long day's labors—Dr. Wrench was already saying how he couldn't wait to tell everyone at the oral-surgeons' convention this winter about this "fishery." How Greenwell had grown to love that word.

It was still barely light as they pulled into the yard beside the cabin, but a horned moon had begun to rise over the mountains. Greenwell was unloading the Suburban and telling his fishers that dinner would be served in forty-five minutes when he heard Mr. Buckram's diesel coming toward the cabin from the lower end of the ranch. Greenwell turned to watch the truck approach, feeling the muscles in the back of his neck begin to tighten for as-yet-unidentified reasons. The king-cab made a wide turn as it came into the yard and stopped broadside, right in front of Greenwell's fishers.

And this is the way it all ended:

Buck Buckram, in an orange vest and stained 7X Stetson, a bottle of George Dickel in a blood-stained hand, dropped from the truck and called out, "How's 'bout a snort?" Julio climbed out of the door behind him; and Buckram's younger, taller, slimmer wife, also invested in orange, got out on the passenger side and came around the front of the truck, cradling a lever-action .243 in the crook of her right arm, a carefully proportioned smile (the product of several formative years at The Miss Francine Academy of Charm) on her freshly glossed lips.

Greenwell could see his fishers stiffen; he felt as if his wading boots had sunk into two feet of mud, trapping him where he stood like a mastodon in tar.

"Our Mr. Greenwell here," declared Buckram loudly, affecting his frozen-food-selling voice, a gigantic grin on his face, "neglected to inform me that you gentlemen were of the fly-fishing persuasion. Julio's the one let me in on it," he added, pointing the neck of the whiskey bottle toward the ranch hand wearing a torn and faded denim shirt. Julio was bobbing his head in a shy nod toward Greenwell's fishers.

"Now you all just step right this way," said Buckram, "because there's something I know you'll want to see."

Greenwell's fishers looked at one another, then moved slowly, flocklike, toward the pickup. Greenwell, in spite of his apprehension, felt drawn along in their gravitational pull.

In the back of the truck lay two better-than-fair field-dressed pronghorn bucks and an exceptional mule deer, well more than thirty inches. Green film covered their eyes and their carcasses were bent around in contorted postures in order to accommodate a 100-quart plastic cooler set inside the tailgate.

"From what I know about you fly-fishing boys," a still-grinning Buckram said, once more trying to press the Dickel onto Greenwell's fishers, every one declining, "you don't ever catch nothing. Now I plain could not stand the thought of any of you, as our very first guests here at the ranch, going home empty-handed, with nothing to show your friends and neighbors. So...." And with that Buckram dropped the tailgate of the truck.

A viscous mélange of antelope and mule-deer blood dripped slowly out onto the ground as Buckram threw open the lid of the cooler. As he did, Greenwell could feel a scream of *No!* catch in his throat.

"Mama and I worked real hard all day after getting our critters down to snag you something nice to carry back with you," said

Buckram merrily, nodding to the contents of the cooler. Packed head to tail from end to end and seemingly top to bottom in a bed of crushed, rose-tinged ice lay dozens and dozens of three- and four-pound trout, their eyes staring back in frigid reproach. Along the wall of the pickup bed lay the spinning rods, blood of both mammals and fish staining them too, lending it all the unmistakable air of a crime scene.

"You be sure and tell your buddies that there's plenty more where these came from, now," said Buckram, lifting the bottle to his own lips and pulling off a string of bubbles while Tawny Buckram smiled glossily on.

Greenwell made himself look away from the back of the pickup in time to see Wrench, back at the Suburban, removing his cane rod from the carrier.

Wrench was heading for the cabin, tearing down his rod like a man snapping kindling. Buckram slipped up behind Greenwell and threw an arm around his cranberry-clad shoulders. To the back of the departing figure of Dr. Wrench, DDS, Mr. Buck Buckram, MBA, shouted, "Hell, we'll even fillet the sonsabitches for you!"

Flash back Hare's Ear

Prince Nymph

George's Brown Stone

the shining path

Michael Doherty

In 1984, seven Shining Path rebels held up a busload of tourists on their way to Machu Picchu. Their haul proved modest—a handful of digital and other watches, some traveler's checks, credit cards, a multitude of small denominations of various currencies and some simple rings. In one purse they might have found instructions, a key to a safebox and an address to a place they would never visit: Cle Elum, Washington.

That purse was Jennifer Robinaut's, and she would gladly have given it up, if she had a little more time. She was in no hurry. Her pilgrimage to this place, like the wonders she had seen before—the Great Barrier Reef, Petra, Easter Island, Mount St. Helens—left her with a greater sense of omnipotence, youthfulness and vigor. She traveled light, two sets of shirts and two sets of slacks, interchangeable, and of muted duns, blacks and olives. What else? A small camera, a money belt, clean underclothes, a wetpack, some novels and her good sense.

Now gray and never married, she carried herself well and struck one of the bandits as elegant and most definitely rich, in part because she didn't slouch or show fear. She was not afraid, and had long ago concluded these men—all men, really—were vessels, experiences and nothing more. Just minutes before the bandits' attack, she'd admired the twilight of the southern solstice, itself a calming milestone. A moment during which she told herself again that travel broadened the mind and the heart, and leaving a place could be just as enlightening as finding someplace new. Here she was, far from the Yakima River, far from Cle Elum, her childhood home, on the roof of the Andes visiting a sacred place.

She found the bandits' impulsivity intoxicating if not a little erotic. This was a most primal experience, perhaps only trumped by what her first and only boyfriend had done with her one afternoon on a runoff bank of virgin gravels, below a meadow on the banks of the Yakima.

One of the rebels saw her thrust chin, her squared shoulders and confident demeanor as insolence. Prone to poor judgment, and in need of close supervision, this bandit grew impatient. He barked commands at her, asked her to speed the emptying of her purse. She smiled at him.

Without the calming influence of his marginally brighter colleagues, the bandit drew his knife and moved it in an arc through the air. His arm blurred, a rainbow whirl of his striped cotton poncho, fast-moving, and at the end of it, a new cut, a bad one, a fatal one, across her throat. The rapture Jennifer had learned of at Stonehenge, the Pyramids and the Holy Cities was finally about to come. And with it, she would move from her great loneliness to a world of the pure and young. She was not afraid, she would be led into the bright light, to green pastures, beside sapphire pools on mountain rivers, to the boy she once loved....

My Father and His Love for Cle Elum

When he learned of Jennifer Robinaut's death, my father took me to the Yakima River, to his favorite stretch. I was maybe 14 or so; it's where he taught me to fly-fish. In that low water, gentle cascades formed braids and pools, and cut-away banks were overhung with tangled woods. This was our version of the great wonders of the world, the Yakima not far from Cle Elum.

He sat on the gravel, his bamboo rod beside him, and never fished a minute. Head hung, yet still encouraging when I showed him the fish I brought to hand. These were solid, young rainbows, confident in their strikes and precise in their fighting. These were my favorite Cle Elum things—the mountains, this great river, him, the pools and runs, the fish with all their brilliant colors.

After I was done, he told me the story of Jennifer Robinaut, in part because he was once her boyfriend, the one who made a move some 30 years earlier on the banks of the Yakima. In part because he needed someone other than my mom to confide in, that he lost a friend he cared deeply for, although he hadn't seen or heard from her in years. And in part because he hoped I would never take such journeys. "Follies" he called them.

"All you need to know about the world can be found within 50 miles of Cle Elum, or up here." He would tap on his head with his index finger, and make a clicking noise when he did it.

Time often heals, but the revulsion of Jennifer Robinaut's passing became a long preoccupation of my father's. He was careful about it, my mom never saw it. But certain sights and sounds triggered his melancholy. The tumble of waters, the gravel popping underneath his truck, the cottonwoods going to seed, the irrigation shifts in the river, the shrieks of summer kids tubing down the canyon. Some days I'd fish and he'd just wander the banks, looking at the stones, the river rocks, sometimes picking one up, the ones with the big lines of quartz, the veins of unknown ores, maybe agates, pocketing them, bringing them home to his small garden. Years later you'd see that look, just for a moment, when the tour buses rolled through, on their way to Roslyn, on pilgrimage to where they filmed a TV show called *Northern Exposure*. I guess that's the second wonder of the Cle Elum world....

Shropshire Lads Deliver Justice

Back to Peru, to 1984 for a minute, the story there is not done. On that tour bus were three members of a British SAS team on leave from a Falkland Islands town, Port Stanley. These men were killers and had watched with some slight amusement the clumsy antics of the Peruvian rebels. They sat at the back of the bus and while not entirely calm, were certainly confident. They were armed, by habit, with knives of Sheffield steel lashed to their legs, and each of them was a little bit drunk and each was now handling his blade and waiting. Signs were passed just as they had learned on Salisbury Plain, and later in combat—Goose Green, Mt. Tumbledown and the bogs and tidal marshes outside Port Stanley two years prior. Semaphored intentions, warrior signs.

The rebels made their way closer to the back of the bus, clumsily pocketing the gems and loot when the shrieks of the passenger beside Jennifer Robinaut alerted all of them to a fundamental shift in matters and intents. The screams that accompanied the exsanguinating Robinaut proved a perfect diversion. During that general confusion, the soldiers rushed the bandits and three minutes later seven peasant rebels were dead, their throats slit similarly to Ms. Robinaut's. Justice was swift. There was an end to these Shining Path fools.

Two weeks later a small package was sent from Stanley to the only address in the small purse of Jennifer Robinaut. In that smudged envelope was the key and instructions to the lockbox and a letter describing the events of that miserable day with the clumsy poetic detail of a former Shropshire constable turned mercenary:

"The perpetrators wore smocks of many colors similar to the natives of the area...."

"The small clasp knife severed the carotid artery in a jagged zed pattern...."

"They were dispatched with precision and a minimum of fuss...."

"All goods were accounted for, excepting of course these possessions, presumably those of one Ms. Jennifer Robinaut...."

"She died in the twilight, with the sun setting...."

"We are terribly sorry for your loss...."

The package was sent to my father. I saw him read it, once, twice and so on. I read it too, when he wasn't around. I knew what those words meant, what the day looked like. I looked up Machu Picchu in the library and saw pictures of that place and thought at least she died in the mountains, near the ruins, near those magic stones. Closer to wherever she wanted to go. It looked like the wilderness near Chikamin and Lemah, where the Teanaway forms from snowmelt and springs and makes its way to the Yak.

A Brief, Disturbing Introduction
to the Pan Flute Leprechauns

There's a lot of water between 1984 and now. I have brought my father to specialists in the big cities, miles from Cle Elum. I have asked for their help and they have run their studies. You might think that Jennifer Robinaut broke his heart, but no, she didn't. My dad wasn't a weak sapling, he had reason and kindness all around him, my mother too, and he knew the dangers of nostalgia, prolonged mourning and imagined sentiment. He did well enough. He fished the big waters, walked the high Cascades.

What's got him now is his mind's going. He doesn't remember much anymore, he can't tell his legs and arms to move fast. He remembers way back, when I was a kid, when he was a kid. He remembers the great holes that held the big trout. He remembers when steelhead and kings were common in the Yakima. He knows why Salmon La Sac is called that. He can tie a fly on a leader with one hand. And he knows how the hills around Cle Elum have everything, gold, gems, coal, granite, basalt, fossils and hill people. He'll tell you how to smelt cinnabar down to mercury and how mercury vapor can make you mad-hatter crazy and set your teeth loose. He can, on a rare day, find an agate, a small Ellensburg Blue, in the river gravel, and he'll tell you how to tickle a trout, though he never showed me how. He'll tell all this to you more than once, maybe a hundred times, and sometimes now they'll get mixed up in a jumbled mess. What he won't tell you is what day of the week it is or the season anymore.

He sees things, he hallucinates. Small and non-threatening things mostly. When we watch the Mariner's game he tells me about the guys in the corner. The pan-flute guys, how they're playing "Danny Boy." At first I laughed, there he would be, humming along. He says the pan-flute guys sometimes carry fly rods, and they're on the way to the water. Apparently they are bamboo purists.

"The fellas are fishing again, good luck little guys...."

"At least they don't mime. They mime, Dad?" (In my mind there is a hierarchy of lousy entertainment capped by mimes, pan flutists, clowns, TV preachers and so on.)

"Whatsat?"

"Mime, you know, white-face stuck in a box?" I showed him.

"No, they don't do that, why would anyone do that...Nothing interesting about being stuck in a box...."

"Can't argue with you there."

It was the third specialist who put the name to it, Lewy-Body Dementia. A slow, indolent, irreversible decline into further stiffness, limited mobility, memory loss and hallucinations. He would die of it ultimately, the doc said that, right there, out in the open with Dad in the room. I wanted to punch him, but Dad didn't seem to care, shrugged his shoulders, he had no fears. We tried some medications, dopamines, phenothiazines. But those things didn't make much difference so I didn't push them.

You know what happens when you fill those kinds of prescriptions? Some jerk gets your address and sells it to a company and six weeks later you're on a mailing list for a magazine called *The Dementia Caregiver*. It's scrape-your-heart-out depressing. They give you prices for bedpans, restraints, chair lifts, Velcro-closed orthopedic shoes, bulk diapers, chux wipes. And to kick you in the nuts? Articles about learning how to balance your care-giving with your social life. Not that I had one. With his band of invisible benevolent midget pan flutists who fished and kept him company, Dad didn't need me. There's a depressing thought.

I was jealous of them, those little flute-playing f—ers. On a bad night when I'd eat too much chocolate, drink too much, smoke one too many, my dreams would turn up strange. These little bastards would march like the dwarves in Snow White, tooting their pan flutes, down switchbacks to the best fishing hole, wearing their ponchos and singing:

Oh Danny boy, the pipes, the pipes are calling/
From glen to glen, and down the mountain side/
The summer's gone, and all the flowers are dying/
'Tis you,'tis you must go and I must bide.

Then one by one, in great precise macroscopic detail, they disassemble their flutes, fit the pipes onto the ends of one another, male to female, and make giant bamboo rods or long wooden knives, and instead of fish, they'd whip and cut the crap out of me. I would wake with a headache and soaked sheets.

(They don't write anything about that in *The Dementia Caregiver* trust me, I look every month the new copy comes. Nothing about nightmares. Nothing about pan flutes, nothing about fishing, waters, gemstones, mountains, youth or beauty. Just things like "Top Ten Tips to Cope With Death and Loss." Sad thing is, I read that magazine cover to cover, and I get antsy when it's not there when it should be.)

I realize I gave these Andean leprechauns way too much thought, they hijacked my mind. But here's my take on them—maybe Dad's Zamfirian brothers were a spin on those rebels, some mental trick to infantilize, dehumanize and neutralize imagined memory. Although he knew her when she was most vulnerable, he wasn't there, he didn't see Jennifer Robinaut in her proudest, strongest and bravest final moments. But he knew demons destroyed her, and there was a time, years ago, when they haunted him too. Surely these pan-flute guys were related, maybe it was their karmic duty to heal him, maybe they were pied pipers, leading his rotten memories away? The thing that bothered me though, that I couldn't trump with better reason, was why'd they lead him away from me?

Resolution

I took him one fall day to the Yakima, just above the canyon, one of my favorite stretches. We went to a place I knew, where we wouldn't have to walk far. I pitched a lawn chair on a small beach near a good hole that came out when the irrigation flows finally ended. I'd fished there many times before, never with him though. It was always a prime spot. I walked him out and wrapped him in one of those Mexican space-invader blankets, poured him two fingers of Scotch and worked the waters while he watched.

There was one fish rising upstream, over and over, a big fat healthy nugget. If I went for him I would no longer be in view of my father. I turned back, looked at him, all wrapped and comfortable in that chair. He waved at me, pushing the air forward, as if to say, "Go for him son, you go get 'em." A paternal wave that right then meant everything and was timeless.

So I did, I cast, I got him to strike, a rainbow whirl, played him to hand, on this great jewel of the river, and released him. Threw a few more times thinking there might be more but there were none.... And then thoughts of my old man back on the beach and that wind coming downstream from the pass and the mountains with winter on it now the equinox had passed, and the old man bitching and moaning about how a cotton blanket is a bad idea.

But when I got back, there he was, humming, not "Danny Boy" anymore, but some tuneless sounds, happy, maybe he was drunk, who knows.

In this last year I put my dad in a nursing home and I miss him more than he will ever know. I'm ready for him to go, I could no longer do him justice, I was regularly ordering from *The Dementia Caregiver* and I caught myself in the mirror now and then and I saw him in me, looking like he did on the river back in those bad times. I couldn't keep doing this and promised myself, when he died, I would leave Cle Elum. I would not be stuck there.

After he left our place, I went through his stuff slowly, room by room. I liberated his flies, Deceivers and Stimulators, from his flimsy box and put them in my wallet. I cleaned his reels, rewrapped the bindings on his bamboo rods, threw out his rubber waders. And reset the clasps of some of his favorite caps to fit me.

And in the last room I came across that letter, that envelope, those instructions. I re-read them, weighed the skeleton key in my hand.

And wondered about what was in the lockbox. In a small inspiration, as though that box contained some amazing chunk of history, of his history, Jennifer's too, I made my way to the bank.

Armed with the key, the letter, the obits he'd saved. I passed them all on to the cashier and asked for her help. She checked with her manager, and the box was opened, inside it a smaller box. The manager didn't even open that one, he wasn't the least bit curious, he handed it over and said not to worry about returning it, he needed more lockboxes and he'd never found a relative of Ms. Robinaut's who wanted to claim her belongings.

I took the box to the nursing home. And after what passed for conversation, me doing all the talking, brought it over to Dad. His head was hung like it used to when he was in a mood. But it was his strength failing now. He didn't seem to have the firepower for moods or muscles anymore. He propped his eyelids open with his fingers when I shouted at him.

"Dad, look at this, we're going to look inside Jennifer's lockbox...."

He shifted in his seat and sat up some. And with both of us looking on, I opened the lid.

A shimmer of bright blue light from inside, rays of it shining out, and there was the most beautiful Ellensburg Blue I ever saw, and with it, my father, first incredulous and then smiling, a great big beam of a smile. I swear he could recognize it from long ago and, in that moment, all was good again.

Love Story of the Trout

author biographies

Rob Brown is a fly-fishing writer who lives in British Columbia.

Michael Doherty was the winner of the 2008 Robert Traver Fly-Fishing Writing Award and received honorable mention in the competition in 2010. He lives in Seattle.

Charles Gaines is the author of *Pumping Iron* and other well-known books. A contributing editor to *Garden & Gun*, he splits his time between Nova Scotia and Alabama and is currently writing a novel.

Jerry Gibbs was the fishing editor of *Outdoor Life* for more than 30 years and is the author of *Steel Barbs, Wild Waters* and other books.

John Gierach is the author of among the best-known books in fly-fishing, including *Sex, Death and Flyfishing*, *Where the Trout Are All As Long as Your Leg*, *Trout Bum*, *Fool's Paradise* and others.

J. H. Hall is writer who lives in Maine. He is the author of *True Stories of Maine Fly Fishermen*.

T. Felton Harrison, a long-time fly-fishing writer, also designed and marketed fly reels.

Cliff Hauptman is the author of *How to Fly-Fish* and other books. He lives in Massachusetts.

Dave Hughes is author of many of the best modern books on fly-fishing skills and fly tying. He writes the "Practical & Useful" column for *Fly Rod & Reel*.

Robert F. Jones contributed frequently to *Field & Stream* and *Sports Illustrated*. He wrote non-fiction books including *Upland Passage: A Field Dog's Education* and such novels as *Tie My Bones to Her Back*. He died in 2002.

Jim McDermott is a writer who lives in Virginia. Of the story published here, he said he originally dedicated "this tale of iconoclasm to the memory of two English setters who stood out."

Thomas McIntyre is a well-known outdoor writer and essayist who lives in Wyoming. He is the author of *Seasons & Days* and other books.

Seth Norman is the author of *Meanderings of a Fly Fisherman* and other books. He writes the book reviews for *Fly Rod & Reel* and is a columnist for *California Fly Fisher*.

Randy Oldebuck is the pen name of celebrated fly-fishing and fly-tying author Dick Talleur. Talleur tell us: "The name Randy Oldebuck was derived from a guy I once knew who always introduced himself thusly: 'Hi! I'm Randy!' Which he always was."

Gary J. Whitehead is a writer who lives in West Nyack, New York, and was the 1997 winner of the Robert Traver Fly-Fishing Writing Award.

Subscribe

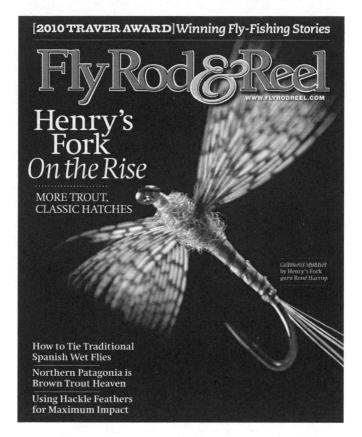

[2010 TRAVER AWARD] Winning Fly-Fishing Stories

Fly Rod & Reel
WWW.FLYRODREEL.COM

Henry's Fork
On the Rise

MORE TROUT,
CLASSIC HATCHES

Callibaetis Spinner
by Henry's Fork
guru René Harrop

How to Tie Traditional
Spanish Wet Flies

Northern Patagonia is
Brown Trout Heaven

Using Hackle Feathers
for Maximum Impact

1-800-888-6890
www.flyrodreel.com